"I landed in…in…a damn mule pie!"

Marcus burst out laughing. He couldn't help himself. Now that he knew it was mostly Amanda's dignity that was injured, he felt intensely relieved. Even when she cursed him and smacked his arm hard enough to make him lose his balance, he couldn't stop laughing.

"That's you, then?" he said, chortling, crinkling up his nose and sniffing dramatically.

"Oh, please." She pitched him a look of pure, undiluted murder. But it was dry murder now. The tears, thank God, were gone.

"I hate you, Quicksilver. I truly, truly do." She shook her fists at the sky. "Just look at me! I'm sitting here all crippled and smelling to high heaven, and all you can do is laugh like a damn, demented hyena!"

Dear Reader,

All of us at Harlequin Historicals would like to wish Mary McBride a warm congratulations on making the *USA Today* bestseller list with her story in our OUTLAW BRIDES collection along with authors Ruth Langan and Elaine Coffman. Mary has a new book out this month, a Western romance called *Quicksilver's Catch*. This delightful story features a runaway heiress bride and the tough-as-nails bounty hunter who is determined to make as much money as he can from his association with the willful young woman, if she doesn't drive him to drink first. Don't miss this warm and funny story of two people who *really* don't belong together.

A devil-may-care nobleman finds redemption in the arms of the only woman who can heal him, in Margaret Moore's *The Rogue's Return*, the next installment in her MOST UNSUITABLE... series set in Victorian England. And *Outlaw Wife* by Ana Seymour is a bittersweet Western about the daughter of a notorious outlaw who loses her heart to the rancher who saves her from jail.

Fleeing Britain and marriage to an elderly preacher, an English adventuress becomes involved with an American spy in our fourth title for the month, *Nancy Whiskey* by Laurel Ames.

Whatever your tastes in reading, we hope you'll keep a lookout for all of our books, wherever Harlequin Historicals are sold.

Sincerely,

Tracy Farrell
Senior Editor

Please address questions and book requests to:
Harlequin Reader Service
U.S.: 3010 Walden Ave., P.O. Box 1325, Buffalo, NY 14269
Canadian: P.O. Box 609, Fort Erie, Ont. L2A 5X3

QUICKSILVER'S CATCH

MARY McBRIDE

Harlequin Books

TORONTO • NEW YORK • LONDON
AMSTERDAM • PARIS • SYDNEY • HAMBURG
STOCKHOLM • ATHENS • TOKYO • MILAN
MADRID • WARSAW • BUDAPEST • AUCKLAND

ISBN 0-373-28975-8

QUICKSILVER'S CATCH

Books by Mary McBride

Harlequin Historicals

Riverbend #164
Fly Away Home #189
The Fourth of Forever #221
The Sugarman #237
The Gunslinger #256
Forever and a Day #294
Darling Jack #323
Quicksilver's Catch #375

Harlequin Books

Outlaw Brides
"The Ballad of Josie Dove"

MARY McBRIDE

is a former special-education teacher who lives in St. Louis, Missouri, with her husband and two young sons. She loves to correspond with readers and invites them to write to her at: P.O. Box 411202 St. Louis, MO 63141.

Prologue

"Miss Amanda says she doesn't want to eat, ma'am." Bridget flexed her knees, as much to steady herself on the moving train as to show proper respect to her elderly and exceedingly rich employer.

"Poppycock." Honoria Grenville snatched a hanky from her black sleeve and waved it brusquely at the maid. "My granddaughter hasn't eaten a bite since we left Denver yesterday. Give her the tray, Bridget."

"Oh, but, ma'am..."

"Now." Mrs. Grenville's voice was as adamant as the rap of her ebony cane on the floor of her private Pullman Palace car.

"Yes, ma'am."

Bridget flexed her knees again, stifled a sigh of resignation, and made her way toward the curtained sleeping compartment. Rich people. They baffled her and made her very nervous.

"Won't you have a bite of supper, Miss Amanda?" she crooned, a bit hesitantly, through the closed drapes as she hoisted the large silver tray shoulder high and slipped it between the brocade folds. When there was no response, Bridget bit her lip and stepped back. *Oh Lord, here we go again,* she thought when a teacup whizzed inches from her nose, to crash against the mahogany paneling on the opposite side of the car. The saucer followed a second later and met with the same shattered fate.

Then, suddenly, it was raining. Peas and carrots! *Saints preserve us!* Forks and spoons! Bridget ducked just as the big silver tray sailed over her head, skimmed the length of the Oriental carpet, and came to rest at the black hem of Honoria Grenville's dress.

"That will be quite enough, Amanda." The old woman's cane came down, denting the tray. "Bridget, did she hear me? Tell my granddaughter I won't tolerate this behavior any longer."

A muffled shout came from behind the curtains. "Tell my grandmother I heard her, Bridget. And tell her the minute she stops keeping me prisoner and lets me go back to Denver to marry Angus McCray, she won't have to tolerate my bad behavior anymore. I'm going to marry him, Grandmother. Did you hear me? Did she hear me, Bridget?"

One look at Mrs. Grenville's livid face proved to the maid that she had, indeed, heard the threat. "I believe she did, miss," Bridget said, her gaze flicking nervously now from her irate employer to the brocade curtains, which were rippling and waving, as if from Miss Amanda's hot breath.

It was a continual surprise to the young Irishwoman that rich people argued. And so vehemently, too. If she had money, she thought, and especially a fortune like the Grenvilles', she'd be as dreamy and contented as a cow in clover, as blissful as a sow in springtime mud. Of course, like Miss Amanda, she'd want to marry the man of her choice, and she'd be furious, too, she supposed, if she'd been snatched from the altar just as she was about to speak her vows, the way Miss Amanda had been yesterday.

"Angus McCray is a fortune hunter and a scoundrel," Mrs. Grenville said in a booming voice.

"I'm still going to marry him, Grandmother."

"What did she say, Bridget?"

"She said…"

"I said—" Amanda's voice rose from the depths of the sleeping compartment "—that I'm still going to marry him. I said you can't keep me under lock and key forever, Grandmother, and the minute your back is turned, I'm going back to Denver. You wait and see."

"What did she say, Bridget?" The ebony cane stabbed the tray again and again. Honoria Grenville's knuckles were fierce white knobs on the handle. With her other hand, she waved her lace hankie again. "Come here, Bridget," she demanded. "Tell me what she said."

"Well, ma'am…" The little maid edged away from the sleeping compartment, picked her way through peas and carrots and flatware as daintily as her brogans would allow, until she stood directly in front of her employer. She curtsied again—out of habit, or from nerves—thinking she'd rather stand between the armies of blue and gray than between these two women. She swallowed hard before she spoke.

"Well, ma'am, putting it in a nutshell, Miss Amanda said she's bound and determined to marry the rogue."

With the hankie, Mrs. Grenville motioned her even closer. The light in the old woman's pale blue eyes struck Bridget now as more like a glimmer of hope than the earlier spark of anger. "And did she say she loves him?" Mrs. Grenville whispered. "Did my granddaughter say anything about love?"

"Love?" Bridget gulped the word, and then frowned. Had she? Had Miss Amanda, in all her righteous fury, shouted a single word about love?

"No, ma'am. No, she didn't. Not as I recall."

The old woman closed her eyes for a moment and sagged into the upholstery. The hankie drifted from her hand. She sighed. "Precisely what I thought."

Bridget felt an unaccustomed tug of pity for her wealthy employer just then, but before she could offer so much as a comforting cluck of her tongue, the old woman stiffened her spine, rammed her cane into the floor once more, just missing Bridget's foot, and bellowed, "Over my dead body, Amanda Grenville."

Chapter One

North Platte, Nebraska
1874

"Shine your boots, mister?"

"Scat."

"Aw, come on. Them boots of yours could do with a little spit and polish, and I sure could do with a nickel. What do you say, mister?"

"You're a pest."

"I'm enterprising."

"Same thing." Marcus Quicksilver thumbed up the hat that was shading his face in order to get a look at the kid who'd been buzzing around him like a gnat for the past five minutes. He expected to see a chubby, apple-cheeked tycoon, but instead his eyes lit on a skinny boy with smallpox scars and a single suspender that was failing miserably at holding up a pair of too-big pants.

"How old are you, kid?"

"None of your beeswax." The boy aimed his pitted chin into Marcus's face as if it were the barrel of a nicked and battered derringer. "Nine, if you have to know. How old're you?"

"Ninety." Marcus grinned, then quit when his forehead felt as if it were splitting down the middle. He muttered a soft curse, offered up another promise never to touch bar whiskey again, and closed his eyes. "Make that ninety-five."

"You could sure use a shave, mister."

Marcus traced his fingers along his jaw, where the three-day growth was old enough now to feel soft, rather than bristly. "Wait. Don't tell me. You're an enterprising barber, too. Right?"

The boy laughed. "Naw. But for a nickel, I'll set you up with the best danged barber in town."

"No time."

"You waiting for the train?"

"Yep."

The boy fished a gold watch from his pocket, clicked it open and studied its face. "Aw, you got a good twenty minutes before the westbound's due. That ain't enough time for a haircut, maybe, but it's plenty for a shoeshine." He dropped the watch back in his pocket and peered at his potential customer. "Well? How about it?"

Shifting in his chair, Marcus unwound his legs and stretched them across the planking. He stared at his boots a moment, wondering when it had ceased being important to him to have shined boots, a shaved face or well-pressed clothes. Wondering if he was as unkempt inside as he was outside. If his heart and soul were as disreputable as the rest of him. Wondering if he cared.

"You win," he said at last, with a sigh of resignation. "Have at it, kid."

"Yessir!" The boy snapped his soiled chamois rag, knelt, then promptly spat on Marcus's left boot and got to work.

"Mighty nice timepiece for a bootblack," Marcus said casually, looking down at the top of the boy's head. The hair there was yellow and wild as fresh pitched hay, and probably hadn't seen a comb all month. "Did you lift that watch from a fella heading east or west?"

"Neither." He stopped working the shine rag long enough to pat his pocket. "This here watch is a legacy from my pappy. He was rich."

"Uh-huh," Marcus drawled. "What was your rich pappy's name?"

"Joe. Joe Tate."

"Mighty poor speller for a rich man."

The boy glanced up now, his eyes big and quizzical. "What...what do you mean?"

"The initials on your watch, son." Marcus winked. "Somebody named N.F.R. is walking around somewhere right now, scratching his head and wondering whether it's ten minutes till or ten minutes after, I expect."

The pockmarked little face flushed with color, and the boy swallowed hard. "You won't tell anybody, will you, mister?"

"Not as long as you promise me you'll quit stealing watches."

The boy released the chamois cloth just long enough to sketch a quick cross over his heart. "I swear," he said. "Honest I do."

Marcus sighed and closed his eyes again. *I swear. Honest.* It wouldn't surprise him one bit if, ten years from now, he was tracking this kid, once he graduated from watches to payrolls, from petty larceny to felony or worse. Now that was a depressing thought—Marcus Quicksilver still in the saddle riding down lowlifes a decade hence, at the ripe old age of forty-four. God almighty. He'd probably need spectacles to read the Wanted posters.

Not that his keen eyesight was doing him any good at the present. His last three bounties had been pure busts. He'd gotten to El Paso on the heels of Elmer Sweet, a rival manhunter, who'd had himself a great guffaw when he led his thousand-dollar prisoner right past Marcus's nose. A month after that, he'd had the hell kicked out of him by a horse thief named Charlie Clay, who turned out of be the wrong Charlie Clay, one with no bounty on his head. And damned if three days ago Marcus hadn't arrived in Rosebud just in time to watch his quarry take a long drop from a short rope in the town square.

He never used to lose bounties before, Marcus thought. Every man he set out to catch, he caught. Over the past decade or so, he'd earned himself a fearsome reputation. Often as not, if a man heard that Marcus Quicksilver was on his trail, he'd know he was as good as done for and just turn himself in to the nearest available lawman.

Ten years. Twelve. How long had it been? Marcus stared at the yellow-headed kid now, thinking the boy hadn't even been born when he collected that first bounty. Suddenly it seemed like the criminals were getting younger and faster with each passing year, while he was getting older and slower and...

"That's not true, dammit." Marcus said it out loud as he jerked his leg and pushed himself straighter in the chair.

"Hey, watch it," the kid snapped. "Who're you talking to, anyway?"

"Nobody. Mind your own business." Marcus settled back in the chair again, attempting to relax his leg and to clear his aching head of such dismal thoughts.

Hell. If he wasn't getting any younger, he certainly wasn't getting any richer, either. It kept getting harder and harder to save that last few thousand dollars toward the land he'd hoped to buy. Even when he did collect a bounty these days, by the time he got back to Denver he'd be honestly surprised that most of it had slipped through his fingers.

Since they'd hanged Doc Gibbons in Rosebud, there wasn't even sand to slip through Marcus's fingers this time out. Still, here he was sitting in the sunshine at a train depot in Nebraska, getting his boots shined for a nickel when his pockets were very nearly empty. That realization made his head ache all the worse.

"Psst."

He opened a single eye at the sound of the nearby hiss but didn't see anyone, so he settled deeper in the chair.

"Psst. Yoo-hoo. Little boy."

The brisk cloth stopped moving across Marcus's boot when the boy said, "You calling to me, lady?"

Marcus hadn't seen anybody—lady or otherwise—but when he opened both eyes now he caught a glimpse of a little female in fine traveling clothes peeking around a corner of the depot.

"Yes, I am calling to you." She smiled and crooked a gloved finger. "I'd like to speak with you. Would you come here a moment?"

The kid dropped his chamois rag and tore off in her direction, leaving Marcus with one boot shined and the other still covered with trail dust. He started to curse, but then he laughed instead. It wasn't the first time a young entrepreneur had let his business go all to hell when beckoned by a pretty smile. He, himself, had lost a bounty or two when distracted by other, softer pursuits.

He leaned forward, picked up the rag, and went to work on the dusty boot, thinking maybe he'd keep the nickel—Lord knew he could use it—but knowing he wouldn't deduct even a penny from the scrawny little hustler's pay.

"There you go frittering away money again, Marcus," he murmured to himself, shaking his head with dismay more than disgust. "When are you going to learn?"

Both boots looked pretty good, in Marcus's opinion, by the time the kid reappeared a few minutes later. But instead of returning to finish the job he had started, the boy walked right past Marcus's chair, toward the door of the depot.

"Whoa. Wait a minute," Marcus called after him. "You started something here, pal. For a nickel, remember? Here's your shine cloth." Marcus waved it at him.

The scrawny boy stopped for a second, his hand on the door, and then he shrugged. "Aw, that's all right, mister. You keep 'em. The nickel and the rag both. I don't need either one of 'em now." He flashed a lopsided grin before he disappeared inside the depot.

Marcus sat there a minute, shaking his head in bafflement while staring at the dirty and now abandoned rag in his hand. Then, just at his shoulder, a throat was cleared with polite insistence.

"Excuse me, sir. Could you possibly tell me what time it is and how soon the train is due?"

Marcus looked up into a pair of eyes the color of money, the shade of greenbacks fresh from the press. They were bright and clear and rich with promise. Below those was perched a delicate nose, and somewhere in his field of vision there was a mouth that struck him as sensual and eminently kissable, for all its primness. It was only when that mouth twitched with impatience at each corner that he realized he hadn't answered the question it had posed.

He balled up the boot rag, tossed it onto the planking, then tugged his watch from his pocket. "It's five past eleven, miss. The westbound's due any minute now, if it's running on time."

"Good. I certainly hope so." Saying that, she whisked her skirt around and walked back to the edge of the depot, where she'd been standing earlier.

Well, not standing, exactly. It was more like skulking, Marcus thought now, vaguely aware of a little flicker of disappointment in his gut. He was used to women making advances toward him, some shyly asking the time, despite the watches pinned to their breasts, others coming right out and telling him they'd never seen a more handsome devil in all their born days and was he married or promised or going to be in town long? None of them, however, ever skittered away to skulk once the connection had been made. Ever.

He didn't consider himself a ladies' man, exactly, but he wasn't a rock by the side of the road, either, dammit. This little lady's obvious disinterest had definitely taken a chunk out of his male pride. He scowled at his boots a minute and rubbed his jaw before getting up, stretching and sauntering her way.

"Nice day."

He might as well have been a rock, the way she ignored him.

Marcus nudged his hat back a fraction. "You headed west, miss?"

Her pretty face tipped up to his, and those green eyes regarded him with cool disdain, less like a rock now than like something that had crawled out from under one.

The hell with her. Marcus would have turned on his heel and bidden her good-day and good riddance then, if he hadn't noticed the tiny trembling of her lips and the way her fingers shook when she reached up to brush a stray wisp of blond hair off her forehead. She was nervous. No. More like frightened. Scared to death. Only you couldn't tell it by her voice.

"I'm not in the habit of talking with strangers," she told him in clipped, cool tones, then added an icy "Go away," just to make sure he got the point.

He got it, all right, and—scared or not—he was about to give her a view of his departing back when she muttered, almost under her breath, "Where the devil is that little boy? What in the world could be taking him so long?"

"Pardon?"

She sighed and spoke as much to the clapboards on the side of the depot as she did to Marcus. "I asked that young shoeshine boy to purchase a ticket for me. I gave him two twenty-dollar gold pieces and told him to hurry. He ought to be back by now."

Or halfway across the state by now. No wonder the little son of a bitch had been in such a sweat to leave Marcus and his boots and his damn nickel behind.

"Excuse me, miss." Touching a finger to the brim of his hat, Marcus turned and walked away.

* * *

Amanda peeked around the building for a last glimpse of the stranger, whose whiskers hadn't totally concealed a strikingly handsome face. Even the shade of his hat hadn't been able to hide eyes that were bluer than a prairie sky at noon. And now, as he walked away, Amanda couldn't help but notice how wide his shoulders were and how his gunbelt hugged his narrow hips. If eastern dandies had the merest notion how the slant of a bullet-laden gunbelt set a woman's heart to pounding, she was convinced that New York and Connecticut would soon be as wild as the West.

"Oh, my." But even as the wistful sigh escaped her lips, Amanda reminded herself that a woman who was engaged to be married had absolutely no business noticing the physical attributes of men. Strange men, too. Ones who, for all she knew, were only interested in dragging her back to her grandmother and pocketing the five-thousand-dollar reward.

She'd only escaped two days ago, tossing her hastily packed valise from the train as it slowed for the Omaha depot, then jumping after it, while her grandmother snored in her big upholstered chair. "Over my dead body," the old woman had blustered. But as it turned out, over her snoring body had been adequate.

Amanda smiled, still quite pleased with herself for outfoxing the stubborn old vixen. She didn't for a minute believe her grandmother didn't have her well-being at heart, but this time Honoria Grenville was wrong. This time—for the first time in all her twenty-one years—Amanda knew what she wanted and, by heaven, she was going to get it, even if it meant slinking around train depots and begging favors from raggedy little shoeshine boys.

And where was that boy, anyway? Surely he'd had ample time to purchase her ticket by now. She'd have gone into the depot herself, but with those reward posters tacked on every available inch of wall, she didn't dare. Her grandmother must have had them printed within minutes of her escape, then hired half the men in Nebraska to post them.

She paced back and forth now, squinting up at the sun, wishing she'd remembered to take her watch with her when she jumped off the train. If she had remembered it, though, she wouldn't have had an excuse to ask that darkly handsome man for the time, though, would she?

A tiny grin itched at her lips. How shocked her grandmother would be at Amanda's bold behavior. Of course, she hadn't expected the man to pursue the brief conversation. Or her. That worried Amanda considerably. What if he had seen one of the posters?

It suddenly occurred to her then that the little boy might have seen one of the dratted posters inside the depot and run for help. Her fingers twitched at the sides of her skirt, ready to hike it up and make yet another escape, when she heard the soft jingle of spurs just around the corner of the building.

"Here you go, miss."

When the handsome stranger held out a ticket, Amanda snatched it from his hand. *Thank God,* she wanted to wail, and had to swallow hard to keep from showing her incredible relief. But before she could subdue her vocal cords enough to offer a single word, the man quite literally chilled her with those blue eyes of his.

"You're welcome," he said with undisguised sarcasm. "Always glad to help a lady in distress."

What did he think she was, an ungrateful, ill-mannered boor? She was a lady, after all. That was practically her sole credential. And as for distress, well, she'd gotten along just fine for the past two days, despite the fact that she was being hunted like a dog. And, like a dog, Amanda could feel her lips pulling back in a snarl when she said, "I'm most appreciative of your chivalry, sir. Keep the change, won't you?"

"Keep the—?"

Marcus dragged in a calming breath as he looked down at the four silver dollars in the palm of his hand. He'd just sprinted a quarter mile to catch a nine-year-old thief, caught the boy by the scruff of the neck, upended him and shaken the two double eagles loose.

"Don't you ever steal from somebody who trusts you," Marcus had warned him. "Especially a lady who's scared and in trouble and is depending on you for help. You got that, kid?"

After nodding and blubbering about how sorry he was, the little bastard had proved just how much the advice meant to him by kicking Marcus in the shin and hightailing it into a grove of elm trees.

And now here he was—Marcus Quicksilver, knight errant, slayer of dragons and shoeshine boys, humble ticket bearer—being told by his damsel in distress to keep the goddamn change!

He was tempted to swipe the railroad ticket right out of her dainty little hand and tell her to walk wherever it was she was headed and good luck to anybody she met along the way. Instead, he reached out for her hand, turned it over and slapped the four coins into the palm of her glove. Hard.

"My pleasure, miss," he said through clenched teeth. "Enjoy your trip." *And here's hoping I get hit by lightning before I ever set eyes on you again.*

Marcus was still muttering to himself half an hour later as he settled into his seat in the crowded railroad car. He'd had the devil's own time getting his horse, a chestnut mare he'd christened Sarah B., up the ramp of the baggage car and into her narrow stall. Like her dramatically famous namesake, Sarah Bernhardt, the horse was temperamental. She rarely acted up when the two of them were alone on the trail, but seemed to prefer an audience, usually one of chortling, tobacco-chawing geezers who took great delight and purely perverse pleasure in Marcus's predicament.

He sat now with his saddlebags on the empty seat beside him, his arms crossed over his chest and his legs stretched out, anticipating a halfway-decent nap once the train got under way and its rocking motion began. It ought to be fairly quiet until the train pulled into the next meal stop, in Julesburg. He listened to the big locomotive building up its head of steam, felt the floor beneath his boots begin to tremble, then heard the conductor bawl out, "All aboard!" Marcus let his eyes drift closed.

With a little luck and a little nap, he hoped his foul temper would dissipate. Maybe his luck would change, too. He hadn't been lucky of late. Not a bit. Now he was just about broke. Again.

Not that it mattered all that much, Marcus thought wearily. A lifetime ago, when he became a bounty hunter, more out of necessity than by choice, his plan had been to collect enough bounties until he had the cash to buy a decent piece of land and try his hand at farming again. Even try his luck at marriage one more time.

He was no closer to that dream today than he'd been a decade ago, and it made him wonder—when he allowed himself to think about the pain of the past and the blank slate of the future—if maybe he really didn't want that dream to come true.

Hell. Maybe a man was only meant to be lucky once in a lifetime, and his all-too-brief marriage to Sarabeth had been his own brief portion of good luck.

He sighed roughly, shrugging off the haunting memories, settling deeper into the upholstery. Even more than good luck now, he needed the healing power of a good, long sleep.

"Excuse me." Someone jabbed his shoulder. "I said excuse me, sir. Would you be good enough to remove your belongings from this seat?"

Marcus didn't even have to look up. That haughty voice was almost as familiar to him as his own now. Her face, as well. Those money-green eyes would be narrowed on him, cool and demanding, and her luscious mouth would be thin with impatience. He hesitated a moment, as if he hadn't heard her, before he reached over to grab hold of his saddlebags and shove them under his seat.

"Thank you."

"Don't mention it." Marcus angled his hat over his eyes once more and crossed his arms, more determined than ever to fall asleep, despite—or maybe because of—the feverish activity in the adjacent seat.

She sat. She sighed. She got up. She muttered under her breath and then she stepped on Marcus's foot.

"Sorry."

"It's all right," he grunted, his eyes still closed.

"I can't seem to get this hatbox properly situated up here."

He'd just about talked himself out of the chivalry business entirely when the train lurched forward and the damsel and her hatbox both wound up in his lap. It nearly knocked the breath out of him, but Marcus knew it wasn't the fall so much as the feel of her that made his chest seize up.

Suddenly he was caught up in complicated silken

curves and corn-silk hair. He remembered now asking to be hit by lightning, and he was fairly certain that his wish had just been granted. When he swore, it came out as a beleaguered sigh.

"Hold still," he told her as she wriggled on his lap.

Somehow a strand of her blond hair had gotten wound around his shirt button, and the more she squirmed, the worse it got.

"I'm caught!" she squealed.

"Hang on a minute." He tried to unwind the silky lock of hair.

"Ouch!"

"Hold still, dammit."

"Ouch!"

"Aw, hell." Marcus ripped the button from his shirt. "There. You're free."

She scrambled off his lap and managed to step on both his feet before retaking her seat. Once there, she fussed with her curls and her clothes, paying no attention to Marcus and blithely ignoring the hatbox, which was still on his lap.

He counted to ten. Slowly. Practicing the patience of a saint. Nine saints. Ten. He sighed. "Your hatbox, miss."

And just as Marcus had known she would, she looked at him with her rich green eyes, flicked him a small but still imperious smile, and suggested he stash the hat box in the rack overhead.

"By all means, Duchess," he muttered under his breath as he got up to cram the box into the wire rack. He half expected her to hand him a nickel when he sat back down, but she didn't. His imperious duchess—the little brat—was already fast asleep.

"Sleep tight, Your Ladyship," he whispered, knowing his own hopes for a nap had been blasted to smithereens by the mere fact of her presence.

Chapter Two

Her Ladyship slept through two scheduled stops to take on water and one abrupt, unscheduled stop when a herd of southbound buffalo took a full five minutes to cross the Union Pacific tracks. She slept with the faith and innocence of a child, even during the commotion when all the passengers shifted from window to window to watch the passing herd. All the passengers except Marcus—former knight errant—whose sole function at the moment seemed to be in serving Her Ladyship as a pillow.

He didn't mind so much. God, she was pretty. Not that he put a woman's looks above other qualities. He didn't. Sarabeth hadn't been a beauty, by any means, but Marcus had loved her sweet disposition and her sprightly wit and—most of all—her ability to turn any grief or sadness into sunshine. This woman appeared to have the disposition of a she-cat, but she was still a pure pleasure to look at. Marcus liked the warmth of her as she leaned against his shoulder, the feel of her soft hair just brushing his cheek and the occasional riffle of her breath on his jaw. He didn't mind so much being used as a pillow.

What he minded, though, was that when the train finally stopped in Julesburg, Her Ladyship awoke all smiling and refreshed, while he felt like and most probably looked like a rumpled bed. A bed that suddenly remembered that its headboard ached like hell.

She sat up and stretched like a dainty cat, then smiled and exclaimed with innocent surprise, "Oh, I must've dozed off."

"For a minute or two," Marcus said, rolling his neck and his left shoulder to loosen the kinks and get the circulation going again.

She leaned across him then to look out the window, apparently unaware that her elbow was digging into his thigh or that her breast was snug against his upper arm.

"This must be Julesburg," she said, gazing this way and that out the window. "What an interesting-looking little town."

Julesburg? It was a patched-together, put-up-overnight railroad town, half clapboard and half canvas, all of it baking in the afternoon sun. Marcus might have called it peculiar at best or downright ugly at worst, but certainly not interesting.

"I guess that depends on where you're from," he murmured.

"Do you suppose there's a dry goods store here?" she asked, still squinting out the window.

"Probably. Yeah. Sure. I suspect there'd be a

mercantile wedged in somewhere between all those saloons and dance halls.''

"Good." She levered off his leg and gave her curls a little toss. "I need to purchase a few items. Tell the conductor I'll be back shortly, will you? Oh, never mind. I see him up there. I'll tell him myself."

"This is a meal stop," Marcus said. That meant the passengers were going to be given maybe twenty or thirty minutes to wolf down a tough antelope steak and some soggy griddle cakes before the train pulled out again. There was barely enough time to eat, much less locate a privy or do any shopping.

She smiled at him sunnily. She spoke with cheerful dismissiveness. "Yes. Well, enjoy your meal." Then she made her way along the aisle, gave the same smile to the conductor and told him to hold the train for her.

Hold the goddamn train for her! Marcus could hardly believe his ears. And the poor, slack-jawed conductor was still scratching his head, Marcus noticed, when the duchess descended from the car and whisked purposefully past the depot and the dining hall on her way into town.

When she traveled west the first time, to join Angus McCray in Denver a mere two weeks ago, it had been in a private railroad car that her fiancé had procured for her trip. The accommodations had been luxurious, quite what she'd always been accustomed to, but Amanda hadn't seen much of the country through the heavily draped windows of that train.

Once again, she had found herself walled off from the real world. It was a shame, really. There was so much to see. Even this half-built town of Julesburg struck her as interesting.

For all her wealth, she thought, she'd actually experienced very little—next to nothing, really—in the twenty-one years she'd lived under her grandmother's stern gaze and firm thumb. Running away to marry Angus was the only way Amanda knew to escape that silk imprisonment and to remedy her inexperience. And she was still bound and determined to do it. In fact, she was more determined than ever, now that she realized how set Honoria Grenville was on keeping her in her gilded little cage and the lengths to which her grandmother would go to achieve her ends.

"Over *my* dead body, Grandmother," Amanda muttered as she walked into the little mercantile on Julesburg's only street. She called a cheerful good-afternoon to the young female clerk behind the counter, but the girl didn't seem particularly enthusiastic when she merely nodded back.

It was probably her appearance, Amanda thought as she caught a glimpse of herself in a cracked mirror hanging from a nail near the door. Good heavens! Her hair was frightful, and nearly two shades darker than normal from all the dust and cinders on the train. She peered closer into the glass and wiped a smudge from her chin with a dirty kid glove.

It had been two—no, three—days now since she had a proper bath. By the time she got to Denver,

Angus would probably find her, well…pungent, to say the very least.

She lifted a vaguely familiar bottle from a nearby shelf and squinted to read the small print on the label. What she had assumed was lavender toilet water turned out to be a tonic for assorted female complaints, but since being dirty and smelling bad was not among them, she put the bottle back on the shelf, easily returning it to the exact spot, because there was a perfect, dustless circle to mark the place. Amanda frowned and found herself wondering all of a sudden what in the world the stranger on the train had thought of his sooty traveling companion or how he'd even been able to sit next to her, when she must reek to high heaven.

Not that it made any difference, but a little part of her wished she looked a bit more appealing to the handsome man with the deep blue, nearly indigo eyes. She told herself she was being vain and silly, and that if she thought dreamily of anyone's eyes at all, it ought to be those of her fiancé. Angus had lovely eyes. They were… What the devil were they? Brown? Green? A muddled shade somewhere in between?

"I was looking for some eau de cologne, miss," she called out to the salesgirl, who was now leaning both elbows on the counter and gazing out the window instead of being of any assistance. It was far from the behavior Amanda was accustomed to from fawning clerks in fashionable shops in New York, who always seemed to know what she wanted before she herself did, obsequious people who did her grandmother's bidding. She'd always detested all that flattery and fuss, but right now she had to admit she wouldn't mind having a bit of it, if it meant finding what she wanted.

"I can't seem to locate any perfumes or eaux de cologne on these shelves," she said, trying to sound a little less helpless than she felt, attempting not to sneeze at the dust she had disturbed in her search.

"Oh de what?"

"Eau de cologne," Amanda repeated, but when she received only a blank look in return, she added, "Toilet water. Any fragrance will do."

The girl, whose face was as pale and as flat as the moon, continued to stare at Amanda. "You're not from around here, are you?"

Amanda shook her head, attempting to reassure herself that the question was simply a friendly one, born of natural curiosity rather than dark suspicion. After all, not everyone in Nebraska would have seen those posters, and half the people who might have seen them probably couldn't read. She hoped.

"So where're you from?" the girl asked.

"Back east," Amanda answered nonchalantly as she continued to peruse the shelves.

"Whereabouts?"

"Such curiosity." Amanda laughed nervously now, picking up another bottle from the shelf. "Just east," she said, instead of the more truthful *I'm that runaway heiress from New York you've certainly read about. The one with five thousand dollars on her head. The one who hasn't washed her hair or had a bath in days and whom you can probably smell all the way across the store. That one.*

"We don't have any," the girl said.

"Pardon me?"

"I said we don't have any of that oh de stuff they sell in the East. There's a bottle of vanilla extract over there by the pickles." She pointed. "Smells ever so good when you dab it on. Will that do you?"

Breathing a little sigh of relief, Amanda walked to the pickle barrel and picked up the small brown bottle of vanilla. Her hand was shaking. "This will do nicely," she said, trying to hide the tremors from the salesgirl as she fumbled in her handbag, found a gold coin and handed it over the counter.

Just as the girl dropped the coin in a metal cash box, the blast of a whistle shook the dry goods store and rattled the glass in the windows, as well as all the bottles on the shelves.

"Train's leaving," the girl said casually while counting out Amanda's change. "How long you staying in town?"

"What? Oh, no. I'm not staying," Amanda replied, with some amazement, and a touch of amusement that she hoped wouldn't hurt the clerk's feelings. It was one thing to do a bit of necessary shopping in a town like this, but the very idea that she would actually stay here was, well...absurd.

The girl, however, didn't seem to think it was so absurd. She was smiling now, angling her head toward a window in the back of the store. "Oh, yes, you are staying," she said, just as the big black Union Pacific locomotive steamed past.

The smile on the clerk's flat face widened, then twisted into what Amanda might almost have called a sneer when the girl added, "You need to buy anything else—toothbrush, toothpaste, a cake of soap—to see you through till the next train comes?"

Outside the depot, Marcus leaned against a roof post and scraped a match on the sole of his boot. He'd declined the antelope steak and the griddle cakes, but accepted a cigar from a fellow passenger as they both stood contemplating the Wanted posters tacked up just inside the dining hall. Marcus had pointedly avoided looking at the posters in North Platte, hoping to forget for a while that he was a bounty hunter who'd just lost his last bounty to a hangman's noose.

"Take a look at that one," the cigar-smoking fellow had said, pointing to a fresh sheet of paper near the bottom of the array of torn and flyspecked notices. "Now that would be some catch, wouldn't it?"

Marcus had been reading the Wanted poster for a bank robber named Ed Caragher, alias Chick McGee, alias Robert LePage, and wondering how the culprit kept his monickers straight when his gaze drifted to where the man was pointing. Reward, it said, in bold black print, and just beneath that Runaway Heiress. Of course, as soon as Marcus read the description—blond hair, green eyes, small stature, delicate build—he knew exactly who his damsel in distress was. Some catch, indeed.

He'd done his damnedest then to hide the predatory smile tugging at his mouth. "She's a hundred miles from here, if she cut loose from the old lady three days ago," he told the man beside him. "Probably already in Denver by now, if that's where she was headed."

The man had sighed, and Marcus had echoed it. A five-thousand-dollar sigh.

"I sure could've used that reward the old Grenville woman's offering." The man had lifted his shoulders in a shrug. "Oh, well. I expect you're right about that girl not being anywhere near here. Enjoy that cigar. Nice talking to you." He'd shrugged again and began to walk away.

"Thanks. You too. And you know what they say," Marcus had called after him. "Easy come. Easy go."

They also said something about a bird in the hand, Marcus thought as he glanced around to make sure no one was watching when he surreptitiously took the poster from the wall, folded it and stashed it in his pocket.

That explained the duchess's imperious behavior, especially her blithe request that the conductor hold the train. Amanda Grenville, described in the poster as the sole heiress to the Grenville Ironworks, was used to riding in private railroad cars that did indeed come or go at her command. Marcus was sure it hadn't even occurred to her that the train wouldn't wait. After all, time and tide and probably even the Almighty tended to stand still for the obscenely rich.

But little Miss Amanda Grenville was way out of her element now, no longer in that ethereal place where beautiful, spoiled goddesses snapped their dainty fingers to halt trains. Little Amanda was without a clue as to how the real world worked. She needed help even more than she knew. Poor little, rich little Amanda.

Marcus smiled. A slow, smooth, self-congratulatory smile. Poor little Amanda was in dire need of a knight in shining armor, and he—Marcus Quicksilver, hero, helper, honest, brave and true—was more than ready to fill that particular bill.

There had been a stampede of diners when the conductor called, "All aboard," but there had been no one rushing from the opposite direction of the town, no breathless heiress hurrying to catch the train, so Marcus had hastily retrieved the hatbox and his saddlebags, and then he had led Sarah B. from her stall in the baggage car. The mare had been so happy to leave the train that she was as docile as a kitten, and she stood at a nearby hitching rail now, placidly whisking her tail at flies.

Marcus felt almost placid himself as he leaned against the post and lit his cigar. Five thousand dollars! The biggest bounty he'd ever brought in had been six years ago, when he captured Herman Culley, a murderer with two thousand dollars on his head. The local authorities in Texas had wanted him dead or alive, but when Marcus obliged them—not to mention spared them the time and expense of a trial—by bringing Culley in draped over his saddle, the politicos had reneged on the two thousand and only paid him fifteen hundred.

Five thousand dollars. There'd be no reneging with old lady Grenville, Marcus was certain. Five thousand was a drop in the bucket to someone like her. And to him? To him it was perhaps the future that he'd spent the past decade avoiding. Five thousand could buy a lot of land. Good land. By God, maybe it was time.

Marcus blew a stream of cigar smoke off to his left and picked a fleck of tobacco from his lower lip. He was intensely aware of the folded poster in his pocket. It already felt like folded greenbacks, and he wondered if the Grenville woman would come across with cash or a check. Of course, he hadn't done anything to earn it yet, he reminded himself. Fantasizing about the reward was one thing. Bringing Miss Amanda Grenville in was something else entirely.

He was glad now that she'd gotten off the train. That saved him forcing the decision upon her. The fewer people who saw her, the better, because it was as sure as sunrise that every manhunter west of the Mississippi had already dropped whatever he was doing and was hot on little Amanda's trail. It was also likely that every amateur with a five-thousand-dollar dream was searching for her, too.

For a minute, Marcus seriously considered tying her up and nailing her in a crate neatly addressed to

Granny Grenville. That would not only garner him the reward, but would also put an end to hatboxes, snagged buttons, sharp elbows and all the other irritations the lady just naturally provoked. But it would also mean the end of those glorious green eyes and that fetching little mouth and...

Well, hell. It just wouldn't be sporting, Marcus told himself. Half the pleasure of being a bounty hunter was the chase, in his estimation. Most of the pleasure, if he was to be brutally honest. The money had never meant all that much to him.

What was even better, he thought now, as he watched little Miss Amanda Grenville come flying down the street in his direction, was having his quarry run right into his arms. Into his *waiting, helpful arms.* Marcus took a last pull from his cigar, then dropped it and ground it under his heel.

"The train left!" She skidded to a halt beside him, and hardly had enough breath to get the words out. Her pretty face was flushed and damp, but those green eyes were dry and hot.

"Right on time, too." Marcus bit down on a grin as he shifted off the post and gestured toward the fabric-covered parcel not too distant from his feet. "There's your hatbox, Duchess. Don't bother to thank me."

If she heard him, she didn't react. Nor did she express a tad of gratitude. Not that Marcus expected a goddess to be grateful to a mortal. Her gaze moved frantically around the platform. She waved her hands wildly. "Where's my valise?"

He shrugged.

"I need my valise!" she wailed, not so much to him as to the Fates in general. "All my clothes are in my valise. And my hairbrush, too. And...and..." Her foot shot out and sent the hatbox flying. "All my money's in my suitcase, dammit. What am I supposed to do now?"

Then she paced back and forth for a minute like a tiny tornado on the platform, before she plopped down in a heap of skirts and started chewing on a nail, muttering to herself as if Marcus weren't there.

He stood silently, watching the way the afternoon sun warmed her hair, wondering what it would look like unpinned and spilling over her shoulders like a yellow shawl, imagining the delicacy of those shoulders, the perfect paleness of the skin, the...

"Did you miss the train, too?"

Her plaintive question brought him out of his reverie and put an end to his foolish, misdirected thoughts. "Yep," he said. "Looks like we're in the same boat, so to speak."

She looked up at him, shading her glorious green eyes against the sun, pondering him with her brow furrowed and the tip of her pink tongue passing over her lower lip. No doubt she was wondering if she could trust him. For a minute she reminded Marcus of a lost little girl, rather than a pampered and spoiled runaway heiress. His heart gave an extra and very peculiar thump, and he suddenly felt like fighting a grizzly bear on her behalf, or stopping a train by throwing his body across the tracks. Doing all those foolish and heroic things he would have done so gladly for Sarabeth all those years ago.

"Help me," she said. "I'll pay you."

Pay him? Marcus's heart gave a tiny pop, like a soap bubble. Pay him!

"Help me catch up with the train," she said. "Then, when I retrieve my luggage, I'll reward you handsomely."

He shouldn't be so put out, he told himself. Or so confoundedly disappointed by her offer. After all, money and handsome rewards were what this was all about, weren't they? He wanted to be paid—and paid well, too, dammit—didn't he?

"You might try a simple thank-you," he growled.

"Then you will help me?" She scuttled up from the platform and looked up into his face eagerly, holding her breath while she awaited his reply.

Marcus made her wait, just because he felt cussed and mean and bruised, even though he had every intention of *helping* her, of sticking to little Miss Amanda Grenville like glue from here on out.

"Say please."

Those big green eyes blinked. "I beg your pardon?"

"I said say please. You know, that little word that often accompanies requests." He arched an eyebrow. "Surely you've heard it before, even if you haven't used it yourself, brat."

Her mouth formed an astonished and perfect little O then, and her eyes flashed.

"Say it," he coaxed.

When her mouth finally closed, her teeth were clenched so hard she could barely get the word out. "Pl-please."

"That's better." Marcus grinned and stepped closer to her. Just then the breeze shifted, blowing up dust and cinders from the track, along with a powerful fragrance that seemed to emanate from Miss Amanda Grenville herself. He sniffed, baffled for a moment. The rich women he'd known—a few over the years, and far less rich than Amanda—had smelled like exotic flowers, jasmine and tuberose and lily of the valley, or like musky she-cats in hot jungles. But this woman suddenly smelled like... like...

Still baffled, he sniffed again, then took a half step back, eying her suspiciously. "What the hell is that?"

"What is what?"

"That smell. That perfume you're wearing."

Her chin lifted imperiously. "It's vanilla, if you must know. I think it's rather nice. Fresh. And...and wholesome."

"Wholesome, huh? You smell like a damn cake."

"I'd suggest that you cease breathing, sir, but since I'm in need of your assistance..."

Marcus shook his head. He'd have to stay downwind of her, that was for sure. Or see that she got a bath. "All right. You wait here while I wire ahead to the next station and have them pull your luggage off the train." He started toward the depot door.

"Wait a minute. I'll need to know what it looks like, this valise of yours. Any identification on it?"

"It's a brown alligator satchel with double handles and the initials *A.G.* in gold on one side."

"*A.G.?*"

She blinked, flummoxed for a second by her admission, before the runaway heiress recovered her wits and called out, "Yes. *A.G. A* as in Alice and *G* as in…as in Green. Alice Green."

"Right." Well, she was fairly quick on her feet, he thought. He would've preferred a slower-witted bounty. "You're sure about that?"

"Of course I'm sure," she snapped.

Marcus touched the brim of his hat, giving her an encouraging little salute from the door. Little Alice Green would probably need it, since she wasn't going to be seeing that monogrammed suitcase again in the foreseeable future. Nor would she be traveling in the style to which she was accustomed. Nor would she be smelling like a rich, rich rose.

Inside the depot, he walked right past the telegrapher to the counter, where he used most of his remaining cash to buy two tickets on the next westbound stage.

Chapter Three

The crowded stagecoach was another new experience for Amanda. She thought she rather liked it. Well, except for the stifling heat and the cramped quarters and more dust than she'd ever dreamed existed, all of which combined to intensify the now cloying scent of vanilla that she had tried so hard to rub off at the depot after being compared to bakery goods.

She and Marcus—he'd introduced himself at last, saying, "Well, Miss Alice Green, I go by Marcus Quicksilver"—had been the last ones to board the stage, and as a consequence they hadn't been able to sit together, which irritated Amanda at first, but now was pleasing her enormously, because it allowed her to look long and hard at the handsome man who had offered her his assistance, albeit grudgingly. Well, she could hardly expect eastern gallantry from such a rugged-looking, gunbelt-wearing, unshaven westerner, she reminded herself.

The minute they settled into their opposite seats,

Marcus had tipped his hat down and, to all appearances, fallen fast asleep. Amanda perused what she could see of his face—the dark whiskers shadowing his cheeks and jaw, the hard curve of his mouth, which hardly slackened in sleep, the sculpted tip of his nose. Her gaze kept drifting lower, to the place where the button was missing on his chambray shirt, where a hint of soft, dark hair showed through the open placket between the edges of his leather vest.

Each time she peeked, a little curl of longing unfurled in the pit of her stomach. That, too, was a sensation she'd never felt before, but then, she'd never seen a man's bare chest before, either. She wondered if Angus was similarly furry, and rather hoped so. Not that it mattered. Not one whit. Only…

"Sorry if I'm crowding you, honey. It's these wide shoulders of mine, you know. They don't make coaches for fellas built like me."

Amanda smiled weakly at the man sitting to her right. Sitting *on* her right was really a much better description, considering that the large man had a good portion of her skirt beneath him. She edged a bit closer to the window on her left, and could have sworn the man followed her over, crunching additional yardage of her skirt beneath him as he moved.

"I go by train ordinarily," he said—as if she had inquired. "More room for my samples and such. I'm a salesman, you know. Ladies' undergarments." A wet laugh burbled up in his throat. "Unmentionables, you know."

Amanda glanced sideways at her seatmate, whose

breath smelled of peppermint and onions, an altogether unpleasant mixture, particularly when combined with her own vanilla scent. A pair of muttonchop whiskers flourished on the man's cheeks. His plaid suit and paisley vest could have clothed a small family, with enough fabric left over to drape and swag an end table. She offered the coolest of smiles, along with a polite little hum, to acknowledge that she'd heard him and to discourage any further mention of unmentionables.

"Yeah," he said, obviously indifferent to her chilly response. "Been in this business going on five years now. The name's Linus Dobson." He stuck out a huge, hammy hand. "Glad to make your acquaintance." Then he winked as he added in a decidedly smarmy tone, "And may I say you smell ever so good, honey?"

Unwilling to be rude, especially in such close quarters, Amanda clasped his hand. It was flabby and damp as suet. "How do you do?"

He smiled broadly. "I do all right, if I do say so myself. So. If you don't mind my asking, what's a pretty girl like yourself doing traveling all alone? Visiting relatives, are you?"

"Well, no. Actually, I'm..." Extracting her hand from his with a determined tug, Amanda cast about in her brain, desperate for a reply. What was she doing traveling alone, other than running away? His guess, she concluded, was as good as any she might invent for herself, so she nodded and said, "Yes, I am visiting relatives, as a matter of fact. A sister and brother-in-law and five nieces and nephews. In... um...Wyoming.''

"Pretty country, Wyoming. I've been there quite a bit myself. Why, given the opportunity, I bet I could show you some sights that'd be like none you'd ever seen before.'' He wedged his elbow into her rib cage then, adding, "Snap your garters, for sure, little lady.''

"My, my.'' It would have been nice to have a book in which to bury her nose, Amanda thought, but since she didn't, and since there was no entertainment other than staring at Marcus Quicksilver's chest, she decided to indulge her hammy companion. She'd had few opportunities to converse with members of the opposite sex, much less to twit one of them. In her estimation, Linus Dobson could do with a bit of twitting.

She smiled and batted her eyes at him. "My goodness. Snap my garters, would they?''

"Yes, indeedy. Why, honey, you might think you've seen some natural wonders back east, but I'm here to tell you—''

He didn't get a chance to tell her anything right then, because the stage lurched to a squealing, bone-rattling standstill.

"Stretch stop!'' the driver shouted. "Everybody out who's getting out. Five minutes you got, and not one second more.''

"Well, I'm for that,'' the big salesman said as he reached across Amanda's lap to open the door. "Pardon me, honey.'' He stepped on her skirt and both of her feet before he squeezed himself out of the coach, then he turned and held out his meaty hands. "Let's go, honey. Here. Let me help you."

"Everybody out!" the driver called again, more insistently this time. Gracious, Amanda would have thought the vehicle was on fire, the way the man was yelling.

By now the other passengers had all obediently exited the coach through the opposite door. All but one. Marcus Quicksilver was still napping under the brim of his hat, and he didn't even flinch when the driver banged on the sidewalls and bellowed another warning. "Four minutes now. Everybody out. Time's a-wasting, and we ain't stopping again till Sidney."

Amanda sighed, deciding if she didn't exit the coach immediately, the driver might be tempted to pull her out by the scruff of her neck. She levered herself up toward the open door, and before she could say, "No, thank you. I can manage on my own," to the salesman, he had already clasped his big hands around her rib cage, with his sausagelike thumbs suspiciously close to her breasts.

"There you go, little lady." He set her down on the ground, but didn't let her go until he'd given her a lusty ten-fingered squeeze. "Well, if you'll pardon me now, I believe I'll just walk a ways and give the old limbs a good stretching."

"Yes. Of course." *Good riddance.* Amanda gave her bodice a tug and smoothed her hands across her wrinkled skirt. What a sight she must be, looking rather like a waffle now, while smelling like a cake.

"Don't waste your time," came a deep voice from behind her. "That skirt's going to look a whole lot worse before it looks any better."

She whirled around to see Marcus Quicksilver leaning against the side of the coach, eyeing her rather peculiarly before he bent and reached to pluck a weed from the side of the road.

"On the other hand, Miss Alice Green," he drawled, "you could always have your fat friend sit on your skirt and get yourself a real good pressing."

Marcus stuck the blade of grass between his teeth, irritated with himself because he was irritated with her. How Amanda Grenville carried on with fellow passengers—men in particular—shouldn't have mattered to him one bit, as long as she didn't give away her identity. How she cozied up to a seatmate or what she said shouldn't have bothered Marcus. But it did. It irked him no end that she'd allow some peddler—some itinerant buffoon like that Dobson—to make advances. Didn't she realize there would be consequences to her flirtatious behavior? Didn't she care?

He kicked a boot into a wheel rim. Damnation. How did little Miss Amanda imagine she'd ever make it to Denver without getting caught if she took up with and made sport of every Tom, Dick, Harry and Linus along the way?

"I see your nap didn't do anything to improve

your disposition, Mr. Quicksilver,'' she said, tilting her pointed little chin up into his face.

"Nope. My mood's about as wrinkled as your skirt.'' Marcus bit down harder on the weed. His head was starting to ache again, and he could feel a vein throbbing in his temple, threatening to burst. Not only was Amanda Grenville a spoiled brat, but now, on top of that, she was proving to be a careless and outrageous flirt. Everything about the little blonde had begun to nettle Marcus, and yet he found her impossible to ignore.

She dismissed him now, quite thoroughly and efficiently, the way a goddess would dismiss a mortal, with a brusque little cluck of her tongue. "I'll be so glad to get my luggage when we arrive in Sidney,'' she said, turning her full attention back to various pleats and folds of fabric.

"Uh-huh,'' he answered noncommittally, thinking she did look a bit more bedraggled now than she had earlier today, when he first saw her skulking outside the depot in North Platte. Traveling, especially by stagecoach, tended to wear people down. Women in particular. This woman, who wasn't used to prairie heat or road dust or old jolting coaches. She'd probably never gone anywhere without at least one maid to see to her every need and comfort.

And yet here she was with no one to take care of her. She'd run away from all that, hadn't she? Or so the Wanted poster claimed. Marcus wondered why. Then he scowled and wondered why he wondered. What difference did it make why she'd abandoned a life of great wealth and perpetual ease? Once Marcus delivered her to her grandmother and collected his well-deserved five-thousand-dollar reward, he'd never see Amanda Grenville again, much less think of her.

He plucked the weed from his mouth, tossed it to the ground and went to see about Sarah B., who was tethered, and not too happily, either, to the back of the coach.

"Two minutes, folks," the driver called down from his lofty perch, where he was all but invisible behind a blue cloud of cigarette smoke. "If we push it, we'll be getting into Sidney just about dark."

While Marcus readjusted Sarah B.'s bridle and reins, he spoke to the mare softly, apologizing to her for making her run behind a dust-making stage, promising her a warm stall and a fat bag of oats that night.

"Mmm… A fat bag of oats," sounded a wistful voice close by. "I'm so hungry even that sounds delicious."

Marcus gave a last yank to the knot in the reins, then braced his forearms on the mare's neck. Bedraggled or not, Miss Amanda Grenville looked beautiful in the mellow light of late afternoon.

"When did you eat last?" he asked her, then watched while her smooth brow furrowed and her eyes turned a deeper, thoughtful green as she pondered his question.

"Yesterday. No. The day before that." She gave a mournful little laugh. "To tell you the truth,

Quicksilver, I'm not sure. But I know I must be famished if a bag of oats sounds appealing."

"Here." Marcus unbuckled his saddlebag and withdrew a piece of jerked beef. "This is a little better than oats."

She took the mahogany-colored dried meat and stared at it a moment, turning it this way and that, before she looked back at Marcus. "What is this? Leather?"

"Edible leather. It's beef jerky. Go ahead. Try it, brat. If it doesn't fill you up, at least it'll keep your mouth occupied for a while."

She studied it some more, bending it, bringing it to her nose and sniffing it. Anyone would have thought he was trying to poison her, Marcus thought disgustedly. Ten to one she'd hand it back to him and refuse to even try it. He watched in silence, then, as her pretty mouth twitched and her front teeth tested the dessicated meat. She tugged at it like a terrier then, to no avail.

Marcus retrieved a second piece of jerky from his saddlebag. "Not that way," he said. "Like this." He clenched the tough morsel in his back teeth and ripped off a good-size portion, which he proceeded to chew.

"Oh." She eyed the dried beef as if it were about to bite her back before she sank her molars into it and nearly growled as she sheared off a piece. Then she chewed. And chewed some more. Soon she was staring off into the distance, grinding her teeth as if that had become her lifelong occupation.

Marcus had never seen anyone quite so dogged about food. Or so unsuccessful. "Spit it out," he told her.

"Mpht," she answered.

He motioned toward a nearby clump of weeds. "Go on and spit it out before you wear down your damn teeth."

She spat as if she'd never done that before, either, and walked back dabbing a hankie to her lips. "That was terrible," she exclaimed. "I believe I'd prefer eating a roof shingle."

"I expect a person has to develop a taste for jerked beef," he said, more amused than apologetic. He wasn't all that fond of jerked beef himself.

"Well, I'd much rather redevelop my taste for rare roast beef or oysters. Now those a person doesn't even have to chew." Her eyes lit up, and she smiled brightly. "Oh, do you suppose there will be a decent restaurant in Sidney?"

"Probably. Do you suppose you can afford to eat in it, brat?"

"Stop calling me that," she snapped. "And yes, of course I can afford it, once I get my suitcase back. I might even consider treating you to supper, Quicksilver. What do you think of that?"

She spun around and walked away, treating Marcus to a view of her haughty backside. He shook his head. Actually, he thought they'd be lucky to eat a boiled egg on a slice of moldy bread this evening, but there was no point in telling her right now, then having to watch her sit and sulk for the next few hours till they arrived in Sidney. The duchess would find out soon enough that her suitcase was still riding the rails west, along with all the money in it.

As was customary on stagecoaches, all the passengers returned to their previous seats when the driver shouted that their stretch stop was over and that anybody who wasn't back inside the vehicle in half a minute would be left behind. "No exceptions, ladies."

Linus Dobson had lumbered back from his stroll just in time to offer Amanda a boost up into the coach, and then the burly oaf had trampled her toes once more before reclaiming his seat beside her. Marcus Quicksilver sat directly opposite from her again, and even though it was now somewhat dim inside the vehicle, he retreated once more beneath his hat brim.

Despite the gathering dark, however, Amanda still had a fairly good view of his half-open shirt, with its exceedingly distracting fur, which, at present, she found much more appealing than his personality. The next time he called her a brat, she decided, she'd show him just how contrary she could be, by launching her foot into his shinbone.

"Well, well. Here we are again," Linus Dobson said, nudging her with an elbow while sending a moist breeze of peppermint and onions in her direction. "Say, I don't believe I caught your name, honey."

Here we are again, Amanda thought morosely.

The gnawing sensation in her stomach had gotten worse after her attempt to chew the dessicated beef, and it didn't help one bit when the hunger pangs were coupled with those peculiar flickers every time her eyes drifted below Marcus's collarbone.

She was missing her grandmother, too, all of a sudden, which struck her as odd, when she was doing her best to escape the old woman's clutches. But she'd lived with Honoria Grenville nearly all her life, ever since her parents—Joshua Grenville and his young wife—perished in a steamboat explosion while vacationing on the Rhine. Her grandmother had really been more like a mother to her for twenty years. She was a stubborn, overbearing mother, however, and one who refused to let Amanda make decisions for herself in even the smallest of matters.

But she had decided, hadn't she? When she wound up quite by accident and quite alone in a carriage with the dashing Angus McCray, and when he proposed marriage on the spot, Amanda had accepted. Just like that. Her decision, she knew, had less to do with love than with independence, but her fiancé was a worldy and very handsome man, and Amanda was certain she would come to love him in time. Anyway, how could she love Angus? Good gracious, she barely knew him.

In all honesty, she probably knew her portly seatmate as well as she knew her fiancé. The salesman was poking his elbow in her ribs again.

"I said I didn't quite catch your name, little lady," he repeated.

She really ought to ignore him, she thought. He

was being outrageously forward, even more so than before, and Amanda would have been perfectly justified in pretending to have suddenly gone deaf to his overtures. But she was eager to be distracted from the heat and dust in the coach, not to mention her growling stomach and Marcus Quicksilver's intriguing chest. So she offered Linus Dobson a tiny, tempting smile.

"My name?" She blinked innocently. "Why don't you try to guess?"

A small chuff of surprise caught in the peddler's throat, and then an oily grin spread across his lips. "Oh, I see. You're one of those that likes to play games, honey. All right. Let me get a real good look at you." He poked his straw hat higher on his brow, then angled his head and narrowed his eyes, studying her. "You don't strike me as a Jane or a Ruth. Not a Mary, either. Am I right?"

Amanda fashioned a smile that told him he was not only right, but amazingly clever to boot.

The salesman's gaze roved from her face to her bodice, paused there for a long leer, then came back to her face. "You're a tiny little female. Real delicate. Mind you, I can tell despite your ruffles and pleats, being in the business I'm in. Ladies' underclothes, remember? But petite as you are, I'd be inclined to guess you've got a longish name." He scratched one muttonchop thoughtfully. "Hmm... Elizabeth, maybe?"

"No."

"Eleanor?"

Amanda shook her head.

"I'm getting warm, though. Right?"

Warm? Yes, Amanda thought the man was getting quite warm, actually. His beefy face was flushed a bright pink now, and several beads of sweat were glistening above his upper lip. Suddenly she didn't think that playing a guessing game with this man had been such a good idea. First of all, he was coming frightfully close to her true name. And second—worse—Linus Dobson seemed to be playing an altogether different game now as he shifted his bulk in the seat and thrust a huge arm around Amanda's shoulders, pulling her closer, very nearly crushing her against him while attempting to suffocate her with the scent of peppermint and onions.

"Whatever your name is, honey, you're the prettiest little thing I've seen in weeks. What do you say when we get to Sidney, the two of us...well..." He bent his head and whispered, his hot, foul breath and indecent proposal both almost scorching Amanda's ear.

She felt her jaw dropping and her mouth framing an indignant but speechless O. She couldn't utter so much as a squeak, but as it turned out, she didn't have to, because just then a low, lethal voice cut through the gathering dark inside the coach.

"How 'bout changing seats with me, pal? I'd like to sit next to my wife."

Linus Dobson moved fairly fast for a man of his enormous bulk. First he wrenched his arm from around Amanda and then he shoved up from the seat, hovering there all scrunched up in his huge plaid suit while Marcus—with catlike grace and speed—slid across the narrow aisle and into the space beside Amanda.

"I…I didn't know," the salesman babbled, cramming his hips and shoulders into Marcus's vacated seat. "How could I have known? She…she didn't say anything."

"I'm saying it." Marcus's voice was as sharp and as cold as the blade of a knife, and then, as if to make his point, he reached out and scooped up Amanda's hand. His grip was hard and tense at first, almost hurtful, but it slackened immediately to a gentle possession.

"I'm…I'm sorry, ma'am," Linus Dobson said. "I'm truly sorry."

There was a tremor in his voice, and the poor wretch looked absolutely terrified, as if he wished he could dig his shoulders so far into the horsehair seat that he'd simply disappear. Amanda stole a glance to her right, toward the man who'd struck such abject fear into the peddler and turned him instantly from boisterous rogue to quivering wreck. Even in the coach's dim interior, she could see that Marcus Quicksilver's face seemed dark and hard as cast iron. His mouth bore a harsh, even cruel curve, and his blue eyes had deepened to a fearful midnight hue. Amanda found herself thinking that she was enormously relieved that this thundercloud in human form wasn't angry with her.

But then it occurred to her suddenly that it was she who had every reason to be angry with him. How dare he interrupt her conversation and interject himself into her affairs! The nerve of the man! The absolute gall! Did he think she couldn't look out for herself when an idiot like Linus Dobson made advances? Did he consider her a helpless dolt? On top of all that, the man had had the sheer, unmitigated audacity to proclaim himself her husband! Her husband, of all things!

"I have a bone to pick with you, Mr. Quicksilver," she hissed.

"Not now, Mrs. Quicksilver," he growled.

Deep in his corner across the way, Linus Dobson gasped, as if someone had just thumped him soundly between the shoulder blades. He stared stupidly across the aisle for a second, then inserted a finger beneath his collar, as if trying to obtain enough air to speak. "Quick—Quicksilver, did you say?"

"That's right," Amanda snapped.

The salesman made a little strangling noise now in the back of his throat. "That wouldn't be the Quicksilver out of Denver, would it? Marcus Quicksilver? The bounty hunter?"

"The—?" Before she could get the next word out, Marcus's grip tightened on her hand, pressing her fingers together painfully.

When he spoke, his voice dropped to a menacing register. "I think we've all done about enough jabbering for a while. Let's just sit real quiet now and enjoy the rest of our ride, shall we?"

It wasn't a question, but rather a cold command that Linus Dobson immediately obeyed, snapping his gaze to the window, apparently discovering a sudden fascination with the dark landscape outside the coach. Amanda, on the other hand, wasn't about to be stifled quite so easily.

"Are you?" she asked in a voice intended for Marcus alone. "Are you what he claimed?" She was hoping—oh, God, how she was praying—the answer would be no. "Tell me, Marcus. Tell me this minute, or I'll scream. I swear I will."

"Yes," he whispered harshly, and his fingers curled more tightly around her hand. "Now be still."

She was still. Small and still as a mouse in a trap, her fingers in the iron grip of his. Amanda felt as if her heart had been punctured. Hot tears welled up and began to sting her eyes. She'd been caught! All along she'd been caught, and she hadn't even known it!

Chapter Four

It was dark when they pulled up in front of the torchlit stage office in Sidney.

"End of the line," the driver yelled. "Everybody out. Don't forget your hats, gents. Ladies, mind your gloves and parasols."

Linus Dobson didn't even say goodbye. After almost exploding from the coach, the salesman snatched up his valise and sample cases the second the driver removed them from the boot, and disappeared into the night. Marcus Quicksilver had let go of Amanda's hand only long enough to grasp her waist and help her out of the stage. Then he led her around to the rear of the vehicle, where he began to untie his horse.

"Don't do anything foolish, Miss Grenville, like trying to run away," he warned her while he drew a leather rein through a round metal hoop.

"Oh, I wouldn't dream of it." Amanda crossed her arms and chewed on her lower lip. For the past hour in the coach, once the shock of her capture— the insult of it!— had worn off, she'd come to a few conclusions about her predicament. Reluctantly, she'd conceded that she'd been outwitted by the notorious bounty hunter. But he was, after all, a *bounty* hunter, which meant that money was important to him. And money, right now, was her only weapon.

Amanda glanced at the gun nestled against his hip, the gun that only hours before had thrilled her with its implied danger. But now the sight of it made her shiver imperceptibly, until she decided that he'd never use it on her. The dratted posters hadn't said Dead or Alive, for heaven's sake, and any reasonable human being would have to know that Honoria Grenville wanted her granddaughter returned in one piece. One unscathed piece. No. Marcus Quicksilver would never use that lethal-looking weapon on her. Amanda was convinced of that. She, on the other hand, had no qualms whatsoever about using her own weapon on him.

"My grandmother is offering five thousand dollars for my return, Quicksilver," she said, taking a step or two in his direction, pinning him with her gaze, unafraid of him now, thinking that perhaps he should be afraid of her. "It's a very generous reward. You already know that, of course. But I'll be even more generous and give you even more if you don't take me back to her."

He didn't answer, but continued to unfasten the leather straps that bound the horse to the stagecoach. The mare nodded her head agreeably, as if Amanda's offer had a certain appeal, but the bounty hunter didn't respond, didn't shrug or even send so much as a questioning glance in Amanda's direction.

"Did you hear me, Quicksilver?" she demanded. "I offered—"

Now he snapped his head toward her and growled, "I heard you. Hell, all of Sidney and half of Nebraska probably heard you. Do you want to get to Denver or not, brat?"

Brat again! Amanda fought down the urge to launch her foot into his kneecap or leave the imprint of her hand on his handsome face. "Yes, of course I want to get to Denver, but—"

"Then shut the hell up." He backed the horse away from the coach, snagged Amanda's arm just above the elbow and started down the street. "Come on."

It wasn't as if she had any choice, she thought, while she trotted along beside him, doing her best to keep her feet from catching in her hem. The town—another combination of clapboard and canvas—was dark, for the most part, except for a saloon here and there where music and yellow lamplight spilled through open windows and doors. The bounty hunter stopped at a hitching rail, where he released his grip on Amanda in order to tether the mare, who whinnied in protest.

Amanda felt like whinnying, too, as she stood nearby, massaging her sore, probably bruised arm. She looked around her for a possible avenue of escape, and her gaze lit on the sign over the building directly behind her.

"The railroad depot," she exclaimed. Thank God. Now she could claim her bag, change her clothes, brush her hair and put some of the gold coins stashed in a satin side pocket to good use. "I'll retrieve my valise and pay you a hundred dollars in advance for your services, Quicksilver. Let's go."

She snatched up her skirts, whisked through the depot door and assumed it was she who was leading the bounty hunter until her feet suddenly went out from under her and her backside made abrupt contact with the hard wooden seat of a bench.

"Wait here," he told her. "Keep your head down and your mouth shut. You got that?"

Amanda got it, all right. How could she not, especially when she saw that his eyes had turned that stormy color again and his right hand had come to rest on the butt of his gun? He wouldn't use it, she reminded herself. He wouldn't dare. The gesture was merely meant to frighten her, to reinforce the notion that it was he who was in control. For the time being, anyway.

"If you'll just get my bag for me, perhaps we can discuss this over a nice supper," she said, as sweetly and as calmly as she could. "My treat."

"Right." Marcus gritted his teeth as he strode toward the stationmaster's window. Maybe he should have wired ahead to have the luggage taken off the train. Even with the telltale initials on the bag, at least there was cash inside. It might have been worth the risk, he thought, but it was too late now.

He glanced back to make sure the runaway heiress was still firmly planted on the bench where he'd left her, then jabbed his finger down on the brass bell on the counter. The stationmaster appeared, looking as if Marcus had just rousted him from a good night's sleep, then took forever to wipe his spectacles and to fit them on the bridge of his nose before he managed to squint through his little wired window. "Can I help you, mister?"

"How soon's the next train west?"

The man yawned and blinked and scratched his jaw. "Lemme go see," he said, just before disappearing from the little cage.

Marcus turned around, angled his elbows back on the counter and surveyed the waiting room of the depot. Her Ladyship was still right where he'd left her, sitting like an aggrieved princess on her wooden throne, glaring an occasional green dagger in his direction. He found himself wishing she wasn't quite so pretty when he noticed how she drew the gazes of the several male passengers scattered through the room. Two young cowhands bent their heads together and exchanged what appeared to be appreciative whispers. Not far from them, on another bench, a weasel-faced fella in a checkered suit seemed particularly intrigued with Amanda, and kept peeking, all beady-eyed, around the edge of his newspaper to get a better look at her.

In response, Marcus could feel the muscles in his shoulders bunch and all his nerves snap to attention, and he wasn't sure whether his reaction was male and territorial or whether it was purely business. Business, he told himself. Professional caution. That was all it could be, after all. Amanda Grenville was his bounty. She wasn't his woman. Thank God.

A sleepy voice came from the wire cage. "Next

train's due within an hour. It's an immigrant train, though. Next regular one's tomorrow morning.''

An immigrant train! Marcus could just imagine Her Ladyship's expression when forced to travel with the teeming masses. He glanced back at her now, then swore when he saw that the weasel in the checkered suit had changed seats and was now attempting to strike up a conversation with Amanda, who didn't appear at all resistant to his overtures. First Dobson and now this. God dammit, did she intend to talk to everything in pants between Omaha and Denver?

''Be right back,'' he told the sleepy stationmaster.

His spurs bit into the soft wood floor as he stalked across the room toward the happy couple. On closer inspection, though, Amanda didn't appear all that enthused. Her face was a few shades paler than when Marcus had last seen it, and her hands were twisting in her lap. Her eyelashes fluttered up to him, and her eyes looked wildly bright when she spoke.

''There you are, dearest. Did you manage to locate my bag?''

Dearest? For a second, Marcus wasn't sure just who she was talking to, much less which bag she was talking about. Was she as crazy as she was rich? Then he noticed that the glad little smile on her face was composed less of teeth than of nervous twitching lips.

He glanced at the newspaper that the weasel clutched in his hand and caught a glimpse of a headline—the word *Runaway*— which gave him a good idea just what the man was up to. No wonder Amanda looked panicky as a deer in the bright beam of a headlamp. But she hadn't panicked, had she? Much as Marcus hated to do it, he gave her credit for her presence of mind and quick thinking in addressing him the way she had. Now it was his turn to do some fancy brainwork.

Marcus leaned down to brush a kiss across her soft cheek and to whisper, "Don't worry," close to her ear. "Sorry, darlin'," he drawled, straightening up. "That bag's nowhere around here." He shrugged helplessly, then grinned at the weasel. "Fine thing for a husband to lose his wife's suitcase the first night of their honeymoon, huh?"

The man's beady eyes enlarged. "Honeymoon? The two of you are married?"

"Just." Marcus smiled with as much husbandly pride as he could muster, then extended his hand. "Glad to meet you. I'm Al Green and this is my brand-new bride, Alice. And who might you be, mister?"

"Doesn't matter." The weasel glared sideways at Amanda. "You're married to this man? Is that right?"

She nodded with enthusiasm, much to the displeasure of the weasel.

"You don't look all that married to me," he said accusingly.

"Well, I haven't had much practice, actually. At marriage, I mean. It's only been..." Her gaze flitted up to Marcus. "How long, dearest?"

Marcus fished out his watch, snapped it open and

pondered the hands. "Three hours and twenty-seven minutes, give or take a few seconds." He smiled down at her, using the sappiest expression he could manage and trying to sound like a lovestruck groom. "The best three hours and twenty-seven minutes of my life."

"Aw, hell," the weasel snarled. "I mistook you for that runaway Grenville girl. I was just reading about her in the Denver paper, then I saw you sitting here and I thought, seeing your blond hair and fine clothes and all, that I had myself that five thousand for sure."

Amanda laughed. "Oh, you silly man. My goodness, I wish I were that Grenville girl. Then I'd have a servant or two to look after my luggage properly for me. My new husband doesn't seem to be doing such a good job."

She batted her eyes up at Marcus now and smiled with all the sweet indulgence of a woman who'd married an incompetent fool, which seemed to thoroughly convince the weasel that they were indeed husband and wife.

"Damn." The man stood, then slapped his newspaper down on the bench and walked away without it, shaking his head and muttering to himself.

The second he was out of earshot, Amanda started laughing. "That's the second time you've married me in the past few hours, Quicksilver. I honestly believe you're fond of me." She batted her eyelashes up at him again. "Either that or you have an incredible lack of imagination when it comes to charades."

"It worked, didn't it?" Marcus growled.

"Beautifully," she conceded. Then she gestured toward the stationmaster's cage. "Now, do retrieve my valise for me, will you?"

"That was no lie, Duchess." Marcus lowered himself beside her on the bench and snapped open the newspaper the weasel had left behind. "You won't be seeing that suitcase again. At least not until Denver. Sorry."

"Sorry! But I thought you wired ahead to direct them to take my suitcase off the train." Her voice rose a notch, as well as several degrees. "All my money's in there. What am I supposed to do now?"

Marcus shrugged. He was only half listening as he read the article on the front page of the Denver paper, the majority of which was an interview with Honoria Grenville, who had returned to that city following her granddaughter's escape in Omaha. The old woman had apparently taken over the top floor of the Excelsior Hotel, whence she was now commanding a battalion of private detectives and newspapermen. That didn't surprise Marcus a bit—not the fact that Granny Grenville was willing to spend a small fortune to have her own way or the fact that there were scores of eager and greedy characters more than willing to assist her.

What surprised him, though, was the reason for Amanda's exit in the first place. She'd eloped from New York to Denver with Angus McCray. Eloped! Marcus wasn't sure what he'd been thinking, or whether he'd given it any thought at all. Women rarely ran away for the pure pleasure of it, and

Amanda Grenville certainly hadn't run away to join any circus. But elopement? With Angus McCray?

It was hardly a secret in Denver that the dapper, slick-haired Scot made his living off women. He'd been down the aisle at least once already, with the widow of a gold miner, but unfortunately for him, it had turned out that the gold miner was really a silver miner on a relatively meager scale, and— worse—for McCray, anyway—the fella wasn't even dead.

"Angus McCray," Marcus muttered behind the newspaper. "Angus damn McCray!"

"Oh, is there something about Angus in there?" Amanda grabbed for the paper, but Marcus held it out of reach.

He was boiling, and he wasn't sure just why, except he hated to see people making stupid mistakes. And of all the mistakes a rich girl could make, this one was probably the stupidest and the worst. "You're figuring to marry that no-account, lily-livered, freeloading snake?"

"Yes," she said with a little toss of her head. "Not that it's any of your business, Quicksilver." Then her gaze played over the assorted passengers in the waiting room. "And I shouldn't have to remind someone in your line of work to be a little more circumspect when discussing certain subjects. Not to mention quieter. If you know what I mean."

She was right, of course. Marcus looked over at the weasel, to find the man's beady little eyes trained on them once more, and an expression of renewed curiosity puckering his narrow face. Several other men were regarding them now, including the stationmaster, who stood within easy reach of his telegraph key, the one that could put him in touch with Granny Grenville and her minions in about ten seconds, leaving Marcus to kiss that five thousand dollars goodbye. That, he vowed, was not going to happen. By God, he already felt as if he'd earned at least half of that five thousand just in irritation and aggravation.

"Come on." He folded the paper, stuck it under his arm, and tugged Amanda to her feet. "Let's go."

"Where are we going?"

"Someplace," he growled.

"A restaurant?" she asked hopefully.

Amanda tried to ignore the rumblings in her stomach as she sat perched on a wooden crate in an alley across from the train depot, watching Marcus Quicksilver pace back and forth and listening to the soft jingling sound his spurs made. Or was that the sound of his teeth grinding? she wondered. The bounty hunter appeared to be mad at the world in general, and at her in particular.

If anyone should be throwing a fit, she thought, it was she. Her hair was filthy. Her clothes were wrinkled, and she still smelled vaguely like cake. Day-old-cake, at that. Her luggage had vanished, and if she had ten dollars left in her handbag she'd consider herself quite lucky. She loosened the braided silk drawstring now and dumped the contents out onto her lap.

For lack of a streetlamp in the alleyway, there was only moonlight with which to inspect the coins that had clattered out. And then even the pale moonlight was blocked by a pair of wide shoulders as Marcus halted in front of her.

"What do you think you're doing?" he demanded, looming above her.

"Just what it looks like, Quicksilver. I'm counting my money." She plucked an errant silver dollar from a fold in her skirt. "Which I wouldn't have to do at all if someone had sent a proper wire concerning my suitcase."

"Forget about the suitcase. It's gone. Anyway, you're better off not having anything with those initials on it." He swiped off his hat and ran his fingers through his hair. "And while I'm giving advice, Miss Grenville, I want to request that you stop taking up with every man who gives you a sidelong glance. Do you think you can do that?"

"Hush. You're making me lose count. Fourteen. Fifteen." Amanda added two silver dollars to the stack of coins in her hand, then sighed forlornly. "Well, I'm afraid that's the sum of it. Oh, no. Wait." She practically dived headfirst into her handbag then and unbuttoned a small compartment in the silk lining. "I'd completely forgotten about these," she said, coming up with two bright twenty-dollar gold pieces.

But no sooner had she discovered them than Marcus snatched them out of her hand.

"Give those back!" she cried.

"You can have whatever's left in Denver. If you

want me to help you, then you're just going to have
to do this my way. Understand?''

His words were comparable to a bucket of cold
water tossed on a fire, and Amanda's anger sputtered
out immediately. He'd just said he was going to help
her, hadn't he? Despite the fact that his face was
dark and menacing as he stood looking down at her,
and despite the fact that he looked as if he'd just as
soon strangle her as look at her, Marcus Quicksilver
had actually offered his aid.

''You've agreed, then? To help me get to my fiancé in Denver, I mean, instead of dragging me back
to my grandmother?''

''I'll get you to Denver. That's all I can promise.
But it's not going to happen if you keep striking up
conversations with every male between here and the
Rockies. Can you get that through that hard-as-a-
diamond skull of yours?''

She bit down on a smile, not wanting to let him
see how thrilled she was or how relieved she was
that she was no longer his captive. ''Yes, I believe
I can.''

''Good. Now give me all the rest of that silver
and we'll see just where we stand.''

Reluctantly Amanda scooped the fifteen silver
dollars from her lap and handed them over.

''Is that it?''

''Yes,'' she said. ''Well, except for the lucky
penny in my shoe. I suppose you'll be wanting that,
as well.''

''You can keep that. At least for the time being.''
He pocketed the coins, and then his stern mouth

relaxed in something close to a grin. "We're going to need all the luck we can get, Amanda Grenville."

Luck wasn't something he usually counted on, Marcus thought when he walked back into the train depot after leaving Amanda outside. Luck was for gamblers and fools. In his line of work, a man depended on his wits and his skills. Of course, that was when he was on the hunting end of the game. This time it was different. Now he and Amanda were the quarry, and he wasn't accustomed to that.

He wondered about all the men he had tracked down and captured over the years. If the poor devils had been just a little bit luckier—if the wind had blown the smoke from their campfires in a different direction, if their horses hadn't had distinctive markings on their shoes, if they'd zigged when Marcus zagged—would it have made a difference? Maybe. Maybe not. But he knew damn well he'd have to do everything right from this point on, now that half the population was on Amanda Grenville's trail.

Part of that population was eying him now from a bench inside the depot. The weasel had obtained another newspaper and was peeking over one corner of it. Even the stationmaster looked more suspicious than sleepy when Marcus approached his wire cage.

"When's that immigrant train due in?" he asked the spectacled man.

"About half an hour."

"Gimme two tickets. Only as far as Bushnell." They couldn't afford a much longer fare, but then, neither could they afford to stay on any train or stage too long. He slapped both of Amanda's double eagles on the counter. "And I'll need to arrange passage for my mount."

"Gonna cost you twice that," the stationmaster said, eyeing the forty dollars on the counter.

"Twice that? To ride a lousy forty or fifty miles?"

"Yep. New policy for immigrant trains. No short fares. Sorry about that."

Marcus cursed and snatched his money back. If they couldn't afford two tickets on the train, then he'd have to come up with another plan. Either that or rob a bank, he thought dismally as he headed toward the depot door.

Just then the weasel hissed at him and gestured toward a deserted corner of the waiting room. What did the little rodent want now? Marcus wondered. To see his wedding pictures?

"You're not fooling me, Mister Whoever-You-Are," the man rasped as soon as Marcus approached him. "You're no honeymooner, that's for sure. And that little gal with you ain't no blushing bride. She's that runaway rich girl. That Amanda Grenville. Right?" He tapped his rolled-up newspaper in the palm of one hand, the way a policeman might tap a nightstick. "Am I right?"

Marcus didn't reply, but merely stared at him as if to say, "so what?" If his silence was an admission, it was also—he hoped—a mute threat.

Either the weasel didn't understand the menace or he chose to ignore it. His rat face cracked in a yellow-toothed grin. "Yeah. I knew it. Damn if I didn't know it the minute I saw her walk in here." Now he poked Marcus in the chest with his paper. "Guess you'll have to share that reward with me now, won't you, mister? Twenty-five hundred ain't as good as five thousand to either one of us, but it sure beats nothing at all.''

Marcus scanned the waiting room before he leaned a little closer to the eager man. ''What do you say we take this conversation outside, partner, so we don't wind up having to split that damn money a half a dozen different ways?''

The weasel winked and grinned like a jack-o'-lantern. ''Sure thing, partner. Can't be too careful now, can we?'' He gestured toward the door. ''After you, partner,'' he said, then he followed Marcus out the door, down the planked sidewalk and around the corner of the building.

''This'll do,'' Marcus said, turning.

''Yeah. It's a whole lot better. More private-like.'' He grinned again, but now there was a thread of wariness in his voice. ''Kinda dark back here, but...''

He was right to be wary, for Marcus had had every intention of decking him, of ramming his fist into the man's sleazy smile and putting out the lights behind his beady little eyes. But while he was leading the eager fellow around the dark and deserted side of the depot, Marcus had reconsidered. Knocking him out would only get rid of him temporarily, and the man—rat though he was—hardly deserved to be put out of commission permanently. It had occurred to Marcus then that he might be able to use the weasel, instead of abusing him.

So Marcus stuck out his hand for a shake, rather than a punch. ''Looks like we're partners, pal,'' he

said, and when the weasel pumped his hand enthusiastically, Marcus added, "How much cash have
you got on you?"

"Some." The beady eyes blinked. "Not a lot.
Why?"

"Well, here's the deal, partner." Marcus grinned,
then looped an arm around the man's shoulders.
"There's no reward coming unless ol' lady Grenville gets her granddaughter back. Right?"

"Yeah. That's what the paper said. Five thousand
dollars."

"Okay. So we have to get the girl to Denver in
order to collect. Only trouble with that is, I don't
have enough cash for two tickets on the next train.
I'm about forty dollars short."

"Is that right?"

"That's right. So here's what I was thinking."
Marcus widened his grin and leaned closer to the
considerably shorter man. "If you could loan me
that forty…"

"Whoa. Now wait just a minute." The weasel
squirmed out of Marcus's companionable embrace
and took a step back. "Who's to say it oughta be
you that gets to take the girl to Denver? I mean,
who decided that?"

Marcus looked thoughtful for a moment. "Well,
I guess I decided that. See…" He eased his .45 from
its holster, nudged his hat back a fraction with the
barrel of the gun and then aimed it almost casually
at the man's midsection. "…I figured, since I've got
this, I'm in a better position to protect our interests,
not to mention looking out for the little lady herself."

Then his thumb slid up to cock the hammer. "What do you think, partner?"

The weasel swallowed hard, gaping at the gun. "Yeah. Sure. No question you're the better man for that part of the job." His hand darted into a pocket of his checkered suitcoat and came out with two gold coins. "Here's my forty. Only problem is, though, that leaves me here in Sidney just about flat broke. You...you aren't leaving me in the lurch, are you? How am I going to get to Denver to split the reward?"

Marcus holstered his gun and took the coins. Now all he had to do was satisfy the man that he hadn't been fleeced. "You got a pencil and paper on you?" he asked.

After a considerable amount of pocket-patting and peering, the weasel brought forth a small notebook and a stub of pencil.

"Write this down," Marcus told him. "Etta James, 200 Grant Street, Denver."

"Got it," the man said as he scribbled. "Who's this Etta? Is she in on this?"

"That's my sister. As soon as I get the Grenville girl safely on the train, you wire her. Collect. You tell her you're my partner and to send you forty dollars right quick. No. Hell. You tell her to send you eighty. How's that?"

"Eighty?" The weasel's yellow smile increased. "Sure. That sounds good. She'll do it, this sister of yours? Is she reliable?"

Marcus smiled, picturing the expression on the face of Etta James, the two-hundred-pound, six-foot-tall madam at the brothel at 200 Grant Street, when the collect wire came. It'd be a pure miracle if she didn't shred the telegram with her teeth and then pistol-whip the Western Union kid who had the misfortune of delivering it.

"Reliable as night follows day, partner." Marcus winked lasciviously. "She's real pretty, too. But you'll see that for yourself in Denver, okay?"

Chapter Five

Amanda waited in the dark at the far end of the platform, watching while Marcus led a reluctant Sarah B. up the ramp and into the baggage car. Little wonder the mare was testy, she thought. The poor animal hadn't had any supper, either. By heaven, once she got to Denver, Amanda swore, she was going to eat breakfast, lunch and dinner all in one sitting. One long, possibly interminable sitting. Angus would probably be appalled at her unladylike appetite. Let him. She didn't care. Glancing at the moths fluttering about one of the lanterns at the depot door, she wondered just how long a person could go without sustenance, and just how hungry a person might have to be to eat, well…anything. A moth, for instance.

It occurred to her that she'd never truly been hungry before. In fact, if anything, she'd complained loudly and frequently about having to sit at her end of the enormous inlaid table in her grandmother's elegant dining room three times a day. She decided that if she learned nothing else from this escapade of hers, it would be an appreciation of regular meals.

"Perhaps I am spoiled," she muttered, then dismissed the thought when she saw Marcus Quicksilver striding toward her now, saddlebags draped over his shoulder, but not far enough to conceal the opening in his shirt. She dearly wished she had a needle and thread to remove the distraction, but then she reminded herself she wouldn't know how to use them if she did.

She sighed and let her gaze fall to the gunbelt still slung across his hips. He had a way of walking, Amanda realized, that said, "Stay out of my way, or else." Even the jingle of his spurs suddenly struck her as menacing somehow, like the muted rattle of a snake. If he hadn't agreed to help her, she decided she just might be afraid of him.

But she wasn't. So, when he took her arm and said, "Let's go," she balked.

"I don't suppose we could stay here, have a bite to eat and take a later train," she whined. "My stomach truly has reason to suspect that my throat's been cut."

He patted the saddlebag on his shoulder. "Your supper's in here, Duchess. I lifted a couple apples from a barrel in the baggage car. Now be a good girl, get on the train quietly, and I'll let you have one."

"You're too kind." The edge of sarcasm in her voice belied her excitement at the prospect of chewing and actually swallowing something. Even a lowly apple.

Marcus led her toward the train and gave her a boost into the car. She didn't even comment on his rather forward hand—that palm flattened on her backside might have been accidental, after all—because at that moment she was preoccupied with thoughts of settling into a big upholstered seat and sinking her teeth into a piece of succulent fruit. She took one step forward into the coach, but then stopped. Surely they were on the wrong train. Or the wrong car of the right train, perhaps.

"Oh, my goodness."

"What's the matter, brat?" he drawled from just behind her. "Haven't you ever ridden on an immigrant train before?"

There was cool amusement in his voice, coupled with an undisguised disdain. He was challenging her to find fault with the less-than-luxurious accommodations before her, daring her to turn up her nose and refuse to travel in a third-class coach. Daring her!

How dare he!

"No," she said, "I haven't, but you know what they say, Quicksilver. There's a first time for everything." Amanda tossed a stalwart smile over her shoulder. "Which are our seats?"

"The empty ones, if we can find any."

Locating an empty seat turned out to be nearly impossible in the crowded, dimly lit coach, where bundles in the aisle proved to be huddled children as often as not, and the question "Is this seat occupied?" was met with a blank stare, a baffled shrug or a lengthy explanation in a language Amanda couldn't identify, much less understand. The stale air inside the coach reeked of tobacco smoke and cooked cabbage and human sweat.

Amanda halted in the aisle, trying to catch a decent breath, but Marcus urged her along with a hand pressed to the small of her back.

"Here."

He tossed his saddlebags onto a backless, unpainted bench near the rear of the car, where the heat from a cast-iron stove felt like the blast from a furnace and where the foul air was so thick he couldn't have cut it with a knife. Marcus wasn't sure whether to curse or congratulate himself for choosing a crowded immigrant train. It was like riding a boxcar to hell. Still, he was pretty certain no one would think to look for a runaway heiress here. He sat heavily, then, just as the train gave a forward lurch, he reached out and caught a fistful of Amanda's dress to prevent her careening back along the aisle.

She plopped down with a sigh—and without a thank-you for his timely assistance—and then immediately began arranging her skirts as if she had just daintily planted herself on a little gilded chair in the fanciest drawing room in New York. She'd primp a minute, Marcus thought, and when she was satisfied with her appearance and remembered her empty stomach, she'd demand her apple from him without so much as a please or a thank-you, without any regard for the fact that he'd sunk to the level of a common thief to get it for her.

Marcus scowled and surveyed their dank surroundings. Most of the wall lamps were broken, and those that weren't had chimneys so black they barely shed any light. There must've been a hundred and twenty people in a car built to accommodate half that number. Men in caps and overcoats—in June!—all of whom needed a shave even worse than Marcus. Women wearing tattered cotton scarves on their heads and what looked to be their entire wardrobes on their backs. Children in patched rags that passed for clothes sleeping under seats and curled up in the aisles. The passengers were probably the entire population of a down-and-out little burg in Prussia or Poland, who had crossed the Atlantic together and were now still locked together in woebegone steerage as they crossed the American plains.

The expression "a sea of humanity" came to Marcus's mind, but this was more like a swamp of humanity, a tattered mass of hopeful innocents lured west with promises of fertile lands and bright futures.

"Goddamn railroad barons," he muttered under his breath.

"Pardon?" Still fussing with the folds of her skirt, Amanda leaned closer. "I'm sorry. It's so noisy in here, I didn't quite..."

"I was cursing Jay Gould and his ilk, Duchess. Friends of yours, no doubt," he added caustically, "all those railroad tycoons."

"I've met one or two." She lifted her chin and met his gaze fully and frankly. "Oliver Ames, Mr. Gould's partner, is a cousin by marriage, as a matter of fact. He's a very nice man."

"I'll bet." Marcus gestured around the crowded car. "He's also nice and responsible for this human swamp that will soon be poured out onto the promised land, only to discover that it doesn't rain as much as the Union Pacific's brochures claimed, or it rains too much, or the grasshoppers demolish their crops overnight."

Amanda's gaze roamed around the car now, pausing here and there on a weary face. "I really don't think cousin Oliver would intentionally deceive anyone." Her voice, crisp and righteous at first, softened considerably as she continued. "Not when their dreams and their very lives are at stake. Not these people, anyway. Just look at them, Quicksilver. They've come so very far."

But Marcus looked at her instead, amazed by the shine and innocence on her face. He would have thought Miss Amanda Grenville would be offended, disgusted, even, by this moving tide of humanity, so out of her element. He would have bet she not only knew of but wholeheartedly approved of the greedy business practices of her cousin Oliver, the railroad baron, and his conniving eastern cronies. He would have staked all of next year's bounties that at heart Miss Amanda Grenville was as heartless as the rest of them.

And he would have been wrong. Marcus admitted that to himself now, but at the same time he decided he didn't like it all that much. Being wrong about people didn't make for successful bounty hunters, and being wrong about this fair-haired beauty was altogether unsettling.

"I'll take that apple now," she said regally, holding out a small gloved hand.

Marcus grinned. Well, at least he'd been right about that. He unlatched his saddlebag, extracted one of the filched apples and rubbed it on his sleeve. No sooner had he placed it in Amanda's hand, however, than a small boy appeared to materialize out of thin air in the aisle beside her, his large blue eyes fixed on the fruit as if it were a fist-size chunk of pure gold. The immigrant kid wanted that apple in the worst way. It was written all over his grimy young face.

Marcus shifted on the bench, leaned his shoulder against the wall and crossed his arms. This, he thought, was going to be good. The hungry duchess and the famished waif. The spoiled brat versus the starving rat. This little scene about to be played out right before his eyes was worth box-seat tickets to the best melodrama.

"Well, hello there," Amanda said.

"*Apfel,*" the boy replied, his big eyes never straying from the fruit.

The duchess glanced from the child to the long-awaited, highly coveted object in her hand. Her fingers twitched and tightened a bit, Marcus noted, without surprise and with some satisfaction.

"*Apfel.*" She repeated the word with a slight catch in her voice, although she was still smiling pleasantly enough. Noblesse oblige, Marcus thought. He wondered just how obliged her noblesse would be.

"In English we call it an apple," she told the boy,

while she kept a firm, now two-handed grip on the fruit under discussion.

"Apfel." The child nodded somberly, then lifted a grimy hand to swipe at the bubble of saliva building in one corner of his mouth. *"Gut, ja?"*

"Gut?" she echoed. "Oh, is it good? Well, I..." Her smile crimped, wavered, then faltered completely. Her fingers loosened perceptibly, and she held the apple out to the urchin. "I don't know if it's good or not," she said with a tiny gust of laughter. "Here. Why don't you try it and tell me?"

The kid didn't need to be asked twice. He grabbed the apple and promptly took a good-size bite. Juice dribbled down his chin and he chased it with his tongue. *"Ja,"* he mumbled. *"Sehr gut. Danke."*

"Ja. Danke. You're most welcome."

She let go of a forlorn little sigh as the boy turned and walked away, still chomping on the fruit. Marcus sighed, too. He'd half expected to see her rolling in the aisle, wrestling the little beggar for her supper, and now the duchess had gone and done something sweet and unselfish, not only surprising Marcus again, but also forcing him to decide just how sweet and unselfish he himself was prepared to be with the single apple that remained.

Well, hell.

"Here." He reached into the saddlebag and grabbed the last piece of fruit. "Take it."

"Oh, no. I..."

"Take it," he growled.

"But you're hungry, too," she protested.

"Nah. I had two or three of these while I was

getting my mare settled. Even gave one to her.'' Which was partly true. He had given Sarah B. an apple, but hadn't had time to partake of one himself, because the baggage master chose that moment to inspect the cargo.

"Go ahead. Take it," he urged. Then, in a last-ditch attempt to rile her and possibly, even hopefully, dissuade her, he added, "Or isn't this fancy enough fare for you, brat?"

Fire sparked deep in her green, green eyes. "Fancy enough, Quicksilver? I'll show you fancy." She swiped the apple from him, and without even rubbing the dust off she sank her teeth into it. Then, as she chewed, the fury on her face dissolved, replaced by an expression of utter delight. Her eyes closed in sheer, unadulterated bliss.

Marcus had never seen anybody—even the immigrant kid—enjoy a lousy apple so much. "Must be good," he said, trying not to focus too much on the way her tongue kept darting out to catch beads of juice on her upper lip or even to listen to the tiny, sensual, murmuring sounds she made while she ate—sounds that seemed to echo in the pit of his stomach—but rather to concentrate on a different hunger and the way his belt buckle felt as if it were whittling away at his backbone.

It was food he wanted, he reminded himself. Not her. All he wanted from Amanda Grenville, all he wanted *for* her was a big, fat reward. Just the notion that he could think of her as anything but his prize bounty was ludicrous. She was a woman, sure, and a strikingly beautiful one, but he'd had his fill of beautiful butterflies in Denver over the years. He'd learned to avoid anything resembling an entanglement with women like that, who thought their money could buy anything, including him. Marcus Quicksilver was not for sale. Not then. Not now. And he most assuredly was not interested in Amanda Grenville beyond the money he was going to collect once he got her to Denver.

He hadn't yet made up his mind just which Grenville he'd be collecting the money from, though. Amanda had promised more than five thousand if he didn't turn her over to her grandmother, but Marcus didn't know if she was good for it. Maybe she had the money. Maybe not. He figured he didn't have to make up his mind on that score until he actually got her to Denver. Then he'd decide whether it would be Granny's lap of comfort or the greedy embrace of Angus McCray.

Angus damn McCray. That was another damn reason Marcus wasn't interested in the duchess. She was engaged to marry McCray. How could he be interested in a woman who was interested in a slick-haired dandy who was as shallow as a creek in the desert?

He looked at her now. All that remained of the apple was a flimsy core and a couple of seeds. She smiled a juicy, glistening smile and lobbed the demolished fruit over his shoulder and out the window into the dark Nebraska night.

"That was absolutely delicious," she said.

"And?" Marcus began the slow and silent count

to ten, waiting for any combination of words that might approach or even partly resemble a thank-you.

While he ticked off the seconds, Her Ladyship gave a sigh and shifted on the bench, bringing her knees up and angling onto one hip. "And now I'm going to take a little nap. I'm so very tired, and it's so awfully warm in here."

With that, she slid down, and her head made contact with his thigh. "You don't mind, do you, Quicksilver?" she asked in a sleepy voice, nudging her shoulder into his leg, the way she would have done with a pillow, and curling her arms up against her chest.

By God, he should have minded, Marcus thought. It should have irked him to no end to be used as a damn piece of bedding, to function as a mere rolled-up saddle blanket. But somehow it didn't bother him all that much as he looked down and noted the faint blue smudges of exhaustion just beneath her long lashes. He lifted a hand and gently brushed a strand of corn-silk hair from her cheek. His touch brought forth a wisp of a sigh that melted into a sweet smile of contentment on her lovely face.

"No, I don't mind, brat," he whispered. "Sleep. You've had a long, hard day."

Amanda woke up on the floor, or more precisely she stopped sleeping on the bench when there was a thunderous crash, but she didn't actually wake up until a series of bone-rattling jolts sent her thumping to the floor. Something solid landed beside her, and when it cursed roughly, she assumed it was Marcus

Quicksilver. Then he was on his feet and pulling her up before she blinked away the last sleepy wisps of fog in her brain.

Once on her feet, Amanda realized that the railroad car was no longer upright, but canted quite dangerously to one side. The crowd of immigrants was a roiling mass of elbows and knees now, as people tried to struggle up from the floor.

"Come on," Marcus said with some urgency above the din of frantic foreign passengers, all of whom seemed to be shouting now.

"What happened?"

"I'm not sure what *did* happen," he said, "but what's *going* to happen is that stove's going to tip over in another minute or two, and then all hell's going to break loose in here."

She glanced at the cast-iron stove now and saw that it had sprung loose from the bolts that anchored it. Its square door was hanging open, and several orange coals had already spilled out onto the wooden floor. In her estimation, hell had already quite obviously broken loose.

"Oh, dear. We must warn everyone."

"Uh-huh. We'll do just that. From outside."

His arm circled her waist then, and Amanda found herself propelled forward through the frantic, babbling crowd, toward the door, which was now a good four or five feet off the ground. Marcus tossed his saddlebags out into the darkness and turned to Amanda.

"We'll have to jump," he said. "You ready?"

Her heart was pounding so hard she thought it

must be audible over the noise behind them. And even though her knees suddenly felt like pudding, she stepped back a few inches from the open door, from the abyss below and beyond.

"Actually, Quicksilver, I believe I'll just wait here until you can locate a stepladder or something."

"I think not, Your Ladyship."

Almost before the words had left his mouth, his arms were moving around her, and the next thing Amanda knew she was sailing into space, locked in a powerful embrace. They landed with a hard thump and a rough curse. She was quite sure it was Marcus who'd sworn, since she didn't seem to be able to drag in enough breath to utter so much as a gasp.

When he ordered her to wait right where she was, Amanda couldn't have argued with him if she wanted to. All she could do was sit there, blinking stupidly up at the tilted car of the train, the black sky above it, and a slice of moon that seemed to be hovering at a rather peculiar angle, as well.

An eerie orange light began to flicker in the train's windows, and behind the shattered squares of glass, shadows were bobbing crazily. There was shouting, but Amanda couldn't understand any of the words.

It was a nightmare, she told herself. Some demented dream brought on by frayed nerves and a significant lack of food. Nothing like this had ever happened to her in twenty-one sheltered years. Maybe her grandmother was right, after all. Maybe she wasn't capable of making decisions for herself.

Maybe she should simply forget that she'd ever longed for independence, if her efforts at seeking it had merely landed her in pandemonium.

People were jumping off the train now, flailing their arms and hurling themselves into space, and coming down all around her like human cannonballs. She scuttled back in the rough grass to escape the assault. Her heart was pounding, and her breath was ragged. She was terrified.

As earlier, when it had occurred to her that she'd never been truly hungry before, Amanda realized now that she'd never been truly frightened before. She'd never felt helpless and lost before. Never felt totally and terribly alone, the way she did now. Panic swept through her in a cold wave, suffocating her, threatening to drown her. She scrambled to her feet, trying desperately to breathe, only to be knocked back down by a hurtling immigrant. Then she sat in the grass, stunned, staring, fighting nausea and blinking back tears, until she heard a low, calm, oh-so-familiar voice behind her.

"Whoa, Sarah B. Whoa now, girl. It's all right. It's all gonna be fine, sugar. There now. There."

"Quicksilver." The name left Amanda's lips on a long sigh of relief. Marcus was close by. She wasn't alone in the dark, after all. She wasn't dying or drowning. She was safe.

"You think you can stand up and get those legs to carry you over here, Amanda? This horse of mine will bolt if I let go of her for more than half a second."

Amanda struggled to her feet and moved toward

his reassuring voice. The mare was pawing the ground wildly and tossing her head.

"Here." Marcus thrust the reins into Amanda's hand. "Just keep a tight hold on those now. Don't let go."

She gripped the leather straps as if for dear life, but when Marcus took a step away from her, Amanda reached out with her other hand and caught his sleeve. "Where are you going? Don't leave me."

"I'll be right back," he said. "I'm just going to help the last of those poor devils get off the train."

"Don't leave me, Quicksilver." She tightened her grip on his arm and screeched, "Please!"

He stood there a moment, with Amanda still attached to his sleeve, just looking at her and not saying a word. Then a grin—or was it slanted white moonlight?—slashed across his mouth, and firelight sparkled in his dark eyes just before he took her chin in one hand, bent his head and kissed her. A slow, soft, astonishing kiss.

"Why, Miss Amanda," he whispered. "I thought I'd die before I heard that particular word pass your pretty little lips. Say it one more time, just so I know I wasn't dreaming, will you?"

She blinked into the warm firelight that danced in his eyes. "P-please?" It came out less a question than a plea, and whether it meant "don't leave me" or "kiss me again," Amanda wasn't sure. Either one would have been fine just then. Both. Especially the kiss. But before she could say anything else, he had loosened her grip on his arm and was walking back toward the burning train.

"Dammit, Quicksilver," she muttered, without much rancor in her tone. Then she called out, "Be careful, will you? Please."

He gave her a little wave over his shoulder, then hoisted himself up and disappeared into the smoky depths of the derailed train.

It wasn't easy convincing a dozen eager, foreign-speaking men that saving their own hides was more important than saving their pitiful possessions or one of Jay Gould's railroad cars, but Marcus had finally succeeded. Everyone was off the train when he finally jumped down from the door. His throat was raw from the smoke and his eyes were burning, so much so that at first he couldn't see Amanda anywhere. It occurred to him then that the reward for his efforts just might be the escape of Amanda Grenville on Sarah B. But after he rubbed some of the smoke and sting out of his eyes, he saw the runaway heiress right where he'd left her. The moon was lighting up her golden hair as if it were a beacon in the night.

He'd kissed her. He'd been so busy haranguing immigrants and hauling them off the train that he hadn't given that kiss a thought, but it hit him now with the impact of a locomotive, and he couldn't think of anything else. He'd kissed her. What a blockheaded, bumble-brained thing to do. He'd only meant to calm her down, and now he'd probably spend the next few days being raked over the coals for his impropriety and gall. Hell. Sweet as that kiss had been—her mouth had felt surprisingly warm and generous—he didn't want to spend the next forty-eight hours paying for it.

Marcus shoved his way through the bewildered immigrants, thinking he was going to have to make that crystal-clear right off the bat. As soon as Amanda Grenville opened her mouth to admonish him, he was going to...

"You're safe." Her lashes fluttered up to his face, and her hand latched onto his arm. "Thank God. I was so worried about you."

It wasn't the greeting Marcus had anticipated, and suddenly he didn't know if he was safe or not. His inclination was to take her in his arms and kiss her again, which would have made him a prime contender for fool of the century. Did she think because he'd kissed her that she had him wrapped around her pinky now, and tied in a neat little bow, or that she had a hold on his reins, the way she was still holding Sarah's? Considering who she was and where she came from, Miss Amanda Grenville probably did. He decided he liked her better when she was being all high-and-mighty. She was safer that way. *He* was safer that way.

"I'm safe," he growled. "We're all safe, no thanks to your *nice* cousin, who's lining his pockets with money when he should be using it to repair his goddamn tracks."

"I really..."

"Don't bother apologizing for him. Just tell him next time you see him that eighty dollars' worth of tickets landed us smack in the middle of nowhere. On fire.'' Marcus snatched the reins out of her hand and swung up on Sarah's back. "Let's go.'' He slipped his foot out of the stirrup and reached down a hand. "Put your foot in there and swing on up behind me.''

Her mouth flattened as if an iron had just passed over it, and she crossed her arms. "I prefer to ride the train.''

"Fine. Suit yourself, Princess. I prefer to ride into the nearest town and find a soft bed and a hot meal.''

He didn't know if it was the bed or the meal that had the more appeal for her. Whichever one it was, however, did the trick, and after a certain amount of skirt-hiking and hopping and several muted curses, she was up on Sarah's back behind him and they were leaving the wrecked train in their wake.

Now if he could just keep Her Ladyship behind him for the next few days, Marcus told himself, he wouldn't have to reckon with the temptation of kissing her again.

Chapter Six

"What do you mean, *our* room?"

"Well, now, exactly which of those two words didn't you understand, Duchess? *Our* or *room?*"

They were standing in the narrow second-floor hallway of a hotel that called itself—erroneously, to Amanda's way of thinking—the Grand. But while she waited downstairs in the lobby for Marcus to arrange for their accommodations, she had decided not to complain. In truth, it almost didn't matter to her that the wallpaper was mismatched at the seams or that the pattern of the carpet was one of muddy bootprints rather than paisley, or even that the chandelier seemed to be missing more than half its crystals. After three hours of sitting astride a horse and clinging to a man's waist while pretending she wasn't touching him, all that mattered to Amanda was the promise of a meal and the prospect of dropping onto a mattress, closing her eyes and falling into blissful, blank sleep.

It mattered enormously, however, that Marcus Quicksilver had just paused in the hallway, inserted a key in a lock and said something that sounded distinctly like "our room." It mattered, too, that he was now looking down at her with one eyebrow arrogantly cocked and another one of those patronizing grins slanted across his face.

"Where's *your* room, Quicksilver?"

He turned the key and pushed open the door. "Right here."

Amanda peered in at a rickety iron bed and a battered washstand and more mismatched wallpaper. "I see," she said. "Then where's *my* room?"

His reply was a slow, almost courtly sweep of his hand across the threshold. "After you."

Her chin came up, pointing at Marcus's throat like a pistol. Then she narrowed her eyes, the better to aim the fiery green ammunition there. "I think not," she said with an indignant sniff. "This is unacceptable."

"For you, maybe." Marcus took off his hat and lobbed it into the room, where it caught and took one spin on the iron post at the foot of the bed. "But since we're doing this my way, I guess you'll have to think again."

He strode across the threshold, leaving Amanda tapping her foot in the hall.

"It isn't seemly," she called. "In fact, it's quite improper."

"Yep. But it's cheap and it'll leave us enough cash for that meal you've been yammering about for the last two hours." He dropped his saddlebags on the bed and turned back to face her. "If you want a second room, brat, you're going to have to pay for it with your supper. It's up to you.''

She entered the room as if the floorboards were mined, as if the worn rag rug were concealing scorpions and snakes, or a trapdoor that could drop out from under her feet at any second.

Marcus wasn't sure if it was the shabbiness that offended her or the knowledge that she'd be forced to endure it with him. Probably both. He almost didn't care. It was two o'clock in the morning, he was dead tired, and there was still Sarah B. to be seen to and some sort of meal to be scrounged. If Amanda Grenville voiced so much as a squeak of complaint about the thick layer of dust on the washstand or the haphazard angle of the paper on the wall, he swore, he'd put her out in the hall and bid good riddance to any reward, no matter the amount. If she breathed a single snippy word about the mismatched bowl and pitcher, by God, he would...

"You win, Quicksilver." She sighed. "I'm much too tired to argue."

In response, Marcus didn't know what to say. Despite his own exhaustion, he'd been prepared—even eager, perhaps—to argue with her. It was, he realized suddenly, a way of keeping his distance both mentally and physically, something he hadn't been particularly successful in doing during the past few hours, ever since he kissed Amanda to calm her down. That damn kiss had been buzzing around in his brain all night, and playing havoc with his senses. It irritated him like a sandbur under a saddle blanket, like cracker crumbs between the sheets.

His glance cut to the narrow bed now, and he told himself it was time to get out of the room until he could get a better hold on his thoughts. Snagging his hat from the bedpost, he jammed it on his head.

"Gotta go find a livery and get my horse settled," he announced as he brushed past her. "I'll see what I can come up with in the way of supper. Stay here. Lock the door after I go and don't let anybody in."

"Yes. All right. Quicksilver, would you—?" The door clicked closed before Amanda could finish her sentence. She sighed. It was just as well. She'd been going to ask him about bathing facilities, but an answer might have slowed him down, and given a choice between a bath and her supper, Amanda had no choice. Her stomach rumbled again, just to remind her.

Funny how being scrubbed and well-groomed had slipped on her list of priorities, she thought as she locked the door. Lowering her head, she sniffed at the bodice of her dress and picked up a whiff of smoke, in addition to three days' worth of continual wear. Smoke from Marcus Quicksilver's shirt, against which she'd been plastered for the past few hours. She remembered the feel of his solid back and the way the muscles shifted under his skin, how they hardened and tensed, how they slackened but still retained their firmness, how vital and strong they were.

It occurred to Amanda then that she knew Marcus Quicksilver's body better than any other person's in the world. Perhaps at one time she'd known the warmth and curve of Honoria Grenville's ample bosom, but that had been long ago, and once Amanda grew up, her grandmother had been more inclined toward brief hugs and kisses that merely skimmed the cheek, if they connected at all. And as for her fiancé…

She stared into the small mirror over the washstand, trying to recall Angus McCray's arms or shoulders or back. She couldn't. It was all she could do to dredge up a vague image of the face of her betrothed, and her fingers didn't tingle with memories of taut, sleek muscles. Her lips didn't twitch with the lingering feel of a kiss. Good Lord. She was engaged to a total stranger. If that fact hadn't been apparent before, it certainly was now. How in the world could she go through with her plan?

"You'll get to know him, silly goose," she admonished her reflection. "You'll come to know the taste and feel of him, just as you've come to know the taste and feel of Quicksilver, and the rough timbre of his voice, and the stormy blue of his eyes, and the way he quirks a dark brow when he's being particularly loathsome." Her mouth flattened with a certain satisfaction. "And you won't miss that at all, Amanda Grenville. I can assure you of that. Nor will you miss being called a spoiled brat. Will you?"

She clucked her tongue and turned from the mirror. No. She wouldn't miss that at all. Once she got to Denver and began her new and independent life as the wife of Angus McCray, she doubted she'd give Marcus Quicksilver—or his biceps, triceps and lips—even a passing thought.

Plopping wearily down on the bed, Amanda

gazed around the room she'd been so hesitant to enter. It occurred to her that she'd sounded more than a little like Honoria Grenville when she used such words as *improper* and *unseemly*. Running away wasn't going to do her any good at all, if she carried her grandmother's prim attitudes with her like so much heavy baggage, was it? And the prospect of sharing a room—no matter how shabby— with Marcus Quicksilver was thrilling, if a little frightening.

Besides, she thought, who would know? She certainly wasn't going to tell anyone about tonight.

Later, when the key scraped in the lock, Amanda's heart bounded eagerly—for supper! Surely that was the only reason. She jumped up from her seat on the edge of the bed with a greedy, almost beast-like grunt of pleasure and anticipation, but the sound dwindled in her throat as soon as she saw the expression on Marcus's face.

"The whole damn town's locked up tighter than a state penitentiary. Here," he said, offering her a lumpy blue checkered napkin. "The man at the livery rousted his wife, and this is the best she could come up with."

Marcus almost tacked on a "sorry" while he watched Amanda peel back the edges of the napkin and stare speechlessly at the pale green pickle and the hunk of buttered bread she disclosed. On second thought, he'd be damned if he'd apologize, after what he'd just been through to obtain the meager meal. He hadn't actually drawn his gun on the old codger at the livery stable, but the threat had been

implicit in his stance. After that he'd held his hat in
his hand, and held his tongue, too, while the old
guy's thin and chinless wife slammed around her
kitchen, calling Marcus a no-account drifter and
worse, waving her bread knife under his nose and
then demanding a dollar for her late-night hospital-
ity.

He'd been so hungry that he wolfed down his
share immediately after leaving the livery stable, but
he doubted that Amanda would do the same. A puny
pickle and a crust of bread wasn't exactly what Her
Ladyship had had in mind when she talked about
supper. But supper it was, and the best he'd been
able to do under the circumstances. If the brat turned
up her nose and refused to eat it, Marcus was more
than ready to do so himself.

She was gazing at the food now as if she couldn't
quite identify it. "Supper," she said a bit uncer-
tainly.

"Yep." Go ahead, he dared her silently. Point
that pretty little nose toward the ceiling and cluck
that pink little tongue.

Her expression was still one of puzzlement, rather
than disdain, when she asked, "This is all of it?"

"Yep."

Amanda contemplated the food a moment longer,
while Marcus contemplated her until, suddenly, he
realized that he was holding his breath, which struck
him as a damn-fool thing to do. The suspense was
real, all right, but it was also ridiculous. What did
he care whether or not Miss Amanda High-toned

Grenville deigned to dine on a pickle and a heel of bread? Except…

…except just then Marcus felt a distinct shifting in the vicinity of his rib cage. Dammit, as much as he'd intended merely to feed the woman, it dawned on him now—hit him like a fist in his midsection, actually—that he'd also wanted to please her. That mattered to him more than he liked to admit. He crossed his arms to make sure his heart wasn't showing as it thumped against his shirtfront, then glowered at her, hoping that would erase the sappy expression he felt oozing across his face. *Go ahead, brat,* he thought. *It doesn't matter.*

But once again she surprised him, by handling the pickle delicately, bringing it to her lips and then biting off a bit, which she consumed with an almost sensual pleasure. As with the apple earlier, she closed her eyes, to savor the taste all the more. Marcus felt a kind of crazy delight in her enjoyment. It was crazy, all right.

"It's not Delmonico's," he said, "but it's a damn good pickle."

"Mmm."

She settled on the bed, drew her feet up beneath her and proceeded to attack the bread with the same fervor. Rather than stand there like an idiot kid unaccountably entranced by the way a woman's mouth moved, Marcus crossed the room to the washstand, poured some water into the bowl and gave his face a healthy splash of the cool liquid, wishing all the while that he could douse the rest of himself with it and put out the fires that had suddenly flared up.

Lord almighty, it was going to be one of the longest nights of his life, even though, at close to three now, there wasn't all that much left of it.

He sighed and turned. "Which side of the bed do you want?"

Amanda quit licking the butter on her fingers and stared at him. "Excuse me?"

"I asked which side of the bed you preferred."

"Which side?"

"Left?" he said, infusing his voice with a patience he didn't really feel. "Or right?"

She shrugged. "I never gave it much thought."

"I'm partial to the left side myself." Marcus sat on the edge of the mattress and started pulling off his boots, trying not to think about that preference being dictated by the fact that he was right-handed and it hampered his lovemaking when he lay on the right side of a bed.

As soon as he sat, Amanda scuttled toward the opposite side, which was fine with him. Whether he made her nervous because he was a bounty hunter or merely a male, he wasn't sure, but he was glad she was keeping a respectable—for her—and healthy—for him—distance.

He tugged off the other boot and let it drop to the floor. Then he stood, took off his gunbelt and hooked it over the bedpost. "Guess I'll take this side, then, if you don't care."

"We're sharing the bed?" She looked as stupefied as she sounded. As if he had just informed her that the earth was flat as a pancake, rather than round. As if he hadn't just quite plainly stated that he'd take the left side and she could take the right. "But I thought... I mean, naturally I assumed..."

"That, being a proper gentleman, I would naturally want to spend the night on the floor," he finished for her, then added, "You assumed wrong, Duchess."

Marcus lay down, staking his claim to his fair share of the mattress. He closed his eyes. "Good night."

"Good night?" she exclaimed.

"Sweet dreams." He reached up to punch the pillow into shape under his head.

"I can't sleep *here*." She thumped the mattress with her fist for emphasis.

"Okay. Then we'll change sides." Marcus knew very well that wasn't what she meant, but—weary as he was—he couldn't resist teasing her. Plus, he was curious to know just how far Her Ladyship would go, whether she'd actually insist on his giving up the bed, in which case he was anxious to tell her a little bit about pigs flying and snowstorms in hell.

"No. I meant, sleep here with *you*. For heaven's sake, Quicksilver. I've never shared a bed with anyone before, not even schoolmates, and I certainly don't intend sharing one with you."

"Fine."

"Fine."

Marcus steeled himself for the ensuing exchange of words—short ones like *well*, and *okay*, and brittle sentences like *Is that so?* He hunkered down into the mattress, prepared to endure the siege all night if he had to, but the next thing he knew, Amanda was jerking the pillow out from under his head.

"What the hell are you doing?" He barely got the words out before she was tugging at the quilt and yanking it out from under him.

"What does it look like I'm doing?" She unfurled the quilt and snapped it like a whip, then let it billow to the floor. "I'm making my bed." Now she tossed both pillows down. "There. I think it's fair that the person on the floor gets both pillows, don't you?"

Marcus, still framing and nailing down his argument for refusing to give up his portion of the bed, couldn't answer immediately. Besides, Amanda's quick capitulation had changed his position. He'd gone from stubborn knight errant to villain so fast he was almost dizzy. Which was probably the effect the woman had striven for. Unsettling him, if she couldn't unseat him. He raised up on one elbow now and glared at the pillows on the floor. "Yeah, I guess that's fair," he said.

"Fine."

"Fine."

She knelt down, her skirts pooling out around her, and began to adjust the corners of the quilt, while Marcus watched in tight-lipped silence. He knew good and well that if he opened his mouth, he'd be talking himself out of bed and onto the floorboards.

After fussing with her clothes and her curls and both pillows a minute, Amanda angled down and drew half the quilt over her. "This is surprisingly comfortable," she said. Then she yawned and added, "You may turn out the light now, Quicksilver. Good night."

Marcus reached for the lamp on the nightstand and turned down the wick. The room became as dark as the bottom of an inkwell, and quieter than a church. Only for a moment, however, and then soft, feathery laughter floated up from the floor.

"This is fun, Quicksilver."

Fun! Marcus bit down on a curse. He didn't think it was so damn much fun feeling like a selfish cur, making a woman sleep on the floor while he made himself comfortable in a bed. "What's fun about it?" he growled.

She sighed. "Well, I told you I'd never spent the night with schoolmates. I always wanted to, but my grandmother wouldn't allow it. She claimed it was unhealthy, sleeping with so many people in a room and breathing in their vapors, not to mention frivolous and something a Grenville simply didn't do."

"Rest assured, Duchess, I won't poison you with my vapors." Marcus rolled on his side and crooked an arm beneath his head. He was dead tired, but right now he wanted to keep listening to the lilting sound that was wafting up from the floor.

"Tell me what else a Grenville simply wouldn't do," he said.

She laughed again. "Half the things I've done today. Most of them. Riding in public conveyances. Eating apples for lunch and pickles for supper and talking to total strangers. I've been having the time of my life, actually." She sighed. "That's one of the reasons I ran away, you know. To escape all the traditions, all the confounded dos and don'ts and shouldn'ts and mustn'ts of the Grenvilles.'' She sighed happily before adding, ''And then, of course, there was Angus.''

''Angus.'' Marcus bit off the Scot's name as if he were shearing off the tip of a cigar and spitting it out.

If she noticed his reaction, Amanda gave no indication as she asked, almost breezily, ''How long do you suppose it will take us to reach Denver?''

''And Angus?'' Just the name left a bad taste in his mouth.

''Yes. That is where my fiancé resides. I imagine it's where I'll be living once we're married.''

Marcus sincerely doubted that. A person could achieve a pretty grand style in the burgeoning Colorado city, but once Angus McCray had his hands on the Grenville fortune, Marcus was willing to bet, the greedy Scot would be setting his sights on grander, more glittery climes. He didn't say so, though. It wasn't any of his business anyway—who Amanda Grenville married or what became of her after that, in Denver or anywhere else. ''Denver's all right'' was all he said.

''Is that where you live?'' Her voice was taking on a sleepy weight, a breathy languor.

''For now.'' Until he collected his reward, he thought, and then he just might be heading for Wyoming or Montana, as he'd planned so long ago. Settling down, perhaps. Perhaps not. He might just stay in Denver. He enjoyed the pleasures of the city when he was in it, and when he wasn't he enjoyed the rootlessness and the risks inherent in the bounty hunting business.

But suddenly, getting out of Denver didn't strike Marcus as such a bad idea, considering that was where Mrs. Angus McCray would be taking up residence, if only for a while. It hardly made sense, since he hadn't even known she existed before today, but the thought of passing her on Grant Street next month or next year, when she was hanging on the arm of the Scot, set Marcus's teeth on edge. Of course, that vision depended, he supposed, on whether he delivered her to Granny Grenville or to the big bad wolf.

"Good night, Quicksilver," came the drowsy voice from beside the bed.

"Good night, brat."

"I'm not, you know."

"Not what?"

"A brat." There was the sound of skirts rustling then, and some pillow punching and one long exhalation. "If I were a brat, Quicksilver, it would be you down here and me up there."

True enough, he thought, even though he'd be damned if he'd give her the satisfaction of saying so, or letting her know how thoroughly she'd outfoxed him by opting for the floor.

"Go to sleep," he said with a kind of gruff finality.

She couldn't. Tired as she was, Amanda was also oddly wide-awake, unwilling to let go of this day that had brought her so many new experiences. This day on which she'd felt real hunger for the first time in her life, during which she'd experienced real fear. And something else. It was a feeling that she didn't even have a name for, but she knew it had something to do with the handsome stranger whose breath she was listening to in this moment in the darkness. Her own breathing seemed to be evening out and taking on the rhythm of his. Suddenly she felt a peculiar and intimate connection that made her smile in the darkness.

"Quicksilver?" Amanda levered up on an elbow. "Are you asleep?"

There was silence for a moment, followed by a soft sigh and an even softer "Nope."

"Neither am I."

There was no reply other than the faint creaking of the ropes under the mattress, but Amanda sensed that he had turned toward her, that perhaps he, too, was finding it difficult to let their long day go. Perhaps not, though. All the experiences that were so new to her were surely old hat for a man like Marcus Quicksilver. Today might have struck him as just an ordinary day in the life of a bounty hunter.

"I've never met anyone in your line of work before," she said.

"Doesn't surprise me."

"You're quite good at it, I suppose."

"Good enough."

She smiled up at the dark form on the bed. In her experience, limited though it was, people didn't shy away from opportunities to talk about themselves or to brag when given the chance. Young men, in particular, seemed eager to let her know what wonderful catches they were. Not this one, though. Of course, he wasn't all that young. "You're not much of a conversationalist, Quicksilver," she murmured.

"Not at three o'clock in the morning, brat." The bed creaked again, this time a bit more impatiently. "Relax. Go to sleep."

Amanda closed her eyes. That was it, really. She couldn't relax. She was alone with a man in a hotel room. Prone. Horizontal. It was scandalous, really, and—a tiny grin inched its way across her lips—it was almost a shame that no one would ever know. A single woman. An unattached man.

"Quicksilver!" Amanda's eyes popped wide open. "Are you married?"

"Nope."

She sighed. "That's good. Neither am I. What I mean is, it wouldn't do at all to create a worse scandal. You're a bachelor, then? Not even promised to anyone?"

"Nope."

"Good. Neither am—" Her mouth snapped closed. What had she been about to say? She *was* promised to someone. To all intents and purposes, she already had one foot aimed down the aisle. How in the world could she have forgotten that, even for a moment?

"I must be more tired than I thought," she said as she turned on her side and tucked the quilt under her chin. "Good night, Quicksilver. Sleep well."

Two minutes later, the soft and even sound of her breathing told Marcus that Amanda was sleeping well, even if he couldn't. At least not until he scooped her up—quilt and pillows and all—and gently deposited her on the mattress before he attempted to carve out a spot for himself on the hard, dusty floor.

Long day, he thought, pulling his saddlebags under his head. With the circuitous route they'd have to take to Denver, there would be two or three more days, each likely to be as long as, if not longer than, this one. Not to mention the nights. Right now he didn't even want to think about those, or the sleepy warmth of a woman's body as he'd laid her in the bed, or the soft, almost grateful sigh that she'd breathed when he tucked the covers around her.

He edged the saddlebags farther under his neck, cocked one leg and crossed his arms over his chest, telling himself that by the time they got to Denver, he'd once again think of Amanda Grenville as a royal pain in the behind and be only too glad to exchange the runaway heiress—warm, soft, little body and all—for a significant sum of cold, hard cash.

Chapter Seven

Somebody was tapping on the door. Somebody who was thoughtless and rude and annoyingly persistent. Amanda jerked the quilt over her head to muffle the irritating noise while she attempted to preserve the flickering images and sweet sensations of the dream that was drifting through her head.

She'd been riding on a train that mysteriously transformed itself into a bed— No, it was a cloud! A warm and vaporous and wonderful cloud. An all-encompassing mist, within which someone had been kissing her and whispering the loveliest and warmest of endearments and...

The tapping intensified.

"Go away," she called, squeezing her eyes closed and digging her hipbone deeper into the mattress. Now where had she been? Oh, yes. The train had turned into a cloud and those stupefying, quite bedazzling kisses that had circled her neck like a strand of perfect pearls, and the hands that had warmed her skin and set all of her senses on fire before descending ever so slowly to...

When the tapping gave way to raw-knuckled pounding and the door began to rattle on its hinges, Amanda muttered a curse into the pillow, tossed off the quilt and watched her dream disintegrate and swirl like dust motes rising in the bright morning sunshine. Bright Nebraska sunshine. She had thought she was in her bed in New York, lost in lovely dreams, but now she suddenly remembered where she was and, perhaps more importantly, with whom. Quicksilver! Those had been dreams she was dreaming, hadn't they? *Hadn't they?*

She stumbled to the door, tripping over her hem and backhanding the hair away from her face. The woman who stood on the opposite side was just pulling her foot back, preparing to give the door a solid kick, when Amanda opened it.

"I figured you'd up and died in there," the woman said matter-of-factly, as if it wouldn't have been the first time a guest expired in this hotel.

"I was asleep."

"Uh-huh. Sure you were." The woman peered over Amanda's shoulder at the jumbled quilt on the bed, staring at it intently, the way a gypsy fortune-teller might scrutinize a palm.

Whatever did she think she was doing? Amanda wondered. Trying to tell her future? Or—dear Lord—looking for clues to her past? And now Amanda, her face burning, turned to study the haphazard coverlet, as well. That *had* been a dream, hadn't it? All those breathtaking kisses, and those throaty murmurs of love, and the exquisite feel of those warm, slow hands?

"It's hot," the woman said.

Amanda's head snapped around. Could the woman read her mind, too? "I beg your pardon?"

"The water." She pointed to a pail near her feet. "It's hot. Least it was when I brung it upstairs. If you'll get out of my way, I'll haul it in."

Amanda was only too glad to step aside and, in addition, to turn her flushed face away from the hotel maid. She walked to the window, skirting the infernal bed and its telltale coverlet as much as possible, and edged back the water-stained homespun curtain. A stage was just pulling up in the street below. It was a battered and mud-spattered contraption that had probably seen better days in the East and was now rolling its last creaking, bone-rattling miles out here on the plains, going from one dreary little town to another.

Two men clambered out of the coach, then stood beside it, brushing dust off their dark suits and their bowler hats. They were dressed identically, and would have looked like twins if one hadn't been exceptionally tall and thin and the other quite short and overweight. Amanda watched them a moment longer, mentally christening them Lincoln and Douglas, and wondering what had brought the urbane-looking pair to this one-street prairie town.

"'Scuse me." The maid angled herself between Amanda and the window to send a stream of washbowl water cascading to the street, missing Lincoln and Douglas, Amanda noticed, by a scant two feet.

"Strangers." The woman clucked her tongue with disgust as she stomped back to the washstand.

When Amanda returned her gaze to the window, those strangers were gone, but coming toward the hotel from across the street was somebody who wasn't a stranger anymore. How amazing, she thought, that she'd only known Marcus Quicksilver one day and yet his walk seemed as familiar to her as her grandmother's. Both possessed a faintly animallike quality, she mused. But while Honoria Grenville used her cane to navigate like a huge and unwieldy elephant, Marcus Quicksilver's graceful, long-legged gait seemed more like that of a great, sleek cat. There was more than a hint of the predator in the ease and smoothness, even the innate stealth of his stride.

In hindsight, she recognized that she should have taken him for a bounty hunter at first glance yesterday. The question now was whether she was his bounty or his retainer. Amanda still wasn't absolutely sure of his intentions. Not in the future. Nor, she thought, was she all that certain of his intentions in the past. Last night, specifically.

She turned to regard the spot on the floor where she had fallen asleep, and then her eyes flicked up to the jumbled covers atop the bed, where she'd awakened. The maid had begun to straighten them now, and when she tucked them in tightly, they looked, well...proper, somehow...if not completely innocent.

How silly it was to have worried, Amanda reassured herself. Of course that had been a dream, and the hunger she felt at that warm touch had been no more than the result of a pitifully empty stomach, and those amazing dream kisses had undoubtedly been bestowed on her by Angus. He was her fiancé, after all, and if she dreamed of anyone's kisses, it really ought to be his.

When she looked back out the window, the stage was pulling away. Lincoln and Douglas had disappeared, and so had Marcus Quicksilver.

"Well, that'll do it," announced the maid. "If you want to wash up, there's a cake of soap in the topmost drawer, and that water I brung you is still plenty warm." She pointed to the pitcher on the washstand. "I can't be climbing those stairs twenty times a day with hot, you know."

Soap and warm water! Now that was a dream come true, Amanda thought. Once she'd bathed, she would probably be able to think more clearly. "Help me out of my dress before you go, will you?"

"I ain't no personal maid." The woman's mouth turned down in a sour curve as she glared across the room at Amanda. "Anyway," she added, "I don't do nothing for nobody 'less they ask me please."

There was that word again. The woman was as bad as Quicksilver, acting as if Amanda had no manners at all, when in fact she'd been laboriously tutored in them, both at school and in her grandmother's home. Why did people out west want to be pleased and thanked all the time, for heaven's sake?

She made a great effort then to look helpless and properly apologetic at the same time. "Please," she said.

"Oh, well. All right."

And when the maid began to wrench loose the

buttons at the back of her dress, Amanda breathed a sigh of relief, along with a soft but genuine thank-you. She couldn't recall ever having been so excited about a simple pitcher of hot water and a cake of soap. If nothing else, her adventure was surely teaching her to appreciate things she had all but overlooked before.

At a cautious distance, Marcus followed the two men from the stage into the lobby of the hotel. Pinkertons. He'd be willing to bet his next three bounties on it. He could usually tell the detectives anywhere, by their dark suits and bowler hats and by the scent of aftershave that reeked in their wake. It was a miracle they arrested anyone at all, the way the idiots made themselves so obvious most of the time. Like now, as the tall one leaned across the oaken counter, scrutinizing the guest book by dragging a finger down the page, while the shorter one showed a picture to the desk clerk.

Obvious or not, however, Marcus couldn't quarrel with the job they were doing right now. If it was Amanda Grenville they were looking for—and Marcus had no doubt that it was—then the damned detectives had virtually found her.

"Looks like her," he heard the desk clerk say while squinting at the photograph, "only she's registered as a Mrs. Green. See. It's right here in the book. Green, Mr. and Mrs."

"Which room?" the lanky detective asked, leaning farther across the counter.

Marcus didn't stick around for the answer. By

God, he knew which room, and he took the stairs two at a time, sprinted down the hallway and burst through the door without knocking.

He should have knocked. That was the first thing that occurred to him as he stood in the doorway staring at a partially clad woman as if he'd never seen so much skin before in his life. And all on one beautifully formed little woman who was staring back at him, her green eyes enormous and her mouth gaping and her wet, soapy arms jerking up in an attempt to cover herself.

"You should have knocked," she said with a rush of breath.

He already knew that, dammit. But what was done was done, and later he'd deal with the astounding sight of her and what it did to his body. Marcus swallowed, and it sounded as if a rock were wedged in his throat. Then he heard footsteps at his back, so he pulled the door closed behind him.

"It's time to play Mrs. Green, Mrs. Green. We've got two Pinkertons coming down the hall this minute who think they know who you are."

Her eyes got even bigger then, as astonishment gave way to fear. Her jaw dropped another fraction. "Oh, my God! What are we going to do?"

Marcus crossed the room in three long strides. "They've got a picture of you, so the first thing we're going to do is make you look different. Bend your head over the washbowl."

"What?"

"Here." Marcus clamped one hand around the back of her neck and brusquely bent her over the washstand. Then he picked up the pitcher and poured its contents over her head.

Amanda sputtered and hissed like a cat, just as he'd expected. But also, just as he'd expected, when she lifted her head and shook the now sopping mass of blond hair, she looked more like a drowned cat than a runaway heiress. It was the best he could do under the circumstances, he figured. Now if she just didn't behave like an heiress...

A sharp rap sounded on the door.

"You're mad as hell at me," Marcus told her in a low voice.

"I *am* mad as hell, Quicksilver," Amanda sputtered while she wrung water out of a sopping hank of her hair. "How dare—"

"You're mad as hell at your *husband*, Mrs. Green. Remember that. And if you don't want to be hauled off half-naked by two of your grandmother's hired henchmen, you'll do the best acting job of your young life."

There was another knock on the door, this time louder and more insistent than before. "You in there! Open up!" someone shouted.

Marcus took one last, appraising look at Amanda. The wet hair had altered her appearance considerably. It hung past her shoulders in sodden blond curls, the water still dripping down her lithe arms and splattering at her bare and shapely little feet. But what he noticed even more was that the finely woven fabric of her underclothes clung to every inch of her now that it was wet. And, God help him, now that the lacy garments were wet, they were nearly— no, clearly—transparent.

For a minute, Marcus couldn't drag his gaze from the pink jut of her nipples, the succulent curves of her breasts, the darker triangle farther down. His mouth suddenly felt as if it had been sandblasted and the rest of him quickened with desire so that he had to force himself to remember where he was and who was just outside the door. Those two private detectives were going to get a very private eyeful if Marcus didn't do something fast.

He whipped the quilt from the bed and draped it around Amanda's damp shoulders. "There," he said quietly, before turning toward the door and shouting back over his shoulder, "Who the hell's here now? More of your old boyfriends?"

Marcus jerked open the door on the two Pinkertons and the desk clerk. "Yeah," he snarled. "What do you want? Come to see my ever-loving wife, did you?"

At his back just then the pitcher shattered on the floor. "That's it, Al Green!" Amanda screamed. "I've had just about enough of your vile accusations."

"Oh, you have, have you?" Marcus smiled wickedly at the rather bemused trio in the hallway. Amanda, it seemed, intended to play her role with unrestrained gusto. *This just might work,* he thought. "Come in, gentlemen. Take a seat. The fireworks are just beginning."

The desk clerk cleared his throat. "Maybe we should come back," he said, but the two Pinkertons shouldered him out of their way and entered the room. The tall one dropped his gaze to the picture he clutched in his hand, then looked up at the sodden Amanda and vaguely shook his head.

"I don't know," he said to his partner.

"He doesn't know!" Amanda yelled, stepping over the shards of broken pitcher. "Did you hear that? He doesn't know. By God, if that isn't the first time I've ever heard a man say that. You've never said it, Al Green. Not once in all the two years we've been married."

She shook a vehement finger at him, almost losing her quilt. "The two *long* years, I might add. I'm guessing you'd bite off your own tongue before you ever admitted you didn't know something."

Marcus shoved past the shorter detective and stomped to within half a foot of his bellowing battle-ax of a bride. "Is that right? Well, for your information, here's something I didn't know, Alice. I didn't know I'd be spending the rest of my days in flaming purgatory the day I married you."

"Purgatory!" She slapped his arm, hard, shook her wet hair and sent a stream of water across his shirt, then poked a finger into his chest. "Purgatory! And I suppose you think it's been just one heavenly day after another for me. A lot you know, you selfish blockhead!"

The desk clerk had crossed the threshhold into the room now, but he maintained a cautious position near the door, one hand clamped on the knob. "Uh, you folks want to keep the damages down a little. The noise, too. We've got other guests who—"

"See!" Amanda screamed. "You're making a spectacle of yourself again, Al. We can't go anyplace decent anymore because of your hot temper and your bad manners and your filthy suspicions."

"We can't go anyplace anymore without running into at least half a dozen of your old flames," Marcus shot back, jerking a thumb toward the Pinkertons.

"Them?" Amanda threw a hot glare at the two dark-suited men, whom she had immediately recognized as her own Lincoln and Douglas. "I've never seen either one of them before in my life. But who knows? Maybe if I had, I wouldn't be married to you, Al, you arrogant pig."

Marcus, who had already impressed her with his acting skills, now proceeded to make decidedly disgusting oinking sounds, which Amanda thought might be taking things a bit too far. The poor desk clerk shrugged and shook his head before stepping backward out the door and disappearing down the hall. The detectives, however, held their ground while they passed the picture back and forth between them and glanced, curiously, from the black-and-white image to Amanda's face.

"I don't know," Douglas said. "There's a resemblance, I guess, but I can't be sure. Not one hundred percent anyway."

"Me neither." Lincoln scowled. "These two seem pretty married to me. Just listen to them."

When she heard this bemused exchange between the Pinkertons, Amanda's confidence soared. She reached out and snatched the picture from Douglas's grasp. After a quick perusal, she exclaimed, "Oh, this is that runaway heiress, isn't it? That...what's her name? Granman? Granville?"

"Grenville," Lincoln said.

"Grenville! That's right."

Peering more closely at the image, Amanda wrinkled her forehead and pursed her lips studiously. It was hardly her favorite photograph, she thought indignantly. She'd been headachy and out of sorts that afternoon two years ago, on her nineteenth birthday, when her grandmother insisted she sit for it. Even worse, the photographer had been an obsequious, simpering fool whose breath smelled of cloves and whose clothes reeked of flash powder and tobacco smoke. It irritated Amanda considerably that her grandmother had chosen this particular picture as an adequate likeness.

"Well, what do you know?" she exclaimed, passing the photograph to Marcus. "Take a look at this, will you? We could almost be cousins, Al, this Grenville woman and me. What do you think?"

Before he looked at the picture, Marcus aimed a sharp, cautionary glance at Amanda, as if to say, *Don't press your luck.* But she laughed and ignored it. She was having a grand time playacting. Her grandmother had never approved of theatrics in any form, preferring instead dull recitations of psalms and essays. This was fun, playing Marcus's wife and pulling the wool over Pinkerton eyes. It was dangerously exciting.

She patted the wet mass of hair on her head now and batted her eyes. "Anyone might take us for long-lost sisters, that Grenville woman and me. Or cousins, at the very least. Of course, I'm a lot prettier.'' She slanted a grin toward Marcus. ''Don't you agree, Al?''

''I wish you had her money instead of her looks,'' Marcus growled.

''Oh, you do, do you?'' Amanda snorted. ''Well, why don't you just leave me and marry her? Ha! As if you could. As if anybody with any real class would have you.''

''That's for damn sure,'' he shot back. ''Hell, I guess that's why I'm stuck with you.''

''*Stuck* with me!'' She jabbed him in the upper arm. ''*Stuck* with me! Go on and leave. See if I care. See how long it takes me to find somebody else. Somebody better.'' Amanda cast a sidelong glance at the lanky Pinkerton and fluttered her eyelids again, flirtatiously. ''Somebody taller.''

''Oh, now wait a minute....'' Lincoln said, while Marcus cursed and drew back his fist as if he meant to hit Amanda full in the face.

She stepped forward, taunting him, thrilled with her own daring act. ''Go ahead, Al. Hit me. Right in front of these witnesses. I dare you. Go on.''

For a brief second, Amanda had to remind herself that this was all just an act, when she saw the murderous look on Marcus Quicksilver's face. A muscle jerked in his cheek, and blue fire glistened in his eyes. He *was* just pretending, wasn't he?

Apparently Douglas didn't think so, because the short man began backing toward the door, well out of range of the domestic rage. ''Sorry we disturbed you folks," he said. Then, with a nervous glance at his partner, he whined, "Come on. Get the confounded picture and let's get out of here while everybody's still in one piece."

"What's your hurry?" Marcus laughed viciously. "Stick around. The fun's just beginning, fellas. Alice here likes to have an audience. Wait'll you see her when she really gets mad. The woman can raise blisters on a rhino's hide with that tongue of hers."

Amanda shook a fist at him. "Well, you'd know, wouldn't you, Al," she shrieked, "since you're about as sensitive as a rhinoceros?"

When Marcus drew back again as if he were going to slug her, Lincoln took the opportunity to swipe the picture from his hand, then moved quickly toward the door.

"It isn't her," he said to his short partner as he gave him a little shove out into the hallway. "And, by God, even if she were the Grenville girl, I'll be damned if I'd spend a day taking her back to Denver. That old lady couldn't pay me enough." He pulled the door closed, calling over his shoulder. "You two sure deserve each other."

"Yeah, and don't you two sons of bitches come sniffing around my Alice again!" Marcus bellowed for good measure.

He stood there a minute then, his heart thundering, his muscles bunched and all of his nerves wired, as if he really were that mad. Beside him, Amanda was breathing like someone who'd just crossed the finish line in a race. Her pretty face was flushed and glistening and her eyes were still bright with bristling ire. She looked to Marcus, just then, like a wild prairie rose.

By God, he was proud of her! She'd run circles around those two detectives. All in all, she'd probably been even more convincing than he'd been himself. What a hell of a woman. What a team the two of them had been. Marcus turned to her and grinned.

Amanda grinned back, and the next instant they both exploded in laughter.

"Did you see the look on that little fella's face?" Marcus said.

"He was so anxious to get out of here, I thought for a minute he was going to go...to go straight through the wall instead of...of using the door." Amanda's words broke apart in giggles. "You were so...so..."

"Convincing?"

She shook her head, trying to catch her breath. "So funny. Especially the part about the blisters on the rhinoceros. I nearly started laughing right then." When she lifted a hand to wipe a tear from the corner of her eye, the quilt slipped to the floor. "Oops." She giggled more as she attempted to step out of its folds, then nearly lost her balance.

"Careful there, Alice." Marcus caught her by the shoulders and steadied her.

"Why, Al! You sweet old thing. You do care whether I live or die!" She batted her eyelashes up into his face. "Don't you?"

Care. The word entered Marcus's brain like a bullet and ricocheted there as he stood with his hands on Amanda's shoulders and her laughing, lovely face turned up to his. Her skin was warm and supple beneath his fingers, while her long, wet hair cooled the backs of his hands. The urge to kiss her shot through him. The need to taste her—all of her— right now—nearly buckled his knees.

All of a sudden, Amanda's laughter subsided in a surprised little gulp. Her green eyes widened perceptibly, signaling compliance, sending Marcus a sweet and undeniable invitation, saying yes.

Marcus nearly kissed her, too, before the thinking fragment of his brain kicked in with a warning that he was about to make a terrible mistake, perhaps even the worst mistake of his life. He realized he had to stop touching her that second, so he gave her shoulders what he hoped was a friendly squeeze, then dropped his hands to his sides and said, "Nice work. You carried that off real well, Duchess. Get dressed now, and we'll get out of here before those two Pinkertons decide to change their addled minds and come back to snoop some more."

In her joy, Amanda had quite forgotten she was standing there in just her wet camisole and drawers. But the moment Marcus stepped away from her, cool air rushed between them. Even so, she felt a flush blaze across her already heated cheeks, part of the heat that had suffused her entire body when Marcus looked at her that way. That breath-stealing, heart-stopping way. That hungry way—as if he were starving and she was meat and mashed potatoes and gravy over it all.

Which was, she decided, the way her knees felt

now, all soft and fluid, as she stooped to reclaim the fallen quilt. She hugged it around herself protectively then, suddenly as embarrassed by her state of undress as she was bewildered by the feelings she'd just experienced.

But Marcus wasn't looking at her hungrily anymore. The expression on his face now, as his eyes narrowed and his mouth flattened out, was closer to impatience. "Don't just stand there, brat," he snapped. "Get dressed. Let's get out of here."

"Yes. All right." She felt more than a little dizzy and disconcerted. Disappointed, too. She'd been wrong about the man and his intentions, obviously. Her experience with passion was nonexistent, after all. Perhaps it was only the remnants of their angry charade that she'd witnessed in his eyes. Or, if it had been passion, then more than likely it had been the sort reserved for money. He didn't want her. Not in that way. He just wanted to get her to Denver and collect his fee. Amanda felt like a dolt now for imagining otherwise.

Tightening the quilt around herself, she echoed his clipped tone. "I'll be only too happy to get dressed, Quicksilver, as soon as I have a little privacy." She freed one hand in order to gesture toward the door. "And the next time, if there *is* a next time, I certainly hope you'll remember that a gentleman always knocks before he enters a room."

Marcus slapped his saddlebags onto his shoulder. His bootheels hammered the floor as he crossed the room, and then he opened the door with such force he nearly ripped the knob from the wood.

"Maybe the next time, brat," he said, "you'll remember that a lady always thanks a gentleman for sleeping on the goddamned floor." He stepped into the hallway then, and just as he was pulling the door closed behind him, he added in a low grumble, "You're welcome."

The door clicked closed then, leaving Amanda standing there blinking at it while she gnawed on a thank-you as tough as beef jerky.

Chapter Eight

Marcus had turned Sarah B. east instead of west after they mounted up outside the hotel, under the suspicious gazes of the desk clerk and the detectives, who lingered in the lobby. The runaway heiress was supposed to be heading west, to Denver, so it made at least a little sense to travel in the opposite direction. Of course, going the wrong way added more miles to their journey, and more miles meant more time being aggravated by her, but Marcus didn't see that he had much choice at this point, considering the multitude in pursuit of Amanda and their own pitiful lack of cash.

Her Ladyship didn't comment on his choice of direction. It was possible that she hadn't noticed, Marcus thought. More likely, though, it was because she was far too busy situating herself behind him, shifting this way and that, alternately wrapping her arms around his middle and then changing her mind and grabbing at his belt. Sarah B. had about had it with her squirming cargo, and the mare was trotting with her head low and a definite hitch in her hindquarters—probably contemplating bucking both of them off—when Marcus finally snarled over his shoulder, "Will you sit still?"

"I'm trying to get comfortable."

"Well, all that bouncing is just going to make you uncomfortable later on, and I really don't want to have to listen to you whining all night."

"I don't whine." She bustled and rustled around another minute or two, then settled down, having found, Marcus assumed, a proper seat, now that her arms were clamped like bands around his chest and her breasts were snug against his back.

"Oh, and by the way, Quicksilver," she said casually, almost airily, at his shoulder, "I meant to thank you earlier."

He didn't respond immediately, not only because her expression of thanks—offhand though it was— had caught him off guard, but also because he meant to milk every last ounce out of that Grenville gratitude, since it would probably be the last he'd ever hear.

"Thanks?" he drawled as he stared off over Sarah B's head at the wide sweep of green prairie before them and the clear canopy of blue sky above. "For what?"

She sighed. "You know. For everything."

"What? Specifically." Marcus felt a wicked smile edge across his face. No mere blanket gratitude for him. No, sir. No puny gratuity. No small change or threadbare castoffs from the little rich girl. He meant to have it all, right down to the last stitch on the quilt he'd let her keep the night before, the last feather in the pillow, and the last damn stripe of ticking on the mattress.

"Thank you for getting me away from those dreadful Pinkertons."

"You're welcome." He waited a second before adding, "And?"

She sucked in a breath, as if she needed more air to fuel her speech, then she let it out, along with "And thank you for letting me have the bed last night."

"And the pillows."

"Yes, and the pillows," she said grudgingly.

"And the quilt." He cast a quick glance over his shoulder, at the same time tensing the muscles in his midriff against the anticipated fist.

"The quilt?" she asked tentatively.

"Uh-huh."

She was strangely silent a moment. "About last night, Quicksilver..." she began, before her voice trailed off in uncertainty.

"What about it?"

"I was merely wondering... I mean...well, I was fast asleep last night, and I'm afraid that I really don't remember..."

So that's what she was worried about! "Are you asking if I did anything more than relocate you?"

"W-well," she stammered, shifting against his back once more, "in a word—yes."

He should have laughed, but for a dizzy second, reality and wishful thinking blurred in Marcus's brain as he recalled holding her warm body in his arms and knowing the feel of her through the curves of the quilt and wanting more than all those folds of fabric would allow. And now, as before, he told himself his reaction was no surprise. Hadn't he been on the trail three weeks? Hadn't it been more weeks than he cared to count since he was with a woman? More weeks than he dared to count. Especially right now.

"Well?" Amanda inquired, less with trepidation now than with undisguised impatience. Her index finger ticked relentlessly on one of Marcus's ribs.

It might have been fun to string her along, Marcus thought. To let her worry about what had or hadn't happened the night before, when she was fast asleep. To set that pretty, pampered head of hers to worrying overtime. Lord knew the brat deserved a little unsettling. But Marcus just didn't feel up to it. Not just now. Not on this subject, anyway.

He straightened up in the saddle, shifting his weight, dislodging Amanda's tight grip on him a little. What the hell did she think, anyway? That just because he wasn't a wealthy man, or a slick dandy like Angus McCray, he was an animal? That because he wasn't a part of her refined social circles, he didn't have anything but the basest, most bestial instincts? Did she think he couldn't possibly be worthy of her?

"Nothing happened, brat," he told her, aiming a glare over his shoulder. "Believe me, if it had, you'd remember it." He shook his head. "If that's what's been worrying you, you can just put it out of your mind. Nothing happened. And nothing's going to happen, either. Frankly, you're not my type."

At the same moment she breathed out a very welcome, if not grateful, sigh of relief, Amanda found herself sucking it right back in. Not his type? Not his *type?* What the devil did that mean?

She was about to ask, to demand an explanation, but before she could utter a word, Marcus announced "We're wasting time here," then jabbed his spurs into the mare and set Sarah B. off at a pace that precluded speech entirely. All Amanda could do after that was hang on and grit her teeth, all the while wondering just what the bounty hunter had meant by that remark. Wondering, too, just what type she truly was, having never been allowed to express so much as a wish or a whim. If anything, she'd been an obedient type for her entire life.

Until now.

Two hours later, after that hard, bone-rattling, muscle-numbing ride, Amanda stood alone outside the livery stable in Kimball, dragging her fingers through her windblown hair and trying—in vain, it seemed—to comb out a few of the knots and tangles. Her effort to ignore her rumbling stomach was equally unsuccessful, especially when her gaze kept wandering across the street to a sign that proclaimed Beer 5 Cents—Hard-boiled Eggs Free For The Asking.

Marcus Quicksilver was nowhere to be seen in the dark interior of the stable, where he'd disappeared with his horse a while ago. The bounty hunter had barely spoken to her, ever since informing her she wasn't his type. His type! Whatever that meant. The comment continued to irritate her. She profoundly hoped she wasn't anybody's type right now, with her hair all tied in knots and her clothes smelling to high heaven and her stomach shriveled to the size of a walnut or, worse, a raisin.

Although Marcus had ordered her in no uncertain terms to stay right where he left her, if he didn't emerge from the depths of the livery stable in the next few minutes, Amanda decided, she was going across the street by herself to the drinking establishment beneath the intriguing advertisement. Propriety be damned. And good luck, when and if Marcus found her, if there were more than one or two of those free eggs left in the entire place. His type or not, she certainly wasn't the type to sit and starve to death in the shadow of a sign that promised free food.

Smoothing her hair back as best she could, Amanda gave one last glance into the stable, then marched purposefully across the street.

Several minutes later, when Marcus walked out into the sunlit street, he had to squint in order to count the greenbacks in his hand. Sixty dollars for Sarah B. and his Mexican saddle. Sixty lousy dollars. Hell. The saddle alone had cost him eighty bucks a few years back, and as for the mare, well…she'd probably be a lot happier staying in one place and getting regular rest and feed, instead of traipsing around and living half the time on prairie grasses and slow creek water.

He glanced at the vacant slat-back chair, distinctly remembering telling Amanda Grenville to wait right there. She had nodded, as he recalled, while she was fussing with her hair, but she hadn't exactly said she'd do it. Not that Marcus would have expected it, either. What was he supposed to do, dammit, short of handcuffing and hobbling her? After he looked left and right along the street, his gaze came to rest on the sign over the saloon directly across the way.

Muttering a curse, Marcus creased the greenbacks and shoved them in his pocket. Sixty dollars. Already he could hear his friendly Denver banker's tight fist coming down on his leather desktop and see the man's eyes kind of pinwheeling in his head when he said, "What do you mean, you need a couple hundred for a new horse and saddle? Where's your old saddle? Where's that obstinate mare you were so crazy about?"

Over there in the saloon. Marcus bent and tightened the leather thong that kept his gun snug against his leg. *She's over there right now, trying to sweet-talk a hard-boiled barkeep out of a damn ten-minute egg. Advertising to the whole town, the whole damn world, just who she is and what she is and how much she's worth. Messing up my plans but good.*

He straightened up, settled his hat firmly on his head, put on his meanest, most low-down look, then crossed the street to the saloon. The double door was wide open, and before Marcus had even set foot inside the place, he heard an all-too-familiar female voice rising like a chill wind out of the frozen north.

"No, my good man. It's you who doesn't understand. I don't want a beer. I want an egg. Your sign expressly states that they are free for the asking.''

"It's you that don't understand, lady," a male voice replied. "Or maybe you can't read so good." Now a chorus of rough bass laughter accompanied the soloist behind the bar as he asked, "Now, do you want a beer or not?"

"I most certainly do not."

Marcus was just inside the door now, in time to see Amanda's spine snap straight as a ruler and her chin come up several determined inches. He could only guess the fiery color of her eyes when she shot back, "I want an egg, you ignoramus. For free. Don't you know what your own confounded sign says?"

The barkeep, a thin fellow with a black droop of a mustache, looked less like an ignoramus just then than someone who would enjoy nothing better in this world than to sink a hard right hook into a certain little porcelain jawbone. Marcus immediately lengthened his stride toward the bar, where he slapped down one of his newly acquired greenbacks.

"I'll have a beer," he said, "and see that my wife here gets some salt and pepper for her egg."

While the barkeep blinked and sputtered out a quick "Sure. I'll see to that, mister," Amanda turned and trained her smoking, double-barreled gaze on Marcus. He thought he'd never seen a more expressive face. In this case, it fairly raced through half a dozen emotions, beginning with hot indignation and concluding in cool, nearly regal acceptance. If even a hint of gratitude was lurking in there someplace—and Marcus sincerely doubted that—Her Ladyship didn't let it show.

"Just salt," she told the man behind the bar. "I detest pepper."

"You might want to try a little sugar," Marcus muttered out of a corner of his mouth.

"On an egg?"

He shrugged and settled a boot on the brass rail, then leaned forward on his elbows. "Might sweeten your disposition."

"Oh, really?" She stiffened like a broom, and those green eyes of hers flared again, but before she could light into Marcus with her sharp little tongue, the bartender slapped down a plate on which one peeled egg wobbled momentarily from side to side before Amanda snatched it up and bit it in half.

Marcus took a long swallow of tepid beer, figuring that that would have to suffice for his own lunch. Sixty dollars wasn't going to go a long way, even in this prairie town, and he already had plans for spending a good portion of it as soon as Miss Amanda Grenville dispatched her free egg.

Staring idly into the mirror behind the bar, he took in the faces of the half-dozen men sitting at tables, checking those visages off against pictures he'd memorized on scores of Wanted posters. Nothing promising here. They were farmers, not felons. Marcus lifted his gaze then and read the sign over the coat rack. In the mirror, backward, it said *GNILB-MAG ON.*

"Anyplace a fella can find a good poker game

around here?'' he asked the barkeep when the man pushed his change across the bar.

''Try down the street at the Double Eagle.'' The man's droopy mustache drooped a bit more when he added in a low tone, ''My wife's half owner here. Durned Baptist. Lucky we still sell beer.''

''Yep.'' Marcus clucked his tongue in sympathy, then asked, ''How 'bout an emporium? Someplace that sells ladies' clothes?''

''Holcomb's,'' the bartender said, angling his head toward the window. ''Far end of town. You can't miss their sign.''

''Thanks.'' Marcus drained his glass of the last few drops of warm beer, then clasped Amanda's elbow. ''Come on.''

Out on the sidewalk, she swallowed the last of the egg and licked a stray fleck of yolk from her upper lip before she said, ''An emporium, Quicksilver? Ladies' clothes? What did you do, rob a bank?''

That had been a distinct possibility, Marcus thought, when the liveryman didn't show much initial interest in Sarah B. or his Mexican saddle. ''I sold the mare,'' he said. ''I've got a plan.''

''Oh, you do.'' She looked up at him skeptically at first, but then her lips spread in a sudden, sunny smile. ''Well, as long as this plan of yours appears to include a new outfit for me, I believe I'll reserve judgment on it for the time being.''

''Much obliged,'' he said, sincerely doubting that she'd be able to keep her opinions to herself for more than a few minutes, especially when Her Ladyship got a glimpse of the new outfit Marcus had in mind. Little Miss Amanda Grenville didn't know it yet, but she was about to be demoted from princess to peasant, from riches to rags.

Holcomb's Emporium, with its glass-and-walnut display cases and its dust-free shelves, might be a step up from the dry goods store in Julesburg, Amanda decided, but it was still a far cry from the fashionable shops in New York City.

She picked up a tortoise hand mirror from a cluttered table and sought her own reflection with some trepidation. Just as she'd suspected, she looked like a woman who'd ridden hatless all morning under a broiling sun. Her nose was pink as a shrimp and, if she held the looking glass slightly at an angle, she could even detect a few freckles on her windburned cheeks. It wasn't so horrible, really, though, and Amanda thought perhaps she looked healthier than she ever had before. By the time she got to Denver—if she ever did—she'd probably look as if she'd walked all the way from Omaha.

Of course, now that Marcus had sold his horse, such a long hike didn't seem entirely out of the question. She set the mirror down, frowning. What was this mysterious plan of his? she wondered. Did it have something to do with getting her to Denver? He was still working for her, wasn't he? Looking around, she discovered the bounty hunter deep in conversation with the aged proprietor of the store. Then, after Marcus gave her a little salute and mouthed the words *Stay right there,* the two of them disappeared behind a curtain into a back room.

Well, of course she'd stay right here. Where the devil else could she possibly go? Amanda shrugged and began going through some limp cotton dresses suspended from a broomstick. When the best of the lot, a blue calico with a white lace collar, turned out to be fashioned for a woman three times her size, Amanda felt a small but distinct yearning for her grandmother's long-time couturière, Mademoiselle Seurat.

Marcus had never seen her in anything but this woebegone, worn-out, wrinkled traveling suit. Well, that and her sopping-wet undergarments this morning, after he dumped the pitcher of water on her head. She wondered if he'd find her more his type if she was wearing something else. Something, if not stylish, then at least fresh and clean. Not that clothes had ever mattered to her all that much, but men— or so it seemed, in her rather limited experience— set great store in the allurement of female clothes.

Angus McCray certainly had the day they met, when she'd been wearing her blue watered silk. His eyes had positively glowed with appreciation, and he hadn't been able to compliment her enough. That sort of adulation didn't seem to come naturally to Marcus Quicksilver, she thought, if it came at all. Wresting a compliment from the bounty hunter would be comparable to pulling hen's teeth, she decided.

While she searched through the dresses one more

time, Marcus reappeared, holding something black and blue and rustling in his hand.

"Here you go, brat. This ought to do just fine."

He held the object up for her inspection, and Amanda could only stare, speechless, at the gaudy black lace and the satin stripes of black and royal blue.

"What in the world is that?" she asked.

He rolled his eyes toward the ceiling. "What does it look like? It's a dress."

Amanda reached out to finger the shiny fabric. There didn't seem to be a great deal of it. "A dress! This is a dress? It looks more like a corset with a three-foot peplum."

The elderly proprietor seemed to take that as his cue for a little salesmanship, so he stepped forward. "Oh, no, ma'am. It's a dress, all right, and a mighty fine one at that. Miss Caroline Carew of the Double Eagle ordered this straight from Chicago. Only thing was, by the time the dress arrived, Miss Caroline had succumbed to a fever, poor little thing, and none of the other girls at the Eagle was able to fit into it. They tried, too." He laughed. "Some of 'em tried twice."

He stuck out a liver-spotted hand now and gave the satin folds a shaky but loving caress. "I been keeping it in back, so as not to upset some of the proper Baptist womenfolk in town."

"We'll take it," Marcus said decisively.

"We'll do no such thing," Amanda countered. "Why, I couldn't wear that. I wouldn't. It's... it's..."

Marcus curved his hand around her arm and pulled her aside, out of earshot of the elderly proprietor. "It's not something a runaway heiress would wear," he whispered. "And that makes it perfect. Right?"

"Oh."

"The less you look like Amanda Grenville, the better off you'll be. That's part of my plan."

"Your plan. I see." Much as she hated to admit it, she supposed he was right. Amanda cast a mournful glance at the black-and-blue frock, then added with a sigh, "I only wish this plan of yours wasn't quite so...so revealing, Quicksilver."

Revealing was putting it rather mildly, Amanda thought later, as she stood before a mirror in a small hotel room and gave another upward yank to the skimpy bodice of the dress. Her grandmother had always referred to Amanda's physical attributes as pleasingly rounded—when the old prude referred to them at all—but then, she had always required her granddaughter to wear frocks that completely flattened and disguised all of that pleasant roundness.

Now, however, Amanda was amazed to discover just how pronounced her curves could be when encouraged by whalebone and tight laces and a definite dearth of fabric. She looked like a different person. And, much to her surprise, she liked it!

Almost as much as she liked feeling clean for the first time in days. With his newfound cash, Marcus had purchased her not only a dress, but a hairbrush, as well, and then he had gotten them a room and two thick ham sandwiches. Best of all, though, he'd left Amanda alone to bathe and wash her hair.

Now that the dust and grime were gone, the natural shine and softness had returned to her tresses. She brushed one long strand around a finger now and pinned it atop her head. Experimenting then, she pinned up the rest in a crown of loose and lustrous yellow curls—a coiffure befitting the dress she wore. Both would surely give the staid and stern Honoria Grenville at least half an hour's worth of palpitations, with vapors on the side.

And Angus? Amanda pondered her reflection in the mirror, wondering what her fiancé would think if he saw her now, like this. Would he think she looked feminine and lovely? Or would he tell her she looked like a tart and insist that she change immediately into something more suitable? Probably.

"What a shame," she murmured, softly and a little sadly, just as a distinct knock sounded on the door. "Who is it?" she called.

"A gentleman of your acquaintance," came the reply from the hallway. "One who knocks. Are you decent?"

"That's a matter of opinion, I suppose," Amanda answered with a laugh. "Come in, Quicksilver."

The key ticked in the lock then, and the brass doorknob began to turn, and as it did, Amanda's heart turned, too. Quite suddenly it was incredibly important—crucial, even—that Marcus Quicksilver approve of the way she looked. No. More than approve. She wanted him to think she was lovely. Beautiful. Beyond compare. She wanted nothing more at that moment than to bowl the bounty hunter over, to make it impossible for him even to speak, to take his very breath away. As her own breath had just been crowded out by the rampant beating of her heart.

"Well?" She held out each side of the short black-and-blue skirt, twirling gaily, as he came through the door. "What do you think?"

Marcus crossed his arms and leaned a shoulder against the door frame. What did he think? He thought he wasn't breathing any too well, the way his heart was thumping and rearranging itself in his chest. He thought maybe the dress hadn't been such a good idea, after all, considering the way he was reacting to it. He thought he wasn't really thinking, not with his head, anyway. And he thought he'd never seen a more beautiful, a more desirable woman in his life.

It had nothing to do with the alluring mass of curls on her head or the ivory column of her exposed neck or the delicate shape of her bared shoulders or the shapely line of her calves. It had almost nothing to do with the pale swell of her breasts and the dusky shadow of cleavage between them. Well, it had *something* to do with those factors, which held him mesmerized and mute.

But what made her truly beautiful was the look of utter joy on her face. Her green eyes were bright as the first day of spring, and her mouth curved up with all the happy anticipation of Christmas morning. All Marcus could think was how much he wanted her. Right then. Always.

He thought he was probably addle-brained from not having enough to eat in the past couple days, from warm beer on an empty stomach, and from being in the constant company of a woman he couldn't, shouldn't—wouldn't, dammit—touch.

So when she stopped spinning around like a shiny blue-and-black top and then pinned him with her happy, expectant gaze and asked, once again, "Well?" Marcus shoved off the door frame with a fairly brusque, "Fine. You look just fine. The dress fits real well."

The light diminished in her eyes, turning from spring to winter. Her Christmas-morning smile faded to a lackluster Monday. But she did her best to hide the hurt and disappointment by busying herself with a stray thread on her skirt, which made Marcus feel like a heel. Worse. Like a callus on a heel.

Whatever had softened inside him at the sight of her was tough again. He was a bounty hunter bringing in a prize. It was as simple and as clear-cut as that. Amanda Grenville was *his* captive, *his* prisoner. It wasn't the other way around. And there was no room in his plan to allow it to be otherwise. The minute he started thinking with his heart instead of his head, he might as well just turn her over to the Pinkertons and kiss that big reward goodbye.

Which, he reminded himself rather brutally, was exactly what Amanda Grenville would be doing to him once he got her safely to Denver. Blowing him a cool kiss and wishing him goodbye and good luck.

And, despite the way his heart was beating right now at the mere sight of her, he told himself that goodbye and good luck was really all there would be for the two of them to say.

Chapter Nine

If it was attention she wanted, or praise in the form of gawking, Amanda received plenty of both at the Double Eagle a while later. The saloon, as it turned out, was part two of Marcus's slowly unfolding plan. With the money that remained after buying the dress and engaging the hotel room, the bounty hunter intended to indulge himself in a game of poker.

Amanda's protests had fallen on deaf ears. "Why risk what little we've got?" she had asked when they strolled across the street toward the saloon.

"Trust me," Marcus had replied, with some irritation.

"Yes, but…"

It was the last thing she'd said before being propelled through a battered door into what her grandmother undoubtedly would have called a low-class den of iniquity. But Amanda rather liked it, once her eyes stopped smarting from the smoke that hovered in the air and her nose became accustomed to beer fumes, not to mention her ears adjusting to language that was coarser than sandpaper.

What she enjoyed especially was being somebody else. Marcus's plan to disguise her in a new outfit worked brilliantly. Not only did she not look like a runaway heiress anymore, she didn't feel like one, either. Amanda felt, well...common, in the best sense of the word. Normal for the first time in her life. She felt free, liberated from all the conventions and pruderies and expectations imposed on her in the past. She felt quite independent. This was, after all, the reason she had run away in the first place.

Marcus had seated her against the rear wall of the smoky saloon, not far from the piano. "Keep an eye on her, will you?" he'd asked the fat piano man, and then to Amanda he'd said, "Stay here. This shouldn't take too long," before he abandoned her for a seat at a table where a grim-lipped, glowering game of cards was already in progress.

Why they called it a game was beyond Amanda. None of the players appeared to be having any fun. Well, Marcus fit right in, she thought. For a man with such a beautiful smile, he certainly kept it under wraps as often as not. Right now, across the room, that smile was merely a dark slash with a thin cigar sticking out from one corner while Marcus contemplated the cards in his hand.

"That's sure a swell dress, honey."

A strapping redhead in pink satin and high red laced boots took the chair next to Amanda's, straddling it as if it were a saddle. "Glad to see somebody finally took it off old man Holcomb's hands. I tried it on myself, but as you can see, I'm a little too broad in the beam."

Amanda smiled politely and said nothing, rather than agree that the redhead was indeed of such ample girth that her pink dress was threatening to explode at a variety of seams.

"The name's Sally, honey," she said. "What's yours?"

"A—" Having barely opened her mouth, Amanda promptly closed it. Oh, dear. Was she still supposed to be Alice? Somehow that sweet and simple name didn't seem to fit the dress.

Before she could answer, though, ample Sally leaned closer and inquired, "You looking for work, honey, or just out for a night on the town with that handsome devil you came in with?"

Her gaze followed Sally's to the table across the room where Marcus sat. He was a handsome devil, wasn't he, with his hat slanted back on his head and a cigar stuck at a rakish angle in his mouth? A little grin twitched across Amanda's mouth as those peculiar twinges started again in the pit of her stomach. It tickled her, too, to be mistaken for a working girl, or whatever it was they called women who made their livings in saloons.

"I might be," she said. "Seeking employment, that is. What sort of positions are available?"

The big redhead snorted with laughter and slapped her knee. "Positions. Now that's a good one. Best I've heard all week." She reached over and clapped the piano player's massive shoulder. "Did you hear that, Harry? Blondie wants to know what sort of positions we got here."

"Does she sing?" he asked, keeping his eyes on

the keyboard and his fat fingers dancing over the keys.

"What?"

"Ask her if she sings!" he shouted over his own loud music.

The redhead turned back to Amanda, leaning closer and nearly shouting, "Harry wants to know if you sing, honey?"

"Sing? Oh, of course. My goodness, I'd better be able to sing, after studying three years with—"

Amanda stopped. The fact that she'd studied voice with one of New York's foremost tenors, Giuseppe Volpone, was a pretty good indication that she wasn't the commonplace young working woman she appeared to be. "Well, only a little," she said now. "I know some German lieder, and a few other songs."

"How about 'Camptown Races'?" the piano player asked, angling his head in Amanda's direction while he continued to play.

"Well, yes. Everyone…"

"Great. Go get her a beer, Sally. Climb up here on the soundboard, Blondie. You're going to have yourself an audition."

Marcus was staring at his cards so hard that the pips began to blur. He could hardly tell a club from a spade. *Concentrate,* he told himself. He'd already lost half his original stake because he spent more time looking across the saloon at Amanda than watching the cards. He and every other man in the place.

The dress had been a good idea, he reassured himself now. The only problem was that while it disguised Amanda's identity, the damn thing revealed her body in a most unsettling way. He hadn't been able to keep his eyes off the pale slant of her shoulders or the delicate line of her collarbone or the lush swell of her breasts above all that black lace. His wandering gaze had cost him plenty, too, so when the farmer in the tattered overalls tossed his last silver dollar into the pot, then threw down his losing cards and left the game, Marcus had taken the man's less-than-lucky seat on the opposite side of the table, where the view didn't include a beautiful woman barely clad in royal blue and black.

It was better, staring at the dirt-streaked window and scrutinizing his cards and the faces of his opponents, rather than at Amanda's face and form. The new location had even allowed Marcus to win back a few bucks. Still, there was plenty more to add to his stack before he could even begin to call his plan a success.

What he needed was enough cash to get them to Denver, by train, tomorrow. All this time on the road wasn't doing anything but increasing the chances that the heiress would be discovered by one of her grandmother's hired men and snatched away from him somehow. He'd never had to worry about a bounty being stolen from him before, but this time the bounty was five times bigger than most, and there were far too many amateurs in the hunt.

Marcus hadn't quite made up his mind yet whether he was going to turn Amanda over to Granny or the Scot, but either way, he figured, he'd collect a handsome reward. He might, he thought, just bank the five thousand for a while and postpone his decision about buying some land. He'd already put it off for a decade, so there really wasn't all that much rush. Maybe he'd just stay on in Denver for a bit—a couple of weeks, maybe a month or two—to see how events unfolded.

But if he didn't focus completely on the pair of jacks and the pretty queen in his hand right this minute, Marcus reminded himself, Denver remained a good few days away and that fine piece of land was still just the misty dream it had been since he left his farm in Illinois to hunt down the bank robber who'd killed Sarabeth.

The memory wasn't a welcome intrusion, especially during a poker game. He hadn't allowed himself to think about that in years. "By mistake," the son of a bitch had claimed when Marcus finally caught up with him in Kansas. Marcus hadn't bothered to dispute the man's contention. In fact, he'd agreed. "The biggest mistake of your life," he'd said, just before putting six hot pieces of lead in the fella.

"Hey. We're getting tired of waiting on you, mister," announced the cowhand across the table. "You in this game or not?"

Marcus blinked, shunted the unwelcome thoughts of his past aside and refocused on the cards in his hand. "I'll see you," he replied as he tossed another silver dollar into the pot. Then, when his handsome pair of jacks held, Marcus raked his own bet back, along with the coins the other players had wagered.

At this rate, he'd be even in another hand or two, and then he planned to raise the stake and make short work of those railroad tickets to Denver.

While the dealer shuffled, the four other poker players shifted in their chairs. The cowhand directly across from Marcus stood up and stretched, then stood gazing toward the rear of the saloon with a kind of moony expression on his face.

"That little gal's got a real nice voice, don't she?" he said. "Kind of puts me in mind of my mama when she used to sing in church back in Sedalia."

"Bet she don't look like your mama," said the dealer. He continued to shuffle, but his gaze cut to Marcus even as he directed his words to the cowhand. "I'd be kinda careful if I were you, son. If I remember right, that pretty little gal came in on the arm of this fellow here."

Marcus was suddenly aware not only that the music had increased in volume, but that the piano player had been joined by a female voice. A bright, happy voice that cut through the smoky room like sunshine through fog. A voice unlike any saloon singer he'd ever heard. An all-too-familiar voice. Before he turned to look, he closed his eyes and uttered a silent prayer that his worst suspicions were wrong.

But they weren't. Not only was Amanda singing, but she was doing it while enthroned on top of the piano, with a small crowd gathered around her, their glasses raised, urging her on, and in between the verses and chorus of her song, Her Ladyship was

swilling beer. Nothing like blending into the wood-
work, Marcus thought disgustedly, as a curse hissed
through his clenched teeth.

"I take it you'll be sitting out this hand, mister,"
the dealer said then, not even attempting to hide the
smirk on his face.

In reply, Marcus scooped his money from the table, stood up and jammed the coins and bills in his
pocket.

"Your wife, is she?" the cowhand asked, a distinct and wistful note of envy in his voice.

"Something like that." Marcus turned and strode
toward the piano, shouldering several appreciative,
ogling fans out of his way.

"You're making a spectacle of yourself, Alice,"
he told her in what he considered a fairly calm
voice, which was nothing short of a damn miracle,
when what he wanted to do was yell, "What the
flaming hell do you think you're doing up there in
front of all these people?"

And even though Marcus considered his tone re-
strained if not downright polite, Her Ladyship took
umbrage at it just the same.

"What I'm doing up here is having a wonderful
time," she said with a lift of her chin and a tilt of
her beer glass at his face. Her perch on the high
piano box put her twinkling green eyes on a level
with his, and her knees were dead even with Marcus's chest, and she proceeded to nudge one of those
rounded, pearly bones into his shirtfront.

"I'm auditioning for employment," she said with
a distinct slur in her voice. "They have a position

open for a singer. I just might make my living as a diva." She laughed brightly, then took a less than dainty sip from her glass. "A chanteuse, Quicksilver."

"Keep playing," Marcus directed the big piano man, whose fingers had come to rest on the keys while the man leaned sideways in a effort to hear. "This is a private conversation."

"Play 'Lorena,'" Amanda called down to him. "I haven't heard that song in years." But then her tipsy smile turned upside down, into a contemplative frown. "Oh, no. You'd better play something else. I'm not sure I can remember all the words."

"It won't matter," Marcus growled. "We're leaving." He reached to grab her waist, but Amanda scooted farther toward the center of the piano, her legs now dangling over the keyboard, mere inches above the piano man's hands.

"I don't want to leave, Quicksilver. You leave if you want. Go on. Just go." She flapped a hand, shooing him away. "Go. Leave me alone. I'm having a wonderful time."

"Quicksilver? Did I hear her right?"

The buxom redhead in the bright pink dress inserted an ample hip between Marcus and the piano. Her black-rimmed eyes bored into his face.

"Quicksilver? That wouldn't be Marcus Quicksilver, would it? The bounty hunter? The same one who brought in Simon Torrance out in Cheyenne a couple of years ago? That Quicksilver?"

Marcus stepped back a few inches, but the redhead's intense gaze didn't let up. He'd learned to be cautious in these situations. Hard telling whether or not the woman held a grievance over some criminal he'd delivered to the law way back when. A brother, perhaps, or a husband or a lover. Or whether she begrudged Marcus himself for loving her and leaving her. Cheyenne, did she say? Good God, there had been so many criminals in so many towns, and so many redheads he'd loved and left, he couldn't even begin to remember.

"Maybe," he said cautiously.

"Maybe," Sally echoed, moving closer to him, tipping her painted face up to his while licking her red lips and fluttering her dark eyelashes. "And just maybe some of those stories I've heard about you are true."

"Maybe."

"What stories?" Amanda had moved back to the edge of the piano top now and was glowering down at them like a vulture. "What stories about him?"

And that was exactly what Marcus himself was wondering when Sally purred over her shoulder, "Oh, some real interesting stories. What I heard in Cheyenne a few years back was that Marcus Quicksilver's not only the best manhunter in the business, but quite the ladies' man, as well. If you know what I mean." She winked, then fingered the placket of Marcus's shirt where the button was still missing, slipping her long red nails inside. "Is it true, Quicksilver, or is that a maybe, too? Or maybe it's just a rumor you started yourself?"

Marcus didn't know whether to be relieved or not to discover that the busty redhead bore him no grudge for a jailed or hanged love, but instead seemed to be referring to an entirely different kind of love and hoping to add her name to a mythical list of his satisfied female customers. Damned if these stories hadn't followed him through half the western territories.

They were downright embarrassing. It never failed to amaze Marcus, this rumor that he was somewhere between a stallion and a reincarnation of Apollo, since, for all he knew, he only did what came naturally in bed. It made him wonder what other men did by comparison. Still, if a man had to be dogged by a rumor, it wasn't a bad one. Despite the embarrassment, it usually worked to his benefit. But not now. Definitely not now.

Out of a corner of his eye, he caught a sudden flurry of black-and-blue satin. Amanda was clambering down from the piano as fast as she could manage, using the keyboard as a step. She missed the piano man's fat pinkie by a fraction, stomped out an angry chord on the lower keys before she hit the floor, and promptly wedged herself between Sally and Marcus.

"You're right, Quicksilver," she snapped. "It's definitely time to go."

Her green eyes were less the color of money now than like hot emeralds, and for a bewildered second Marcus couldn't figure out what he'd done to rile her so. But then he realized it wasn't anything he had done. It was what the redhead was doing to him. The duchess was caught in the fierce grip of the monster with eyes as green as her own. She was jealous!

And damned if that didn't please him in some dark and primitive portion of his being. At least it did until he reminded himself that Her Ladyship probably just thought she owned him—lock, stock, barrel, and rumor, too.

Amanda caught his hand then and began tugging him away from the redhead, toward the saloon door, glaring at everybody in her path and her short black-and-blue skirt whipping like a flag in a stiff breeze around her legs.

"Come on, ladies' man," she muttered, throwing a few visual daggers at him over her bare shoulder.

"Now wait just a damn minute," Marcus started to say, but he stopped. He wanted Amanda out of here, didn't he? Well, didn't he? Why put up an argument? The fact that she was dragging him along like a misbehaving three-year-old wasn't going to make any difference in the long run. And the leers from the fellows straggling along the bar and the laughter coming from the poker table wasn't much more than a moment's irritation when he considered that he was, after all, getting his way.

Whatever emotion had inflamed Amanda—whatever fire had swept through her when she watched Sally not only making eyes at Marcus, but making a blatant assault on his person through his buttonless shirt—it seemed to die down with each step she took from the saloon to the hotel across the street. Like that unexplainable fit of temper, her stride slowed down, too, and her frenzied heartbeat was almost back to normal once she walked through the door of their room. What the devil was wrong with her? She'd never behaved this way in her life.

"I'm sorry," she said, whirling around to face Marcus, her hands knotted at her sides. "That was rude and quite uncalled-for and I'm ashamed of my behavior. I truly don't know what got into me back there."

"Don't you?" He grinned as he pulled the door closed, then leaned against it.

"No," she insisted. "I don't." It was the truth. Never before in her life had she been so overwhelmed by emotion. Even the apparent impetuousness of her elopement with Angus had been deliberate and well thought out. Well, she was a Grenville, after all. They were not emotional people. But it had been different tonight, when her behavior boiled up out of nowhere. It had been like being possessed. The instant she saw that woman's long, painted fingertips disappear into the front of Marcus's shirt, something had exploded like fireworks inside Amanda.

Something was sizzling inside her now as she looked across the room at the bounty hunter, who didn't appear the least bit angry, or even chagrined, about being dragged from the saloon, but seemed to find Amanda's current befuddlement amusing.

She, however, was not amused in the least.

"What stories was that woman talking about?" she asked him now, trying to sound offhand and only mildly curious. "What did she mean when she referred to you as a ladies' man?"

He shrugged. "It's nothing that concerns you, brat. You sure played hell with my poker game over there tonight. I was on my way to winning enough for two tickets to Denver. First-class. And then some."

"Don't change the subject, Quicksilver." She sat on the bed, grabbed a pillow and jammed it against her midsection. "I asked you a question. Just what did that Sally woman mean about your being a ladies' man? Tell me what stories she was talking about."

"Why?" One dark eyebrow arched, a perfect match for his devilish grin.

Why? Because Amanda couldn't stand the way Sally had touched him, as if she wanted to own him, as if she wanted to consume him right there on the spot. Because Amanda had seen a spark in Quicksilver's dark blue eyes when that happened. Because, dammit, she herself wanted to touch him that way and kindle that same fire. She nonchalantly tossed the pillow in the air and caught it. "I'm just curious. That's all. And since we're traveling companions forced to share a room, I think I have a right to know, don't you?"

"If you want to know anything about that kind of reputation, then ask your fiancé," he said coolly. "Better yet, just search your own memory."

Amanda blinked. Her memory? "Of what?"

"Of Angus McCray making love to you, for starters."

"He didn't," she said, truly shocked by the suggestion. "He hasn't. Not really, I mean. Well, you know. Not…not *that* way."

"What way?" His voice dropped to a deeper register with the question, and Amanda couldn't help but notice that his eyes seemed to darken, too. And somewhere, surprisingly, in that deep midnight blue, she thought she detected an indigo flame. A shocking and very beguiling spark.

Her heart did a little handspring in her chest and her own gaze fluttered away, no longer able to withstand the heat of Quicksilver's. She heard him—felt him—lever away from the door and move in her direction. Panic flickered through her. And wild, wonderful anticipation.

It was a challenge Marcus couldn't resist. He crossed the space between them, aware that a brick wall or iron bars couldn't have stopped him just then, even as he knew he was about to do something as foolish as it was impetuous, something stupid, if not downright dangerous.

"This way." His voice was rough with need. He hardly recognized it. But the second his arms encircled Amanda's body, there was a familiarity he couldn't deny. As if he'd held her a million times before. This way. As if he'd already encountered that initial shock that stiffened her spine and tensed her lips, and then—an instant after—felt all that resistance melt in the heat of his arms while her mouth surrendered to his.

But what began with a challenge and a hot impulse immediately flared out of Marcus's control. If

he'd meant to show her how being kissed *this way*
could feel, if his intention had been to give her a
quick and cool lesson in passion, he discovered suddenly that he still had a lot to learn himself. It had
never been like this. Never.

No woman had ever tasted so sweet. No kiss had
ever driven every sane thought from his head or
filled his body with such need.

"And this way." His tongue teased her lips farther apart, while his hands rose to the satin warmth
of her breasts.

"And here." He left her mouth to trace the firm,
pale flesh above the black lace of her dress.

"Oh, my," she breathed, her skin shimmering,
shivering, as his tongue skimmed it.

"Or this." Now his hands slid around, cupping
her backside, bringing her closer— God! Not close
enough and much too close, all in the same moment.
When the little words she was exhaling turned into
a wordless, deep-throated moan, Marcus had sense
enough—somehow—to quit.

It took a second for Amanda's eyes to focus and
for her brain to register that whatever storm had
raged over her, it had suddenly subsided, leaving
every fiber of her body feeling as if she'd been hit
by lightning. Although Marcus had taken a step
back, his hands remained on her waist, as if he
thought she required propping up.

She did. Her knees had turned to warm liquid, but
she'd be damned if she'd let him know that, especially since he'd broken the kiss so abruptly and
without so much as a warning, when she wanted it

to continue. For hours, if not forever. Her lips felt swollen and numb, but she forced them into a stiff imitation of a smile. Her head was still reeling from the beer she had consumed, but she managed to sound somewhat sober.

"That was quite a demonstration, Quicksilver. I suspect everything Sally said about you is only too true. And I assure you, if my Angus turns out to be equally adept as a ladies' man, I'll consider myself one extremely lucky lady."

His smile appeared almost as forced as hers when he said, "You be sure and let me know, Duchess." Then he slid his hands from her waist, turned on his heel and headed for the door. "I'll just leave you to your thoughts about your fiancé and your lucky future now, while I go back to that poker game and win you a quick ticket to Denver. Don't wait up. I might be late."

Then, before Amanda could summon up so much as a "Wait just a confounded minute," he had slammed the door behind him and his spurs were making jangled music as he retreated down the hall.

Damn the man! She had a good mind to throw open the window and screech at him, once he appeared out on the street below, that no gentleman kissed a lady that way. And surely no gentleman kissed a lady that way, then simply quit before she was done kissing him back. Why, it was like leaving your partner on the dance floor in midwaltz. Like snatching a plate of cookies away from a famished child. Like throwing a person overboard, head over heels, in the middle of the Atlantic Ocean.

Marcus Quicksilver wasn't a ladies' man at all. He was a rogue. A scoundrel. A callous and cruel cad. And, damn him to hell and back a dozen times, he'd just made her feel more wonderful, more alive, than she'd ever felt in her entire life.

Chapter Ten

"You lost *how much* money?"

Marcus thought Amanda's voice was oddly, even exceptionally calm, considering that it was seven in the morning and that he'd just awakened her with the news that they were once again flat broke. He'd been ready for a tongue-lashing at the very least—especially after the way he'd abandoned her last night—and most likely the only reason she didn't shriek at him now and shake both fists in his face was that she was trying to manage the buttered biscuit and the cup of hot coffee he had brought for her breakfast. A meager breakfast, compliments of the poker dealer at the Double Eagle, who was a wealthier man this morning than he'd been last night.

"All of it," he replied between sips of his own coffee. Sitting with one hip angled onto the washstand, Marcus was enjoying a view of the bed and its tousled occupant. The hair she'd pinned up the evening before was half-down this morning, and she was still spilling out of the top of the black-and-blue dress. He hated like hell to see that go, he thought.

"When you're done with your breakfast, you'll have to give me your dress," he said.

She bit off a chunk of dry biscuit, then chewed it thoughtfully a moment before asking, "Give you my dress?"

"That's what I said."

She washed the biscuit down with a swallow of coffee. "Do you mind if I ask why?"

"No. I don't mind. I sold it."

"You sold it." Amanda echoed his casual tone, obviously straining to stay calm, but green fire was beginning to flicker in her glare. Marcus suspected that some of that fire was left over from last night, when he'd walked out on her in the middle of that blazing kiss. He figured he deserved to be scorched, or worse, for doing that to her, to any woman. But if he hadn't walked out on her when he did, well...he'd have been in far worse trouble this morning. They both would.

"You *sold* my dress?" she said again as if she hadn't heard him the first time.

He nodded.

"To whom?"

"The bartender at the Double Eagle."

"Ah." Casting a glance down at the black lace and the satin stripes, she shook her head and muttered, "Well, I hate to tell you this, Quicksilver, but it's not going to fit him."

"He's got hopes of hiring somebody to fit it." *Who'll fill it out as well as you do,* Marcus was thinking. Funny how she still looked rich and refined, even in such a cheap getup. Hell, she'd look rich and refined if she were naked. He chased that thought out of his head the minute it occurred to him.

"Well, at least you didn't give it to your redheaded admirer," she said. Then her eyes narrowed, concentrating their increasing green heat on his face. "I take it you renewed your acquaintance with dear old Sally last night when you returned to the saloon."

Marcus shook his head. He'd planned to, God knew. After he kissed Amanda, every nerve in his body had felt like banjo wire too tightly strung and all too ready to snap. His plan had been to win a little extra at poker and then suggest that the redhead confirm those rumors about him for herself. He hadn't won, though, which was a pretty rare occurrence for him, and he'd chalked his losses up to too damn many distractions, not the least of which were his brain's constantly remembering that kiss and his body's continual response to the mere memory.

Even if he'd won, Marcus admitted to himself now, he probably wouldn't have gone upstairs with Sally. Not that the redhead wasn't pretty, in a rawboned sort of way. And not that he didn't feel the need. But for the first time in a long time, that particular need seemed to be focused on one woman. One particular woman. The one who was glaring at him right now.

"I wish you'd consult me before you make decisions that affect my well-being, not to mention my wardrobe,'' she said with some irritation, while she brushed biscuit crumbs from her lap. Then she shrugged. "I suppose I should be relieved that you didn't sell me, Quicksilver.''

He laughed softly, levering himself up from his seat on the edge of the washstand, locking his gaze on hers. "Trip's not over yet.''

After an indignant snort, Amanda clambered out of the bed. "I look like the cat's breakfast,'' she said as she leaned toward the mirror, scowling at her reflection while she attempted to rearrange her curls. To Marcus, who was looking over her shoulder, she said, "And you, my friend, look like the dog's dinner. Did you get any sleep last night?''

He shrugged and glanced at the whiskers shadowing his jaw, the dark hair straggling over the collar of his shirt, and the shirt itself, with its ancient sweat stains and its missing button. "The dog's dinner" seemed almost complimentary. Hardly the sort of fellow to strike the fancy of a woman like Miss Amanda Grenville. Hardly a slick-combed dandy like Angus damn McCray. Why did he keep forgetting that she was already promised to somebody else? That she considered him just an employee—a damn lackey—whom she was paying to take her to Denver and McCray?

"I'll wait downstairs while you change into your old clothes,'' he said grumpily. "Then, after I deliver the dress to the Double Eagle, we'll be on our way. Two days, brat, and you'll be right where you want to be.''

Would she? Amanda wondered after Marcus left the room.

Where did she want to be? Two days ago, her answer most certainly would have been Denver, but now she wasn't quite so sure.

Marcus was leaning against a hitching rail, long legs slung out and hat slanted against the bright morning sun, when Amanda emerged from the hotel.

"Here's your frock, Quicksilver." She flung the wadded blue-and-black satin at him. "Half the money you get for it is mine, you know. Just how much are you getting for it, by the way?"

"Five dollars."

"Five dollars! You must be out of your mind! We paid twenty for it!"

"That's right," he growled. "If you've got anything else you'd rather donate to the cause, Duchess, be my guest. My horse is gone. And my saddle. All I've got left is my gun, and I'm keeping that just in case I get an irresistible urge to shoot you."

Amanda sniffed. "Five dollars isn't going to get us on a train or a stagecoach."

The flat, hard stare Marcus gave her said he was already well aware of that, but he didn't bother to volunteer any alternatives regarding transportation.

"Well?" she asked.

"Well what?"

"Are we walking to Denver?"

"Partly."

Amanda raised an eyebrow. "And what's the other part?"

"The other part is acting like pleasant but destitute people and catching a ride on a wagon that's headed west." Marcus straightened up from the hitching rail, jammed the dress under one arm and glowered down at her. "Now, I've already seen you act destitute, brat, but I've yet to see much more than a trace of pleasant. Think you can handle that?"

Amanda strained a thin, pleasant smile through tightly pressed lips. "You mean like this?"

"Sort of. Keep practicing," he said, "while I take this satin concoction over to the saloon. And keep an eye out for any wagons that look like they might be leaving town."

She glanced up and down the street. "What about him?" she asked, pointing to a large, battered wagon parked in front of Holcomb's and a large, battered man who was loading a bale of hay onto its bed.

Marcus looked and laughed. "That old buffalo hunter? He'd probably just as soon roll his vehicle over you as give you a ride in it."

"Why's that?"

"I know the type, that's why. Old geezers like that get used to being alone. Often as not, they just quit liking people altogether. He's not about to share his wagon with anybody, and especially not a woman, pleasant or unpleasant."

Amanda looked back at the old man. In his seat-sprung denim pants with holes in both the knees and his faded flannel shirt, he looked rather more unfortunate than unsociable. "I don't know. I expect he'd welcome a bit of company," she said.

"Like a toothache." Marcus took Amanda by the shoulders and backed her toward a chair. "Sit here," he told her. "Don't talk to anybody. Don't smile at anybody. Don't move."

"May I breathe?"

"Only if it's absolutely necessary," he growled. "I'll be back in a few minutes."

She watched the smooth swing of his stride and the fine sight of his posterior for a moment before her gaze moved back to the old man across the street. He was yanking on harness straps now, and seemed to be deep in conversation with the pair of mules that were hitched to his wagon. Anyone who enjoyed the company of mules would certainly find Marcus Quicksilver a boon companion, she thought. Then she gathered up her skirts and crossed the street.

"Good morning." Her cheerful greeting seemed to breeze right past the buffalo hunter. Either that, or he didn't hear her. "Good morning," Amanda said again a little louder.

The man raised his head from the harness rigging and stared at her incredulously, as if she had just materialized from street dust and sunbeams.

"You talking to me, lady?"

Between his battered hat and his bushy eyebrows and his salt-and-pepper beard, Amanda could barely see his face. She could smell him, however. Oh, dear. Well, perhaps that was the mules.

"Yes, I am," she said brightly. "I was wondering if, by any chance, you and your wagon were heading west."

"Me and my wagon." His eyes were the same color as his mules—an undistinguished brown. They fixed on Amanda while the old man rubbed his chin and scratched his cheek and took so long to reply that she began to wonder if he actually understood English.

"Yep," he drawled at last. "Me and my wagon are heading west."

"Oh, good. Would you like company?"

"Company?"

For heaven's sake. If he was going to repeat everything she said, they'd be here all morning. "I need to get to Denver, but I haven't enough money for the fare. And I thought if you're going west...well..." She sighed—a long, pitiful exhalation—dispensing with logic and language, since they didn't seem to be working anyway, and hoping that the old goat would find some appeal in her sad plight and her apparent helplessness.

"You want to ride with me?" He aimed a grimy thumb toward his chest. His bushy eyebrows climbed toward his scalp, all but disappearing under the brim of his battered hat. "With me? In my wagon?"

Amanda nodded, fashioning the brightest, most pleasant smile imaginable. Yes, she wanted desperately to ride in his wagon. The wagon that Marcus Quicksilver had said was impossible. For Amanda, it was as much a matter of principle now as it was of transportation. And she wanted to show the bounty hunter a thing or two, one of which was that she didn't need his help—such as it was—or his kisses, either, for that matter. She could damn well get to Denver on her own. She'd be there now, kissing Angus, if not for Marcus's interference.

The buffalo hunter stared at her blankly while he scratched his cheek. Then he looked up at the sky, as if to consult the sun, after which he contemplated the nearest mule. He shook his head, which worried Amanda considerably until his matted beard and mustache broke in the middle. They seemed to crack open, quite literally, like a shaggy coconut, to reveal a smile that was distinctly unpleasant. It was, well...brown, and his teeth—the few he still had— were little more than stained stumps.

"Well, hell, yes," he said, reaching for her with both hands. "Here you go. Lemme help you up."

Amanda stepped back. Maybe this hadn't been such a good idea, she thought. Perhaps she'd been too hasty. But then her panicky gaze lit on the door of the Double Eagle, where Marcus seemed to be taking his sweet time selling off her wardrobe, while she was supposed to be out here waiting like some poor old horse tethered to a rail.

She jerked up her skirts, gritted her teeth and tried not to breathe the same air the buffalo hunter was breathing while he lofted her into the wagon's rickety front seat.

Marcus punched the saloon door open, squinting in the bright, sudden sunlight outside, glad he made his living hunting men instead of dickering with them. The barkeep, who'd been so eager to buy the dress the night before, had turned into a cheap, reluctant son of a bitch by morning. First he'd offered to reimburse Marcus with two weeks' worth of beer and whiskey. When that didn't work, he'd said he'd let Marcus take it out in trade with Sally, who was dusting bottles behind the bar just then and giving Marcus a look that said she'd certainly see he got his money's worth and more.

"No offense, darlin'," he said, "but I'm leaving town today. With five dollars in my pocket." He aimed a hard glare at the barkeep. "We had a deal, remember?"

"I don't recall you saying anything about cash money," the man replied.

"I'm saying it now." Marcus took his foot off the rail and straightened his stance, while letting his hand hover briefly in the vicinity of his gun. Hell, he hated having to resort to such a threat for a lousy five bucks. It was an embarrassment, but he figured he didn't have much choice.

Still, even with the implied threat of violence, it took another twenty minutes of haggling before the cheap bastard forked over four silver dollars, plus a shot of rye. The liquor and the financial drubbing he'd just taken were still burning in Marcus's gut when he pounded out of the door and into the blazing prairie sunshine.

"There he is. That's my husband. Pull the wagon up right here."

"I thought it was gonna be just you. I mean, just you and me."

"Oh, good heavens, no."

Marcus found himself standing nose-to-nose with

a flea-bitten mule. Glowering down at him was the flea-bitten buffalo hunter he'd seen earlier. And perched beside the old coot on the wagon seat was Her Ladyship, happy as a lark and smug as a cat with a live canary tenderly tucked inside its cheek.

"This gentleman has agreed to let us accompany him west," she said. The "I told you so" was more in the delivery than the actual words. But Marcus heard it all the same.

He tipped back his hat and smiled as affably as his temper would allow. "Much obliged, mister, but..."

"Oh, don't be a stubborn goose, dear," Amanda interrupted. "He's going west. We're going west. It's no imposition." She turned her bright smile on the greasy old codger. "Is it, Mr....? Mr....um. I'm afraid I didn't get your name."

"Raze."

"Mr. Raze?"

"Just Raze."

Raze. Marcus groaned inwardly. Already he knew he'd have to haul the brat kicking and screaming down from the wagon seat where she was so proudly ensconced, drawing more attention to them than he dared. He was doomed, he figured, to travel at least fifteen or twenty miles now—hard miles, smelly miles—with a man who called himself Raze, a monicker that in all probability wasn't short for *raisin,* but for *razor.*

About three hours and ten or twelve miles later, when the sun was beating down from directly overhead, old Raze had apparently had it with Her Lady-ship's persistent pleasantries and dauntless conver-sational skills. Maybe she was nervous, Marcus guessed, sitting up there with the unwashed, taciturn buffalo hunter. Maybe she confused sociability with continual noise. Maybe she kept her tongue wagging to distract her nose from her pungent seatmate. Whatever the reason, Amanda Grenville had talked a blue streak that was ten or twelve miles long, at least that wide, and all one-way.

Where was he from and did he still have family there and what a peculiar name and however in the world had he chosen buffalo hunting as an occupa-tion? Wasn't it dangerous? What about wild Indi-ans? Which part of the beast was particularly good to eat? Tongue, she had heard, or so she believed. Was that true? And, my goodness me, wasn't the weather lovely today?

All the while the old man stared straight ahead at the flea-bitten rumps of the mules, offering an oc-casional grunt but mostly just working the plug of tobacco in his cheek and spitting out into the weeds.

For his part, Marcus had made himself reasonably comfortable in the jolting wagon bed by using a bale of hay as a backrest and his hat brim as a shade against the broiling sun. Despite the animated monologue taking place up front, he'd even man-aged to drop off to sleep for a while. Until the wagon jerked to a stop.

''Get out,'' the buffalo hunter grunted.

''I beg your pardon?'' Amanda was dabbing at her damp neck with a hankie.

"Get out."

After a quick blink, Amanda smiled at the driver and said, "Oh. Yes. I see. I suppose you're stopping here to give the mules a rest. Poor old things. That makes perfect sense." Then she ventured a little laugh—a polite teatime sound, a my-aren't-these-scones-divine sort of burble—while gathering her skirts, looking down to her right and estimating the distance to the ground. "Well, I could use a bit of rest myself, actually."

Right. But Her Ladyship wasn't going to get it today, Marcus feared, not judging from the volume and bluntness of old Raze's command. There wasn't so much as a hint of a "Get back" in his gruff "Get out." There was also a double-barreled shotgun stashed under his seat, and the old man's grimy fingers were twitching impatiently on the reins while Miss Amanda Grenville, runaway heiress, babbled on happily and helpfully about getting out but made no discernible effort to do it.

Marcus sighed, then shouldered off the bale of hay and vaulted over the side slats.

"Come on." Without giving Amanda a chance to hesitate or even to speak, he reached up, clasped his hands around her waist and lifted her down from the seat. And no sooner had her feet connected with the ground than old Raze cracked the reins over the mules' backs, bawled, "Giddyup," and took off with a speed that—even considering the advanced age of the animals and the dilapidated condition of the vehicle—didn't surprise Marcus in the very least. The buffalo hunter had probably had more civilization—and more chatter—in the past few hours than he'd had in the past dozen years. And enough to last him the next dozen, to boot.

Amanda gaped at the tailgate of the retreating wagon. "Well, don't just stand there, Quicksilver!" she cried. "He's leaving us high and dry!"

"Yep." Marcus was watching the tall grasses spring back in the wake of the heavy vehicle, obliterating its passage to the unskilled eye, thinking that he or any decent bounty hunter could trail the old man for days if he wanted to. Which he didn't.

"Are you just going to stand there?" she squealed.

"Uh-huh."

She threw him a look of supreme disgust, hissed a distinctly unladylike curse, and then Her Ladyship hiked up her skirts and took off running before Marcus could hold her back. She did pretty well, too, considering she'd probably never in her life had to run after anything more than a flyaway tennis ball or a disobediant lapdog. Her lacy underskirts boiled up around her feet, and that mass of blond hair streamed out behind her like a golden banner. Marcus smiled, enjoying the sight.

And then, when she'd nearly caught up with the tailgate of the retreating wagon, all of a sudden her feet seemed to get tangled up in tall grass and twisted ruffles, and Her Ladyship went facedown—splat—in the weeds.

Old Raze was a mere speck in the distance by the time Marcus sauntered up, his thumbs hooked loosely in his gunbelt, fully prepared to deflect a hail of curses and a firestorm of accusations. Possibly even a flying fist or knee. He expected the duchess to be in a royal, rip-roaring rage. But she was crying.

Crying! Tears big as crystals were tumbling down her cheeks and dripping off her chin. Her eyelashes were wet and all clumped together in soggy spikes, and she couldn't sniff fast enough to keep up with her nose. Aw, hell. Hell and then some.

"Here. Come on." Marcus tried to soften his naturally gruff voice as he reached down to help her to her feet, but she batted away his open hand.

"Leave me alone," she sobbed. "Get away. Just get away."

He squatted, then swiped his hat off and dandled it between his knees a minute before he reached to pluck a weed. Given his choice—and he wished he had one now—he'd take a spitting, hissing female over a weeping one every time.

"Come on now. It isn't the end of the world, Amanda," he said at last. Quietly. Lamely. Uselessly, as far as he could tell. "Stop crying, all right? We can do just fine without that old coot and his wagon. I'll get you to Denver. I said I would, didn't I? And, dammit, I will. You can count on that."

When the tears showed no evidence of subsiding, Marcus added, though it galled him to say the words, "Why, I'll bet that fiancé of yours is waiting for you in Denver right this minute with a brass band and a big bouquet of roses. Maybe even a preacher, too. Yeah. Definitely a preacher. And a fine gold ring tucked in his pocket, just waiting to be slipped on your finger. So quit your crying now. It'll only be another day or two before..."

Amanda's chin snapped up, and she glared at the bounty hunter through a film of tears. "Stop it. Just stop it. That's not why I'm crying, Quicksilver."

"You're not?" He blinked, shifting uncomfortably on the balls of his feet, clenching the brim of his hat. "But I thought..."

"Well, just quit thinking. All right?" Now Amanda straightened, fumbled for a clean length of hem and wrenched it up to dry her face. Maybe she didn't know exactly why she was crying, she thought, but at least she knew it wasn't about the delay in getting to Denver or the fiancé who was supposedly waiting for her there. It wasn't about that at all.

She wasn't crying because she was sad, dammit. She was mad. And she hadn't yet decided whether her anger was directed at the deceitful, smelly old buffalo hunter or at Marcus Quicksilver or at herself. All three, more than likely.

She swiped a fresh tear away, then slammed a fist in her lap. "I'm crying because you're always right and I'm always wrong. I hate that. I truly do. Go ahead. Say it. You were right about that horrible old man and I was wrong. Say it. Go on. You're entitled."

"Well, now, I—"

She cut him off with a loud sniff. "And, for your information, I'm also crying because I twisted my confounded knee when I stumbled."

Concern flickered in his eyes then, and he edged

closer, reaching out to her, but Amanda stopped him with a furious, boiling glare.

"But most of all I'm crying because, when you were being right and I was being wrong, and when I stumbled and twisted my confounded knee, I landed in…in…" She bit down on her lip to discourage a fresh onslaught of tears before she wailed, "…in a damn mule pie."

Marcus burst out laughing. He couldn't help himself. Now that he knew it was mostly her dignity that was injured, he felt intensely relieved. Even when Amanda cursed him and smacked his arm hard enough to make him lose his balance, he couldn't stop laughing.

"That's you, then?" he said, chortling, crinkling up his nose and sniffing dramatically. "I thought it was just your old friend, Raze, still kind of hanging around on the breeze."

"Oh, please." She pitched him a look of pure, undiluted murder. But it was dry murder now. The tears, thank God, were gone.

"I hate you, Quicksilver. I truly, truly do." She shook her fists at the sky. "Just look at me! I'm sitting here all crippled and smelling to high heaven, and all you can do is laugh like a damn demented hyena."

It wasn't easy, but Marcus managed to smooth his features into some measure of sobriety as he got to his feet.

"Now that's not altogether true, Duchess," he said. "I mean, yeah, I guess you are crippled and smelly. And I guess you're about the wrongest, stubbornest woman I've ever encountered, but I can do a little more than just laugh. Come on.''

He lifted her wriggling, resistant body off the ground in one smooth motion and set her gently on her feet. ''Let's get you up and figure out the damage.''

Chapter Eleven

As it turned out, the damage to Amanda's knee was slight and temporary and nothing that a little walking around didn't dispose of in a few minutes. The damage to her dress, however, was considerable, and not to be disposed of quite so easily.

"Take it off," Marcus said, stepping around her so that he was downwind of the stench of the mule droppings that caked the front of her skirt. He wasn't laughing anymore, either, Amanda noticed with some satisfaction.

An indignant refusal was poised on the firm brink of Amanda's lips, but she contained it. Her silence wasn't so much the result of her grudging recognition that—so far anyway—Marcus was always right and she was always wrong and so perhaps, in light of that fact, she really ought to behave sensibly and be a bit more compliant. Rather, she didn't voice her refusal because she decided she was going to be sick to her stomach if she took in even one more breath of the foul air wafting up from her clothes.

"Oh, all right," she said finally, trying not to

breathe while reaching around to undo the buttons at her back. "Turn around."

He did, laughing again. "I'll close my eyes, too, brat, for all the good it'll do you. Don't forget I've already seen just about everything that the good Lord gave you."

"And don't you forget he didn't give me what he did purely for your amusement, Quicksilver." She wrenched the final button, and then her voice became muffled by yards of fabric as she carefully worked the soiled dress over her shoulders and head. "Or for your enjoyment, either."

"Just where'd you get the idea that I enjoyed it?" he asked.

Amanda sniffed, remembering the moment when Marcus had gazed at her with eyes full of hungry appreciation and desire, then remembering, also, how he'd turned off that emotion as abruptly as if he were twisting a spigot closed. Once again she felt the same dull ache of disappointment that she'd felt earlier, when she realized that the bounty hunter's desire had more to do with her fortune than with her person. And once again Amanda did her best to mask her hurt with an arch, almost acid, reply.

"No, I gather you didn't enjoy it," she said. "So I suppose, in light of that, it doesn't make much difference now whether you look at me or not."

Marcus turned around just as Amanda dropped the soiled garment onto the ground and then stood there almost defiantly in her thin, lacy undergarments with her feet planted apart and her hands fisted on her hips.

"There, Quicksilver. You see." She gave her long hair a shake that sent it tumbling over her shoulders and spilling over the firm swells of her half-concealed breasts. "I'm not the least bit embarrassed, now that I realize you're not enjoying the view, and that you're looking at me the same way you'd look at a lamppost or a flagpole."

Well, not exactly. Marcus figured if they shaped lampposts and flagpoles the way Amanda Grenville was shaped, most men would have a hard time getting from one end of town to the other. Tiny-waisted flagpoles and hip-flaring, bosomy lampposts in sheer cotton lawn, with pert nipples winking beneath soft ruffles and lace, might just spell the end of civilization as they knew it. He dragged his gaze away, bending to snatch up her dress, which he shook viciously and then proceeded to fold inside out.

She turned away from him then, facing west and lifting a lithe, bare arm to shade her eyes from the sun, which was just beginning its long afternoon slide. "How far is it to the next town, Quicksilver?"

"Ha!"

When Marcus laughed again, Amanda whirled around to face him, echoing his terse exclamation. "'Ha!'? What does 'Ha!' mean?"

"It means there is no next town," he said as he secured a corner of the dirty dress. "Not today, anyway. It means we're smack in the middle of nowhere, and a good ten or fifteen miles from anywhere else, and if you've never slept out under the stars, Duchess, you're going to have a whole new experience tonight."

Ticking off the seconds while this information sank in, Marcus waited for her pretty face to turn petulant, for her brow to crumple and her luscious mouth to slide into a spoiled, distasteful curve. He thought she might even cry again. But she smiled instead. Smiled, hell. The woman fairly gleamed, while clapping her hands together like a little girl.

"Oh, how wonderful!" she exclaimed. "Sleeping out under the stars. That's something I've always longed to do."

Stars! Stars and more stars! Amanda had never known there were so many of them. After the sun sank like an orange rock, thousands of stars—perhaps even millions—twinkled and glittered on the black dome of the sky. Having spent her entire life in the city, she had never known the night had so many stars. Or so many sounds. There were crickets. There were cicadas and hooting owls. There was the rush of wings and the low hum of wind in the tall grass and mysterious things splashing softly every now and then in the trickling river nearby.

She'd never eaten without a knife and fork before, either, not to mention without a plate. She'd never sucked a rabbit bone clean. Imitating Marcus now, Amanda tossed the bare bone into the fire, then licked the last bits of grease from her fingers.

"You're an excellent cook, Quicksilver."

"I'm an excellent shot, anyway. It's not easy pegging a rabbit with a pistol." As he spoke, he loosened the thongs that kept his gun secure against his leg, then unbuckled his belt. "The only trick with the cooking is not to burn the little critter to a crisp."

Amanda dried her fingers on her underskirt then combed them through her damp hair. While Marcus was hunting their dinner, she'd done her best to clean her filthy dress in the river, along with her filthy self. The dress was hanging on a cottonwood branch now, stirring lightly in the evening breeze.

"If anyone had told me two weeks ago that I'd be sitting down here while my clothes were up there," she said, pointing to the tree, "I wouldn't have believed them."

"No, I don't suppose you would have," Marcus answered quietly, while he folded the ends of his gunbelt carefully around the holster, then laid it aside.

Still within reach, Amanda noted, watching her companion lean back, stretch out his long legs and hook his arms beneath his head. Half of him was lit by the golden light from the campfire. Half of a burnished smile twitched on his lips.

"Best settle down now and get some sleep," he said, his words trailing off in a yawn.

"Oh, not yet." She lifted her gaze to the starry sky. "I want to enjoy every second of this lovely night. And I'm not the least bit tired."

"You should be. You walked a good five miles this afternoon."

Plaiting her hair in a loose braid over her shoulder now, Amanda sighed. "A *good* five miles. And I enjoyed every inch of them, too. You're quite a pleasant companion, Quicksilver, when you're not preoccupied with trying to prove what a spoiled brat I am.''

His mouth hooked in a grin. "You're a pleasant companion yourself, Miss Grenville, when you're not doing your worst to prove me right."

"I'm not, you know." Her tone was solemn now, thoughtful.

"Not what?"

"Spoiled."

"Uh-huh."

"I'm truly not." She leaned toward him, inflecting her voice with all the earnestness she suddenly felt and needed desperately to express. "I've always *had* things—toys when I was a little girl, then knickknacks and jewelry later on, when I got older—and more fancy outfits than I could ever wear, season after season, year after year—but I never demanded them. None of those things. Ever. They were simply there. And in all honesty, I can't say I miss them, now that all I've got are the clothes on my back.''

She didn't even have those at the moment, Marcus thought, casting a look at the damp dress that was decorating the cottonwood. At least not on her back.

Not on her front, either, for that matter. As the day wore on, Amanda had seemed to overcome her modesty completely, but Marcus had yet to overcome his reaction to so much exposed, lovely female flesh.

"I've reconsidered that," he said rather grudgingly now, "and I don't think you're all that spoiled.''

"You don't?"

"Nope."

God knew he wished he could go on regarding her as just a petulant, pampered pet. That original opinion of his—wrong as it was—was a whole lot safer than regarding her as a beautiful woman who discovered delight in adversity, one who could look nearly any challenge in the eye without flinching.

Amanda Grenville, in his revised estimation, was a strong woman, despite her lack of experience. Resilient. A woman who rarely complained. Even now, with her hair still wet and wearing skimpy underclothes, she wasn't moaning and groaning, but was smiling wistfully into the fire, quietly rubbing her arms to keep warm. She reminded him a lot of his late wife. Sarabeth would be well over thirty now, but he still pictured her as Amanda's age. He couldn't remember now if she'd been twenty or twenty-one when she was killed. There was a lot he couldn't remember anymore, and he wasn't sure whether he was glad or sad about that.

"You best come over here," he said softly, rolling onto his side and patting the ground between himself and the campfire. "Closer to the fire."

For a second then, Marcus caught himself wishing that Amanda would stubbornly decline his invitation. Especially when he saw, what?—a sudden and distinct flicker of anticipation in her eyes, a heat in her gaze not so different from the sudden flames that were kicking up deep in his groin? Then, almost before he realized it, she had scrambled beside him. Shivering, her skin dotted with goose bumps, she fit

herself against him, her back to his front, her damp
hair flung over his face.

"This is better," she said as she rooted around
like a happy pup making a fireside bed.

"Warmer, anyway." Marcus lifted a hand to remove the wet, flyaway tresses from his eyes and
mouth. Having accomplished that, though, he didn't
know where to replace his arm. Damned if he'd ever
had a woman in his arms before and been so muddled about what went where. Or been so unnerved—
scared, even, of the consequences of that geography.
At last, and with a rough sigh of resignation, he
draped his hand on the curve of her hip.

"There. Go to sleep now," he murmured. "It'll
be morning all too soon." *Lord, let it be soon. Even
sooner. Soonest.*

All too soon. Amanda closed her eyes, savoring
the warmth of the bounty hunter's body. No downy
comforter, no velvet cloak or ermine cape, had ever
offered her such all-encompassing heat, such absolute protection. She'd never, in all her life, felt quite
so safe, so secure. Or—oh, dear!—so suddenly and
inexplicably sad. Not only would morning come all
too soon, but so would the rest of her life.

"Denver." She sighed. "I suppose we'll be there
in a day or so."

"Yep."

"And by this time next week, I suppose I'll be
Mrs. Angus McCray."

Though his lips were close to her ear, his voice
sounded far away. A bit like the distant rumble of
thunder. "That's what you wanted, wasn't it?"

She nodded, none too enthusiastically.

"Well, then…"

A dry twig popped in the fire, sending a small shower of sparks up against the dark sky. Amanda watched them go out, one by one, as they fell back to earth.

"What I wanted," she said with quiet deliberation, "was my independence. I wanted—no, I needed—to get out from under my grandmother's great big thumb and away from all the restrictions of the life she had me living. Marriage, it seemed to me, was the logical, if not the only, way to accomplish that."

"Your logic's about as sound as a boat with a hole in it, Amanda."

She glanced over her shoulder at him. It was only the second time he'd called her by her Christian name, instead of "duchess" or "brat." The first time had been when she was crying earlier that day. Both times, she'd loved the sound of her name in his roughened bass voice. Not that she cared for his criticism of her mental powers. "Why? What's wrong with my logic?"

"Well, for starters, I don't think I've ever heard the words *marriage* and *independence* used in the same sentence." He chuckled deep in his throat. "'Course, I could be mistaken about that, since it's not a subject I've discussed too much myself."

"I can't say that surprises me," she said with a little sniff. "So you think I'm wrong, then? You think I'm making a mistake by marrying Angus?"

He didn't answer immediately, only moved his

hand slightly on her hip while he breathed a soft curse close to her ear. "It's your life," he grumbled at last.

"Well, I'm glad we agree on that. But you didn't answer my question, Quicksilver. You didn't tell me whether or not you think I'm making a mistake, running off to marry Angus?"

"It's none of my business."

"But if it were your business," Amanda urged. "If you were…oh, I don't know…perhaps if you were my guardian angel." The notion was close enough to the truth to make her smile suddenly. And then her smile flourished into a laugh. "You probably are my guardian angel, Quicksilver, come to think of it."

Marcus didn't feel particularly angelic just then. "What's the difference what I think?" he asked. "Does my opinion matter so much to you?"

She nodded.

"All right, then. Not that I think too highly of your intended, but I guess I'd have to say it's not a mistake if you love him."

"Love him!" She laughed again, but this time not so brightly. There was a nervous, almost uncertain undertone in her voice. "Love Angus? Why, I hardly know him. But I expect that I'll learn to love him. Once we're properly married. Once we…" She cleared her throat. "Well…you know."

Marcus knew, all right, and the thought of this beautiful, vibrant and, yes, innocent woman in the well-practiced and far-from-innocent grasp of Angus McCray—not to mention the thought of her in the greedy Scot's bed—was almost more than he could tolerate. Especially now, while she was lying in his arms so trustingly. Now, while his hand had moved without his even realizing it and was smoothing up and down the soft, cool flesh of her upper arm.

Well, hell. She was cold, wasn't she? He was just keeping her warm. Just taking care of her and guarding her as any dutiful angel would. It was, he told himself, innocent enough, for all practical purposes. And he was, by God, perfectly capable of ignoring his body's response to the situation.

"I never did give much credence to that 'learning to love' business," he said. "Seems to me love happens. More accidental than planned. I expect that's why they call it 'falling in love.'"

She sighed softly. "That's quite a romantic notion, Quicksilver."

"Maybe. Still, it's what I believe." He wanted desperately to change the subject, but for the moment, his brain was empty. There was just the chirring of the crickets, the riffling of the wind above them in the cottonwood, the soft flapping of Amanda's drying dress, and the warm, womanly, wonderful feel of her beneath his fingertips.

"Have you ever?" she asked.

He blinked stupidly, trying to focus on their previous discussion. "Ever what?"

"Have you ever fallen in love?"

"Who, me?" He laughed, or tried to, anyway, but it came out sounding less like laughter and more like the gulp of a man on a gallows, just before the rope was slipped around his neck. He couldn't remember falling in love with Sarabeth. From childhood, it seemed, she'd just been there to love, a warm fixture in his life. If he'd fallen, he hadn't felt it. Not the way he felt now, as if he were standing on the edge of a fifty-foot cliff, about to lose his damn balance.

"What kind of a question is that?" he asked gruffly.

"An easy one." She glanced over her shoulder again. "My goodness, Quicksilver, if you wanted a hard question, I could ask you…well, I could ask you the name of that star up there." She raised a slim, bare arm to point to a bright, nearly blue dot of light on the black sky. "Or ask you how far away it is."

Marcus angled his head, squinting at the sky. "That's easy enough. It's Polaris," he said, recognizing the North Star, which had guided him so many nights while he was tracking murderers and thieves. It seemed to be winking at him now, mocking him, and although he had no idea how far away the star was, he wished he was on it right then.

"The other question's easier," Amanda insisted. "All it takes is a yes or a no."

The truth was that after Sarabeth died, and in spite of his reputation as a ladies' man, Marcus not only hadn't fallen in love, he hadn't allowed himself anywhere near the edge of that particular cliff. After Sarabeth, there had never been a woman Marcus couldn't easily bid farewell to, or one he wouldn't have been relieved to see vanish into thin air once the sweet necessities of pleasure had been dispensed with.

Until now.

Maybe it had happened—the falling—the first minute he saw Amanda Grenville skulking around the depot in North Platte, trying to look brave and strong as an oak, when she was shaking like a leaf. Maybe it had been when the starving heiress offered her treasured apple to that little immigrant boy on the train. Or today, when she climbed out of a pile of mule manure and her tears turned to laughter. Or maybe it had been when he kissed her for the very first time, or perhaps it was happening this very minute, as he held her warm little body so closely to his own and felt he never wanted to let her go.

He couldn't have determined the when or the why of his feelings any more than he could have counted the stars above him.

Not that the when or the why made a damn bit of difference, though. Amanda Grenville, as well as being a wealthy woman with certain expectations from life that a bounty hunter could never meet, was promised to another man. The truth was that next week, in Denver, she would be Mrs. Angus damn McCray. Then Marcus Quicksilver, the fallen fool, would be picking himself up, most likely from a saloon floor, dusting himself off and getting on with his life.

And that was the answer to her easy question. The hard truth of it was lodged like a rock in his gut right now, and maybe always would be.

"No," he said. "I never have." He supplied a casual sort of laugh for emphasis, to make his lie sound more convincing. "I don't expect I ever will."

Staring at the stars overhead, Amanda watched them blur for a moment before she blinked hard. Well, she'd asked, hadn't she? She'd wanted an honest answer from the bounty hunter, and she'd gotten just that, even if it hadn't been quite what she wanted to hear. Not that she was sure just what it was she was longing for him to tell her.

She'd have been better off asking herself how a woman who was betrothed to one man could be entertaining such traitorous feelings for another. Such headlong, dizzying, altogether unsettling feelings. Her heart was fluttering wildly somewhere in the vicinity of her throat. Her breathing was ragged. It felt, she thought, a little like falling. A lot like falling. Falling head over heels, even as she was tightly wrapped in Marcus's arms.

Edging around within that warm, protective circle, Amanda brought her gaze level with his. Light from the campfire glittered in his eyes, making him appear less guardian angel now than tempting devil as his gaze veered toward her mouth. Her heart picked up speed, ticking inside her like a clock gone wild. A timepiece that was surging ahead toward the future, when all Amanda wanted was for the present to last forever. This moment. This man and this woman, gilded in firelight, lying beneath ancient stars, speaking of love. This warm and wonderful moment. This perfect, perfect now.

Nothing else in the world seemed to matter anymore. Just this. No one else mattered. Just him. Him.

"Kiss me, Quicksilver."

His breath hitched in his chest.

"Kiss me," she repeated, bringing her face closer to his. Then, with her lips just brushing his, she whispered, "Please."

He might have withstood the tempting sight of her lush mouth, just inches away. He might even have been able to back off when her lips made sweet, tentative contact with his. But her hushed little plea undid him. It had hardly been spoken when Marcus did exactly what she asked. How could he not?

He kissed her. Gently at first, a succession of soft nips from one corner of her mouth to the other, a sampling, a cautious expression of his fierce need. A kiss he thought he surely could control. And he might have, too, if he'd been kissing someone less surprising than Miss Amanda Grenville.

Instead of greeting him with dry, virginal pecks, her moist lips yielded to his instantly, and her mouth opened in sweet invitation. The sweetest Marcus had ever encountered. His heart was pounding in his chest. His blood was hammering in his veins. And that little voice in the back of his head that should have been telling him *Beware* was utterly drowned out.

He wanted her more than any woman he'd ever known. God forgive him, even more than Sarabeth. He wanted to take her, here and now, to make her his. His hands were already learning her, the firmness and the warm, sweet give of her flesh. The soft moan that broke from her lips only urged him on, setting fire to whatever caution Marcus still possessed. He had to have her.

Here. Now. Tonight. He'd figure it all out later. He'd deal with the consequences afterward, once his brain began working again. Except.

"Yes," she whispered. "Oh, Marcus, I never knew…"

"Shhh…" he rasped, then kissed her harder to quiet her. His brain apparently wasn't quite as useless as he'd thought, and his senses hadn't been wholly obliterated by his fierce desire. There was something in the night sounds around them now that he couldn't account for. What? A chirping that wasn't birds or crickets. A humming that wasn't the wind. A squeak, shrill and distinct, that didn't come from any beast. What?

Amanda heard it then, too. Her arms tightened around Marcus. "Listen," she whispered against his mouth. "What is that? A wagon?"

As if in reply, the squeaking increased and a rough voice cut through the night air. "You sure it was around here, old man? You sure all that whiskey ain't got you confused?"

"I damn well know where I been, sonny, give or take a couple miles."

"It's Raze." Amanda's eyes widened, locking on Marcus's. "What in the world—?"

"Well," a third voice said, "I don't see no signs of no runaway girl, rich or poor. I don't see nothing but the damn dark."

Suddenly Marcus had rolled himself over Amanda's body and was dousing their campfire with handful after handful of dirt. When the light had vanished, he stood, jerked her dress from the tree with one hand, then reached to pull Amanda up with the other. She could hardly see the bounty hunter now, in the darkness, but she could hear the sound of his gunbelt being buckled, along with a gruff chorus of muttered curses.

Amanda felt like cursing a long blue streak herself. Her perfect moment had become even more so with that stunning, bone-melting kiss, only to be quashed by that smelly old buffalo hunter and his smelly old mules and his no-doubt-smelly companions. It was bad enough that the old man had abandoned them rudely in the first place, but now he'd returned with comparable rudeness, not to mention horrible timing. He'd spoiled everything.

Amanda, her ardor having turned to anger, had a good mind to tell the old man just that. At the very least, she intended to collect for the damage done to her clothes, and in the process, perhaps, also recover a bit of her lost dignity.

"Quicksilver," she hissed as she snapped her fingers in his direction. "Pass me my dress."

"Shhh..." he warned her.

"I will not *shhh*..." she said. "I intend to speak to that nasty old Raze. Then, after I've given him a piece of my mind along with the back of my hand, he's going to regret that he ever—"

Marcus silenced her with a firm hand over her mouth just as rough voices sounded, all of them much closer now than a moment ago.

"Damnation, it's dark. I can't but see my hand afore my face."

"Aw, quit your complaining."

"I'll complain if I damn well want to. And I'll tell you something else, too. When we find her, that runaway gal sure better be pretty as her picture, old man. I never had me a pretty, rich gal before. No, I ain't. Nor gotten paid five thousand dollars to poke her a couple times."

"Half that money's mine, Aaron, and don't you be forgetting about that, dammit. Half the damn money, along with half those damn pokes."

"Pokes?" Amanda gulped the word. "Oh, surely they can't... They don't... Do they mean what I think they mean, Quicksilver?"

"Yep." Marcus had bent down to fasten his holster to his leg. He straightened up now. "They mean every last, nasty word of it. Now do you want to stand here a half hour and debate what we're going to do, Duchess? Or do you want to do what I tell you?"

Amanda swallowed audibly. "What—whatever you say, Quicksilver," she croaked. "Only, if you please, be quick about it."

"Right. Let's go." He grabbed her hand and raced through the darkness for the riverbank.

Chapter Twelve

When the rising sun glanced off the tin roofs and windowpanes of a town, Marcus thought he'd never seen a prettier, more welcome sight in his life. They'd walked all night. Twice the buffalo hunter's wagon had come within a hundred feet of them while Raze's companions continued to speculate on what they would do with the runaway heiress once they got their hands on her. Twice Marcus had reached for Amanda's hand and hustled her through the darkness, out of harm's way.

He was used to being the hunter, not the prey, and he hated running away. It was more his nature to stalk, or, if necessary, to turn and meet his enemies head-on, even when the odds were not in his favor. But risking his own life was one thing. Amanda Grenville's life—not to mention her innocence—was part of this bargain. She had christened him her guardian angel, and Marcus had every intention of following through with the job, even if it meant slinking through the dark night and the tall prairie grass like a turn-tail dog.

Now that it was daylight, he was glad to see the town up ahead. If he was gritty-eyed and dead tired, he could only imagine how Amanda must be feeling. She hadn't complained, though. In fact, it occurred to him now that she hadn't spoken more than a word or two for the past hour or so.

"We'll find a place where we can rest for a while," he said, turning toward her. She'd clambered into her damp dress on the run sometime during the night, but right now it looked more as if she'd fallen headlong into a ragbag and climbed out wearing half the contents. Her face appeared especially pale in the morning light—deathly pale, in fact—and her lovely green eyes were glassy with fever.

"Come here," Marcus commanded quietly. He was relieved that for once she obeyed him without an argument. But that relief was coupled with concern. If this woman didn't argue, she must truly be ill. So, when he pressed his palm against her forehead, it came as no surprise that it felt as hot as a stovetop. "You're burning up, darlin'."

A wisp of a smile touched her dry lips. "I think I must've taken a chill during the night," she said in a voice that was as flimsy as a reed. "I'll be fine. I'm sure I will." She shivered now, and her smile faltered. "Well, I'll be fine as soon as I warm up a bit."

Warming up, Marcus thought, meant a bed, a blanket or two, and a lot of steaming liquids. It might even mean a doctor. And if Amanda's fever turned out to be more than the four-dollar variety, they were going to be in big trouble. Judging from the looks of her at the moment, they probably already were.

He slid his fingers around her wrist, gauging the pulse that fluttered beneath her delicate skin, a little astounded that somebody else's well-being mattered so intensely to him, a bit baffled by the stitch of fear that pulled tight in his chest. Fevers could ravage the strongest of bodies, and Amanda's small and delicate body hadn't been strengthened by being half starved for sleep and sustenance these past few days. No thanks to her so-called guardian angel.

"You just need a few hours of sleep to put you right back in the pink," he said, trying hard to sound as if he believed it. "Come on, darlin'. Let's find you a nice warm bed."

The bed, in a room above the saloon, wasn't all that nice, with its lumpy stuffing and stained ticking. It wasn't all that warm, either, Marcus concluded while he watched Amanda shivering beneath two tattered quilts and an old army blanket. Considering what the pitiful accommodations had cost him, this should have been a suite at the confounded Palace Hotel.

It had turned out that the little town didn't even have a hotel. "There's one coming," the man at the mercantile had told them, "but it ain't here yet. Miz Henderson's got a room she rents. You might try her. It's that yellow clapboard just down the street."

Miz Henderson, however, had taken one look at Amanda, glassy-eyed and sagging against the yellow porch rail, and promptly informed them that she only took in healthy boarders.

Which had left no alternative but the single and rather seedy-looking saloon on the far end of town. As far as Marcus could tell, the place didn't even have a name. Just *Saloon* painted—and poorly, at that—on a weathered board nailed to the building. Marcus sat Amanda by the door, a healthy distance from the suspicious gaze of the bartender, before he sauntered up to the bar and asked about accommodations.

After the bartender grudgingly conceded that, yeah, he guessed there was an available room, the fella had immediately demanded twenty dollars for it. In advance. His girls, he claimed—meaning the two dispirited-looking middle-aged females draped at a table in the rear of the bar—would have to double up in the only other room, and their income would be seriously constrained as a result.

It was tantamount to robbery, and Marcus had told him that. And the barkeep had agreed, almost cheerfully, giving his wide waxed mustache a twist for emphasis. But when all was said and done, it was the only room in town. Amanda needed its comfort desperately, and the four silver dollars in Marcus's pocket weren't going to procure it. All he'd had left was his gun.

A week ago, he thought bleakly, if anyone had told him he'd be skulking around west Nebraska on foot, he'd have laughed. If anyone had had the gall to suggest he'd be afoot without the gun that was as much a part of him as his right hand, he wouldn't have believed it. But there it was. When it came right down to it, he might even have considered giving up his right hand to insure Amanda's health and comfort.

He must've been plain crazy.

Instead of shooting the greedy barkeep right between the eyes, as he was so sorely tempted to do, Marcus had undone his gunbelt and placed it on the bar.

"That ought to get us permanent residence," he'd said. "And three hot meals a day."

"Three days," the barkeep had countered while he slipped the .45 from its holster, squinted to check the sighting, then rolled the well-oiled cylinder smoothly down his sleeve. "Hot coffee and biscuits and bacon."

Marcus had been in no position to argue while Amanda was in such a feverish condition. She needed rest, and whatever he could provide in the way of medication. "Lemme have a shot of whiskey for my wife, will you?"

Obviously pleased with his deal, the bartender had stashed the gun under the bar, then poured two full shots. After downing his, Marcus had carried the other glass of whiskey to Amanda at the door. Then, after she tossed the liquor back without so much as a whimper of protest, he'd carried her up the stairs and gently laid her on the sorry bed, where she immediately fell into a deep sleep.

She'd be better, he told himself now, settling in a chair at the foot of the bed and propping his legs on a corner of the mattress. She'd be better. For all her delicacy, Amanda Grenville was a strong woman. She'd get through this. By God, he'd see that she got through it if it was the last thing he did.

He hadn't been able to stop the bank robber's bullet from taking Sarabeth away all those years ago. Maybe, he figured, this was a small way of making up for that.

Marcus drifted off then into his own much-needed sleep, with something close to a prayer on his lips. Not that he was a praying man, exactly. Not hardly. Hell, Sarabeth, in the short time they were married, had always been after him to go to services, saying Marcus ought to bend his knee in prayer once or twice, if only just for the exercise.

Well, if slumping in a chair counted as kneeling, and if the good Lord even listened to a man who made his living with a gun, and if a single word qualified as a prayer, then so be it.

Please.

"Quicksilver."

Amanda's voice was as parched as her lips. She wasn't sure if the frail light in the room was dawn or dusk, but she recognized the broad-shouldered, long-legged shadow in the chair at the foot of the bed. His mere presence made her feel safer, better, even though she ached to the marrow of her bones.

She'd never been sick a day in her life, and of all her new experiences during the past week, this fever was her least favorite. For a while it had felt as if it were consuming her, trying to eat her alive. She remembered feeling as if she were in an oven, roasting in her own juices, turning this way and that. Then lying still, chilled and limp as an oyster on a bed of shaved ice.

She remembered sweltering heat and chilling cold, daylight changing to dark, night breaking up into day, quilts wrapped around her and the same quilts pushed off, again and again. And dreams. Terrible dreams of burning trains, starving babies, huge black wagons that lumbered through tangled masses of burnt grass. Mostly she remembered a touch as cool as a cloud, a voice as soft as an angel's. Her guardian angel. She wanted to feel that touch again, to hear that voice.

"Marcus," she said, infusing a bit more breath into her own voice in order to make it more than a dry whisper. "Are you awake?"

If he wasn't, he woke quickly. And just as quickly he was at her side, slipping a warm and solid arm beneath her shoulders, raising her for a cool taste of water. After she sipped awkwardly, his gentle hand dabbed the liquid that slid down her chin, then pressed against her forehead.

"Nice," Amanda murmured, closing her eyes briefly. She tried to smile, even though her lips felt like two strips of scorched bacon.

"You're cooler," he said, softly, calmly. "The fever's breaking, I think."

He hoped. But Marcus had hoped before during the past thirty-six hours, when Amanda's rallies—those moments of cool lucidity and fragile cheer—were followed by worse bouts of fever and delirium. She'd been so sick, and he'd felt so damn helpless.

He couldn't even locate a doctor. The best this town had to offer in the way of a medical man was a barber with a jar of leeches, so the only help Marcus had gotten was from the two whores who called the saloon home.

Maybelle and Rose—he kept forgetting which was which, since both women obviously shared the same bottle of red hair dye and painted their faces alike—had been reluctant to get involved until Marcus confided in them that Amanda was a soiled dove herself, one he'd plucked out of a bawdy house in El Paso and married on the run. The lie had not only concealed Amanda's true identity, but it had seemed to spark some long-lost notions of romance in the two haggard prostitutes, and they'd turned into regular Florence Nightingales between customers and behind the barkeep's back.

Still, two well-meaning whores and a bounty hunter—no matter how much he cared—weren't the medical attention the runaway heiress required and deserved. Marcus had just about decided to wire old lady Grenville in Denver and ask for her help when Amanda suddenly, thankfully, appeared to have turned the corner.

It had been the worst thirty-six hours of Marcus's life—not to mention Amanda's—but, by God, it looked as if she'd pulled through.

''Why, Marcus Quicksilver!'' Amanda exclaimed softly now. ''Is that a tear I see sliding down through all those whiskers?''

He took a brusque swipe at the telltale drop of

moisture. "It's sweat," he said, with a gruffness he didn't feel. "You had me worried for a while, brat."

Amanda edged her hand from beneath the quilts and tucked it into his. Her voice was weak and her smile just a wisp. "I wasn't worried. Not for a minute. I knew you wouldn't let me go."

He wouldn't, Marcus thought, if she was his. But she wasn't, dammit, and she never would be, and there was no use in pretending she didn't belong to Angus McCray, or that Marcus himself meant anything more to her than a paid escort. A guardian angel, perhaps, but one on the payroll nevertheless.

"Go back to sleep," he told her, giving her hand a squeeze and then tucking it back under the covers. "You need to get your strength back. It's still a long ways to Denver."

When he moved to return to his chair, Amanda once more caught him by the hand.

"Promise me something, Quicksilver." There was a wet glaze to her green eyes now that had nothing to do with fever. "If I die..."

"You're not going to die."

"I know that, but just in case, will you promise me something?"

"What?" he asked, with some reluctance, because he was a man who kept his promises. No matter what.

"If I die..."

"You won't, dammit."

"Hush. Just listen to me. *If* I do, will you promise to see that my grandmother doesn't take me back to New York? The Grenville family crypt is there."

Her eyes sank closed now, and her voice became even more wispy. "My grandfather's buried there. My mother and father, too. But it's a terrible, dark and dreary place, and I...well, I wouldn't want to spend a few minutes there, much less all eternity. Will you do that for me?" Now her mouth twitched in a small, thin smile. "I mean, even though I'm not going to die, will you promise me that?"

Marcus smoothed a stray lock of hair from her pale cheek. "It's a promise you won't be needing."

"Just promise me. I trust you, Marcus Quicksilver. With my life. And I trust you with my death."

"All right," he whispered. "I promise, but..."

She cut him off with a long, painful sounding sigh. "Thank you, Marcus. I'll rest much better now, knowing I'll always be near you."

"You're welcome, brat," he whispered, tucking the covers about her. "Rest now."

She did rest better during the next twelve hours, Marcus thought, although he gave the credit to the laudanum supplied by Maybelle and Rose, rather than to any promise he'd made. When she opened her eyes shortly after dawn, those eyes were lucid, and once again as green as a fine spring day.

She was even strong enough to sit up in bed, which was good, because Marcus was too tired to get out of his chair to help her.

"I'm much better," she said with a full-fledged smile. "But you're not looking so good, Quicksilver. Perhaps you're coming down with a fever of your own." Her green eyes narrowed as she studied his face more closely. Her tongue clucked softly. "You do look a little peaked, Marcus. Maybe it's you who should be lying down here now, instead of me."

She tossed back the quilts and blanket, then gasped and quickly drew them back again. "Good Lord, I'm...I'm..."

"Unclothed," he finished for her calmly.

"Buck naked!" Color shot into her pale cheeks while she tugged the quilts up another few inches and tucked them firmly, and to all appearances permanently, under her chin. "Was that really necessary?"

"Uh-huh." He laughed softly, not so much at her distress as at her determination to mount a show of indignation, even in her weakened condition. Now he was truly certain she'd recovered. "But don't let your britches get all twisted over it, Duchess."

"What britches?" Weak as she was, she still managed to infuse her tone with haughtiness. It should have irritated him, but it purely tickled him. His brat was back. Thank God.

"Where, may I inquire, are my clothes?"

Marcus cocked his head in the direction of the washstand. "In there. All laundered and pressed, thanks to the two ladies who work downstairs. They were the ones who undressed you. Not me."

"Oh." She contemplated that information for a moment, while gnawing on her lower lip. Then, instead of a glare, she surprised Marcus with a grin. "Well?"

"Well, what?"

Her eyebrows lofted quizzically. "Did you look, Quicksilver?"

Had he looked? Of course he'd looked. He was a man, wasn't he? And the truth was that the two whores must've been a lot better at undressing men than they were at taking underclothes off delirious women, because he'd had to step in when Maybelle and Rose almost rolled their semiconscious patient off the bed. Hell, he'd done most of the stripping himself, while the ladies jabbered at him to be careful and not tear any of the pretty lace.

"No. I didn't look," he said, his gaze sliding evasively to the window as he remembered the intriguing coppery color of her hair against the creamy smoothness of her thighs. A newly minted penny embedded in white velvet. The mere memory set his body aflame now, the way he hadn't allowed to happen earlier, when Amanda was so ill.

"I was just curious," she said with a little sigh. "Under similar circumstances, I'd've looked at you."

Marcus swung his gaze back to discover an impish tilt to her lips. Too impish for her own good. Or for his. It was time, he figured, to put a little more distance between them. He'd made promises beyond her burial wishes. He'd said things, even spoken of love, when she was sick. But that was then. She wasn't sick anymore. There would be no more talk of death. No more talk of love.

Marcus stood up now and reached for his hat.

"I expect you're hungry, after not eating for a

few days. I'll go downstairs and see what the ladies can come up with in the way of a meal.''

Downstairs, Maybelle and Rose came up with a beer for Marcus first. Ever since he told them he'd carried Amanda away from a fate worse than death in a Texas bawdy house, the two women had treated the runaway heiress like a long-lost sister and Marcus like a knight in bright armor.

After a long pull from his beer glass, Marcus asked, ''Where's Jubal?'' He glanced around for the surly barkeep who'd taken his gun in exchange for the three-day room and probably wouldn't hesitate to use that weapon now, if he saw Marcus drinking a free beer. There was also the little matter of their time in that little room being about to run out, which would be no problem if Amanda was well enough to travel by tomorrow. But if not...

''Gone.'' Maybelle gave her hennaed hair a shake. ''Thank God.'' She took Marcus's half-empty glass and filled it to the brim again with beer. Filling a second glass for herself, she added, ''Jubal said he had business in Cheyenne and he trusted us to watch things here while he's away.''

Rose laughed, exposing an array of broken or missing teeth. ''And while the cat's away...''

...the mice will probably drink the inventory, Marcus thought, though he didn't express it. Dependable or not, the two women had been good to him. Without their help, he might have lost Amanda forever. Not that he wasn't going to lose her anyway, as soon as he got her to Denver, he thought

bleakly. But losing her to death had to be worse than losing her to Angus McCray. Didn't it?

"Hey, girls, if you're handing out free beer, don't go forgetting about me."

The voice came from the table by the door. Until then, Marcus had only been vaguely aware of the saloon's only other customer. Hell, he'd been so worried about Amanda for the past two days that he hardly glanced at people as they came and went. But now he took a good look at the man who sat with his head bent over a game of solitaire.

For a moment, Marcus thought he recognized the long-haired, mustachioed customer, who bore a stunning resemblance to General George Armstrong Custer, with his center-parted locks and his long, narrow nose. Or was it Wild Bill Hickok the fella put him in mind of? There was something so familiar...

"How's your pretty missus?" Maybelle asked now, interrupting Marcus's train of thought and reminding him of the reason he'd come downstairs in the first place.

"Hungry," he said.

"Well, now, that's a damn good sign." Rose slapped the flat of her hand on the bar. "Let's see what I can do to a mess of bacon and eggs."

"I'd be much obliged, Rose. I intend to pay you back one of these days, you know." In fact, even now Marcus was thinking of how he could sign over a portion of his reward to the two bighearted whores.

But Rose and Maybelle both shook their heads. "We already got our reward," Maybelle said, jerking her thumb toward the stairs, "and that's seeing one of our own getting out of this business."

Rose held her beer on high. "Here's to runaway whores," she said.

Well, it was close, Marcus thought, as he lifted his own glass and then drained it. "Here's to runaways."

"Here's to my guardian angel."

Feeling human again and healthy—not to mention dressed, in freshly laundered clothes—and having just sipped her very first beer, Amanda decided a toast was in order. She sipped again and concluded that she much preferred beer to sherry and champagne, though she'd barely even been able to sample those under her grandmother's sober and eagle-eyed gaze.

Not that Marcus was looking any less sober and watchful at the moment, as he stood in front of the washstand and concentrated on his own lathered face in the mirror. Earlier, when Maybelle and Rose brought the beer—good medicine, they said—and a plate of bacon and eggs for Amanda, they had also handed Marcus a razor and a foam-filled shaving cup and told him that, now that Amanda was feeling better, he no longer had any excuse for, as Maybelle put it, "looking like a damn derelict."

His shagginess hadn't bothered Amanda at all. She had gotten quite accustomed to his soft, dark whiskers during the past several days. She even rather liked the slightly dangerous look his beard conferred on him. Still, she had to admit she enjoyed watching him shave, and was more than a little curious about the results.

After another taste of the warm beer, she sighed, leaned back on a pillow, and told him just that. Then, when he failed to respond, she asked, "Did you hear me, Quicksilver?"

"I heard you," he drawled, not to her but to his own lathered image in the mirror. He scraped the razor along his jawline, then wiped the soapy blade on the washcloth before he scraped again.

"I'm ignoring you," he said. "Or trying to," he added under his breath.

"And a fine job you're doing of it, too." Much as she wanted to glare at the face in the mirror, Amanda found herself smiling. Lucky looking glass, she thought, getting to possess that strong, handsome face, getting gazed into so intently by those deep blue eyes.

"You're a remarkably handsome man, Marcus Quicksilver." Her voice was warmer and breathier than she'd intended, like a sultry breeze coming from the south. "I'm awfully glad I've come to know you."

Those dark blue eyes shifted their focus and found her face in the mirror. Marcus's hand held still, the blade poised just above his cheekbone. For a second, pinned by the sudden intensity of that gaze, Amanda was unable to move. Only her heart moved, manufacturing an odd, thoroughly unexpected beat. Then the whole room, perhaps even the entire earth, seemed to shift imperceptibly, and the temperature increased. Considerably. For a moment she thought her fever had returned.

Whether the moment lasted a second or a century, Amanda wasn't sure. But she knew for certain the instant when it ended. The blue flame in the bounty hunter's eyes turned to ice. The set of his mouth hardened, and he returned his attention to the task of shaving, slowly gliding the sharp blade down his cheek.

"Save your compliments for your intended, brat," he said in a distinctly gruff voice. "And don't trick yourself into thinking you know a man just because you've shared a room with him and watched him shave."

And don't practice your newfound charms on somebody you'll walk away from the minute you get to Denver. It hurts too much, dammit.

Flicking his gaze to her reflection in the mirror, Marcus saw that his harsh words had apparently fallen on deaf ears. Amanda was still smiling at him between sips of her beer.

"You don't have to tell me I'm naive, Marcus. I'm perfectly aware of that. For heaven's sake, that's one of the reasons I ran away. I was sick to death of being inexperienced and naive."

He snorted, and then cursed when the razor bit into his cheek.

"Be careful," she said.

Careful? That was the problem. He didn't know how to be careful anymore. With his face or with his goddamn heart. Best put the razor down before you slit your throat, he told himself, but when he reached for the washrag, Amanda already had it.

"I may still be a bit naive, Quicksilver," she said as she stood on tiptoe and dabbed away the soap on his cheek, "but I'm not the inexperienced child I was a week ago."

Not a child, anyway, Marcus thought woefully, feeling her breasts brush against his chest and her warm, beery breath on his neck.

"And," she continued, "believe me, I realize I don't know you. Not the facts of your life, anyway. But that doesn't seem to make much difference." Her fingertips touched his cheek now. "You see, I'm falling in love with you, Marcus Quicksilver. I'm just dizzy with it. Isn't that the most amazing thing?"

Amazing? Marcus stepped back and stared at the pretty, eager and—yes—lovestruck face turned up to his. He was amazed, all right. Amazed and dumbstruck. Amazed and dumbstruck and absolutely terrified.

He grabbed for his hat and jammed it on his head, then just stood there like a fifth bedpost until he could think of something to say. Something that made sense. Or not.

"If you're dizzy, you best lie down," he muttered finally. "I'll be back in a while."

And then it was only dumb luck that led him in the right direction and had him using the knob instead of walking right through the damn door.

Chapter Thirteen

A while later, down in the smoky saloon, Maybelle filled his glass for the third or fourth time. It might have been the fifth or sixth or, for all he knew, the seventh. Marcus wasn't even counting. He drank most of the beer before the foam had a chance to settle, then stared into the amber dregs. A few more of these and he wouldn't be able to think clearly enough to even know he had a problem, much less try to come up with a solution to it.

I'm falling in love with you, Marcus Quicksilver. I'm just dizzy with it. Isn't that amazing?

Amazing.

A week ago he'd been fairly happy with his life. Well, hell. Maybe not happy, exactly. Happiness wasn't something he ever thought about anymore. He'd been content with his lot. He'd been reconciled to his solitary existence. But now...

"You're real different, Quicksilver."

Maybelle was leaning toward him across the bar, twisting a lock of red hair around one finger, her red lips curved in a knowing grin as she contemplated

Marcus' face. "Real damn different," she said again.

"Is that so?" He tossed back what was left of the beer and set the glass down with a thud. "You're supposed to be a sporting girl, Maybelle, and a substitute bartender, not a damned Gypsy fortune-teller."

She laughed. "It's true. You are different. And it's more than just the shave. It's something else, but I can't quite put my finger on it."

"Well, while you're deliberating, darlin', put your finger on that pitcher over there and pour me another glass."

The saloon was fairly crowded, and after Maybelle refilled his glass and kept eyeing him peculiarly, as if he were some specimen in a jar, Marcus was glad when she sauntered away to attend to the various thirsts and needs of other customers.

Different! What was so damn different about him? He was Marcus Quicksilver, bounty hunter. That was what he'd been yesterday and what he'd be tomorrow. It was what he'd always been.

No. Not always. There'd been a time he was something, somebody, different.

His gaze lofted to the mirror behind the bar now, and for an instant Marcus felt as if he were staring at a stranger. Maybe Maybelle had been right. It wasn't the shave that accounted for the difference, although that did make him look a bit less threatening. But there was something... He struggled for a word to describe what he saw in his features....

Something...what? Gentle? More relaxed? Less haunted?

One thing was for sure. He no longer had the look of a hard-bitten, hell-bent manhunter. And why the hell should he? He didn't even have a damn gun anymore. Not to mention the fact that he hadn't even bothered to get a look at the faces around him in the saloon tonight. All he'd been thinking about was Amanda.

He surveyed the room now, discovering a few old faces and several new ones, none of which was familiar. One particular face was absent.

"Where's Wild Bill?" Marcus asked Maybelle when she came back to plant herself before him on the other side of the bar.

"Where's who?"

"Wild Bill." Marcus gestured toward the table where the long-haired man had been playing solitaire earlier in the evening.

"Oh, him." Maybelle shrugged. "He got tired of playing by himself and went upstairs to play with Rose instead."

"You know his name?" he asked her.

"No. Why?"

Marcus shook his head. "No reason. He just looked familiar."

"Everybody looks familiar to me," Maybelle said with a husky laugh. "Hey. I just this minute decided what it is about you, Quicksilver."

"What's that?" he asked.

"I just figured out what it is that's so different about you."

"It's the shave," he told her sullenly, hoping to end the conversation.

"No. It's more than that." The whore cocked her head and grinned. "You're in love, honey. I shoulda seen that right off the bat."

Now Marcus laughed. "I'm a married man, Maybelle. Of course I'm in love. It goes with the territory."

"Not hardly," she said with a sneer. "You might've thought you were in love when you stole that pretty little gal away from the bawdy house in Texas. More than likely, though, you just figured you were being a hero and saving her. But you weren't in love with her. No, sir. Not till tonight." Maybelle closed one eye in a slow and all-knowing wink. "Trust me on this, Quicksilver. You might say love's my business, and I've seen hundreds of men not in love, so I reckon I can tell the real thing when and if I see it."

I'm falling in love with you, Marcus Quicksilver. I'm just dizzy with it. Isn't that amazing?

Amazing.

Marcus felt dizzy for a second. He told himself it was merely the effect of the beer while he shifted his weight and tightened his grip on the bar. He told himself he couldn't be in love with a runaway heiress, a woman he couldn't have. Only a damn fool would do that. He'd been a lot of things in his life, but a damn fool wasn't one of them. Then he tried to summon up one of those old easy grins that had stood him in such good stead as a ladies' man all these years, but it felt a little lopsided, as if he were wincing instead of smiling.

"Maybe I'm in love with you, Maybelle," he drawled.

She gave him one of those flinty looks that whores were so good at when they smelled deception. "Sure you are, honey. Sure you are. And maybe pigs fly, too."

"I can't marry you, Angus. I'm sorry."

Amanda shifted her stance in front of the mirror. She tried to erase the smile that kept curling the edges of her mouth. It wouldn't do to break Angus McCray's heart and then burst out laughing.

"Angus, I'm very, very sorry. I'm afraid I simply cannot marry you."

She burst out laughing. It was as if she had swallowed a feather. She'd always been under the impression that love was a serious and sober business, yet here she was, wildly in love and laughing like a loon.

Deciding she'd rehearsed her farewell speech to her fiancé quite enough, Amanda sauntered back to the bed and straightened the quilt one more time. Rose had brought clean linens shortly after Marcus left. She had offered to make up the bed, but Amanda had insisted she could do it herself.

Even though she'd never made a bed before in her life, she hadn't done such a terrible job, she thought now as she regarded the tight corners and the ruler-straight counterpane. For a first time, it was a perfectly acceptable effort. She wondered if Marcus would be surprised when he returned from wherever he'd rushed off to. If he returned...

Suddenly unmindful of the well-made bed, Amanda plopped down on the mattress, drew her legs up and hugged her knees.

What if he didn't come back? No, that was silly. Of course he'd return. If for no other reason, Marcus Quicksilver would come back because she was worth at least five thousand dollars to him. Oh, but she wanted to be worth so much more.

"I can't marry you, Angus," she whispered. "And if I can't marry Marcus, I don't know how I'll live the rest of my life."

Marcus stood in the doorway a long time, watching Amanda, who was curled up like a soft kitten on the bed. She'd turned down the lamp, he noticed, to a warm golden wash of light. It was, he thought, the perfect illumination for lovemaking.

He wished he hadn't drunk so many beers. Or he wished he'd drunk more. He didn't know what he wished. Maybe for turning the calendar back a week and then, when he'd left Dakota, turning Sarah B. southwest instead of due south. He wished he'd never met Amanda Grenville, at the same time he wished he could spend the rest of his life loving her and being amazed, day after day, by her loving him.

God almighty! He'd felt more alive this past week, with this woman, than he'd felt in a dozen years, and yet here he stood, wishing he was dead.

Isn't that amazing?

Amazed. Maybe in love for the second time in

his life. Maybe—probably—drunk for the two-thousandth time. Marcus no longer knew what he was, only that he was standing here on the threshold, unable to walk away and unwilling to move forward.

Just then, in the adjacent room, he heard a burst of husky laughter from Rose, followed immediately by a rough growl from Wild Bill and then the distinct creaking of mattress ropes and the rhythmic thud of an iron headboard against the wall. Damned if his own heart didn't take on that same primitive beat then. And damned if the noise didn't wake Amanda from her curled-up-kitten sleep.

She unwound—slowly, sensuously—stretched her arms over her head, then blinked and brought them back down to her sides when she saw Marcus standing in the doorway.

"You're back," she said, more sleepy than surprised. "I thought I heard somebody knocking on the door." She frowned then, confused, as the iron bedstead next door continued to pound the wall behind her. "What's all that racket? What in the world do you suppose they're doing at this hour of the night?"

"Moving furniture," he said, trying not to grin, and almost succeeding, while he felt himself being irresistibly drawn into the room by the look of complete innocence on Amanda's beautiful face. Amazing.

"Oh." She smiled sleepily, trustingly. "I was waiting for you. I didn't mean to fall asleep. What time is it, Quicksilver?"

"A little after midnight."

"Midnight!" She looked at the wall, where the rambunctious goings-on next door were now making the framed sampler on their side of the wall start to shimmy and jiggle on its nail. "My goodness. That sounds awfully strenuous. Do you think we should offer to help?"

Marcus shook his head, even as the wall-banging increased in volume and tempo.

Then, with a soft thump, the sampler dropped onto the pillow behind Amanda. She scooted closer to the foot of the bed, as if she were afraid the studs and two-by-fours would be coming down next. "They can't keep that up all night, can they?"

Not at that rate, anyway, Marcus thought. "I expect they're just about finishing up now."

No sooner had he spoken those words than Rose and Wild Bill proved him right by invoking the name of the Lord in a succession of lusty shouts, loud and heartfelt enough to rival any preacher on the tent circuit. In the silence that ensued, Marcus suddenly realized he was sweating, which probably explained why his mouth felt so damn dry.

"Moving furniture, Quicksilver?" Amanda tilted her head and cocked an eyebrow. She might have believed him, if Rose hadn't stopped in earlier on her way to the room, if she hadn't seen the long-haired, wild-looking man twisting his hat so impatiently out in the hallway, if Rose hadn't said how lucky Amanda was to be giving her favors instead of selling them, and to the same man night after night, too, instead of a parade of dirty strangers.

"Seems to me that was a bit more like moving heaven and earth."

He didn't answer her, but stood there, dark in the doorway, staring at the toes of his boots as if they were the most fascinating objects in all creation, his chest rising and falling as if each breath were a hard-won battle, as if he were afraid to look at her. And right that moment there was nothing Amanda wanted more than for Marcus Quicksilver to look at her with his dark blue eyes on fire. For her.

She brushed the fallen sampler aside, picked up the pillow and hugged it to her chest, hoping to quiet her wild heartbeat. Through the wall now, she could hear the muted laughter of Rose and her wild-haired lover, and the celebratory clink of glasses. She thought of how shocked she should be. She thought of all the shoulds and mustn'ts and don'ts that had comprised her life up until just recently. She thought that Rose and her lover sounded like the happiest people in Nebraska right now, perhaps in all the world, and she envied them their bliss. Oh, how she envied them.

"I didn't know," she said almost dreamily, as much to herself as to the man still standing in the doorway. "I had absolutely no idea. No notion at all."

"About what?"

"Moving furniture." Amanda grinned, gesturing toward the wall. "I was always under the impression that making love was serious, even somber. I never knew it was supposed to be so much fun."

"Well, it depends."

"On what?"

Marcus cleared his throat. "On who's doing it."

She gazed at him then, golden lamplight burnishing her lovely face, turning her hair into spun yellow silk, flickering in her emerald eyes. "I wonder," she said wistfully, "what it would be like, Quicksilver, if you and I..."

"This isn't some damn game, Amanda."

Marcus stepped across the threshold and pulled the door closed behind him. "We're not exactly children spending a pleasant evening in the parlor playing parlor games right now." He aimed a dark glance toward the room next door. "And neither, for chrissake, are they."

She sat back, blinking. "I didn't for a moment think that—"

"And another thing." Marcus stalked across the floor now and stood towering over her. "You need to be a whole hell of a lot more careful about what you want, Duchess, and who you want. One of these days—or one of these nights—you might get a lot more than you ever bargained for."

Her face crumpled for a second, dark shadows digging where the smooth lamplight had been just a moment before. The disappointment, however, quickly flared into anger, and she clambered up onto her knees, the better to aim her hot gaze right between his eyes.

"If you think I'm playing a game, Quicksilver, you're sadly mistaken. I don't know how to play games. Not hide-and-seek nor anything else. I was never allowed to play games in my grandmother's house. I was never allowed to laugh or to be happy. I was never allowed to live.''

Her fists came up to her hips now, and her chin ratcheted up another notch, along with her voice. ''And if you think, just because I'm inexperienced, that I don't have the vaguest notion what I want or who I want, you're very, very wrong. Dead wrong.''

They glared at each other then, blue eyes burning into green, the air between them charged with a fierce, almost electric heat. Amanda's lips were compressed in a thin, white, furious line. A muscle jerked in Marcus's cheek.

''A week ago you wanted Angus McCray,'' he said through clenched teeth.

''Not Angus,'' Amanda insisted. ''It was my independence I wanted. It was my confounded life I wanted. Angus was the only way I knew how to go about getting it.''

''And now that you've been independent and you've experienced life for all of one week, you want me.'' Marcus threw up his hands. ''Amanda, you don't even know me.''

''I know I trust you with my life.''

''I'm a bounty hunter, for chrissake. My job is keeping you alive so I can collect my goddamn reward!'' It wasn't true, of course, Marcus thought, but it made for a good argument. The only one he could think of just then.

Only Amanda wasn't buying it. The look that crossed her face was pure challenge.

''If you were doing your job, Quicksilver, you'd have had me in Denver the day after you caught me and you'd be rolling in greenbacks right now. Five thousand of them from my grandmother, or even more from me. If you were just doing your job, you wouldn't have kissed me the way you did the other night. Or you would have kissed me more, and the hell with the consequences, as long as you got your reward.'' Amanda paused only long enough to draw in a breath. ''If you were just doing your job, Marcus Quicksilver, you wouldn't have cried when you thought I was dying of fever.''

She was right, of course. Every word of it was true, but Marcus would be damned if he'd admit it, so when she demanded that he tell her that she was right, he merely shrugged.

''Tell me you don't have feelings for me,'' she demanded then.

''It doesn't matter,'' he said quietly.

''Of course it matters,'' Amanda protested. ''If we share those feelings, then...''

''Then what? We're going to live happily ever after, like two characters in some damn fairy tale?''

''It's possible, isn't it? If we care for one another? If we love one another?''

After cursing sharply, Marcus stalked over to the window and aimed his hip at the sill while he aimed the hardest, coldest look he was capable of at the woman on the bed. ''I don't think so, sweetheart. And if you'll use your head instead of your eager little heart, you won't think so, either.''

''So you don't have feelings for me, then?''

''I didn't say that,'' he growled.

Amanda made an exasperated, strangling sound

in her throat and rolled her eyes heavenward. "Then just what are you saying, Quicksilver?"

"I don't know what the hell I'm saying. You've got me so I can't think straight anymore."

Her whole face—mouth, eyes, even her pert little nose—lofted in a smile. "I'm so glad."

She scuttled off the mattress and walked toward Marcus. Sashayed toward him was a better description, he thought, as he noted the extra little slink she put into what was ordinarily a prim and pretty elegant stride. She was all subtle slither and oncoming grace, but this wasn't any pretty ingenue walking with an encyclopedia on her head for practice now. This was a beautiful, infinitely desirable woman who was moving inexorably toward a kiss. A kiss and more.

It was a good thing the window at his back was closed, because Marcus was briefly tempted to lean back and take the long two-story drop to the street below. Even so, his heart had begun to beat as if he were indeed taking that fatal plunge. Amanda advanced, and halted only when she could advance no farther, when her thighs made contact with his knees. But even that didn't stop her completely, for she wedged her skirts between Marcus's legs and then simply kept coming.

The lamplight at her back cast a golden aura around her. She smelled of lavender now, rather than vanilla. Almost against his will, Marcus lifted his hands and let his fingertips skim her soft cheeks, her slim neck, where the skin was smooth and cool, all traces of her fever gone, or replaced now by a fever of a different sort. It pulsed just beneath her skin and glittered in her green eyes as she leaned forward and touched her lips—softly, tentatively—to his.

"Kiss me the way you did the other night, out under the stars," she whispered. "Please."

"Shhh..." He pressed a finger to her lips. "A beautiful woman doesn't have to say please to a man when she wants him to kiss her."

"All right." A tiny grin flirted with the corners of her mouth. "Then kiss me, dammit."

Placing both hands at her waist, Marcus brought her even closer. He pressed his forehead against hers and answered with a sigh that felt as if it were welling up from the soles of his feet, "If I do that, darlin', it won't just be a kiss. It'll be a whole lot more. Do you understand that?"

Amanda nodded her head against his. "I... Yes, I think so."

"There could be consequences."

"Con—?"

Before she could get the rest of the word out, Marcus drew back his head and riveted her with a hard gaze. "A child, Amanda. Make sure you know what you're asking for."

A child! Amanda blinked. It wasn't as if she hadn't been informed of where babies came from. Several years ago, Bridget, her grandmother's maid, had spent an entire rainy November afternoon apprising Amanda of the various ins and outs, so to speak, of conception. The young Irishwoman had seemed to have a good grasp of the necessary facts. But somehow, in the heat of her desire for the bounty hunter, and in the hot pursuit of his kiss and his touch, Amanda had put all those facts aside.

A child! Marcus Quicksilver's child! The thought alone suddenly made her insides quicken with heat and made her heart perform a gay little handspring somewhere in the vicinity of her throat. What a lovely, lovely consequence that would be.

She was just about to tell him that when all hell broke loose in the room next door.

Chapter Fourteen

Marcus stood in the hallway just outside Rose's locked door, listening intently, wanting to make damn sure he didn't bust in on some rough but willing sex games. He'd told Amanda to wait right where she was, but naturally she hadn't. She was crowding up against his shoulder now, her ear pressed to Rose's door.

"He's hurting her," she whispered urgently. "Oh, Marcus! Do something!"

What Marcus wanted to do was get Amanda the hell away from whatever was going on in there. Not that he'd done such a great job himself tonight of preserving her innocence, but if she never learned about the darker, more violent side of love, to his way of thinking, she wouldn't be missing anything of any importance.

Maybelle came tearing down the hall now, her kohl-rimmed eyes blacker and her rouged mouth redder for the fearful whiteness of her face. She tore frantically at the doorknob, and when it wouldn't

give, she screamed, ''We've got to get in! He's kill-
ing her!''

Out of habit, Marcus's hand moved to his hip,
and he swore harshly when he remembered he'd bartered away his gun.

Breaking into a room where a fight was going on
was a good way for an unarmed and overeager hero
to collect a hot piece of lead, but he stifled his in-
stinct for survival, told Amanda and Maybelle to
stand clear and then put all his weight into one well-
placed, wood-splintering kick that sent the door
crashing inward.

Wild Bill, apparently satisfied with the damage
he'd done to Rose, as well as the room, was in the
process of climbing out the window when he turned
and fired his pistol at the intruders. Fired wildly,
thank God. The bullet grazed Marcus's upper arm,
then thudded into the hallway wall behind him. He
looked back over his shoulder just long enough to
make certain neither of the women had been hit before he took a flying leap across the room, connected
with the long-haired man and shoved him the rest
of the way out the window.

The two-story drop should have broken the bastard's neck, but there was enough of a crowd gathered below on the sidewalk that it was only Wild
Bill's fall that was broken, and maybe—with luck—
his ankle. Marcus watched as the man peeled himself off the planking, shook a fist up at Marcus, who
was halfway out the window himself, and then hob-
bled away. Then, after waiting for a minute to make
sure the culprit was truly headed away, instead of

back inside the saloon, Marcus hauled his shoulders
back through the window frame and turned to see
the havoc Wild Bill had left in his wake.

Rose sat crumpled in a heap on the bed, her broken nose and split upper lip bleeding profusely onto
the ripped sheets and the stained mattress ticking, as
well as onto Amanda, who sat holding Rose in a
protective embrace and crooning softly to her. Marcus stood there a moment, marveling at the sight of
the privileged debutante ministering to the battered
whore. If he had any lingering doubts about Amanda
Grenville's innate goodness or her strength in the
face of adversity, those doubts were dispelled. And
if he hadn't fully acknowledged before that he was
head over heels in love with this astonishing woman,
he did so then and there. At the same time, though,
he cursed himself for allowing her to be in this situation in the first place. He was doing one hell of a
job of protecting her.

Maybelle reappeared then, with a few clean rags
and a bowl of ice. She clambered onto the bed, taking Rose's bloody chin in her hand.

"All right, Rosie. Stop your blubbering now,
honey. He's gone." Maybelle touched a chunk of
ice to a dark purple welt beneath her friend's eye.
When Rose winced and tried to pull away, both
Maybelle and Amanda held on tight.

"Hold still, dammit," Maybelle said. "I know it
hurts, but quit your sniveling. This isn't the first time
you've been beat up, you know. You're only making
it worse on yourself, Rose, by letting that long-

haired, no-good son of a bitch make you cry. You hear me?''

Rose attempted to sniff through her smashed nose, then muttered as best she could through a torn lip. ''I'll see that that bastard pays for this if it's the last thing I ever do. I'll see that he pays for it with his rotten, worthless life.''

Maybelle clucked her tongue sympathetically and continued to dab ice on Rose's welts while Amanda nodded her head.

''You think I don't mean it, Maybelle?'' Rose screamed as she swiped at the blood on her face. ''You just wait and see! I want Frank Scobey full of lead and six feet underground! He's already got a price on his head, but I'm going to add every penny I've ever saved to that sum! Here! Just watch!''

Rose twisted away from the women and managed to pull up one corner of the stained mattress. Then, from its straw depths, she extracted a small metal box. ''Listen!'' Rose shrieked, shaking the box, which clattered wildly. ''There's ten double eagles in here! That's two hundred dollars more on Frank Scobey's head now, and I'm going to make sure every gunman in the territories knows about it, too!''

She turned her battered, blood-wet face toward Marcus. ''You first. It's yours, Quicksilver, if you want it. The whole two hundred. Every cent. Just bring me Scobey dead.''

As soon as Rose mentioned the name, Marcus had felt his memory spark and his jaw slacken. Frank

Scobey. No wonder that face had been familiar, he thought. It wasn't because the character resembled Wild Bill Hickcok at all. It was because Marcus had seen that long sweep of almost girlish hair and that mean, slit-eyed expression time and again, on countless Wanted posters. It stunned him now, and worried him considerably, too, that he hadn't recognized Frank Scobey the first time he laid eyes on him, downstairs in the saloon. He should have known him at first glance, especially since he'd considered going after the stage robber several times in the past few years in order to collect the big reward that Wells Fargo was offering, but other, easier bounties had always seemed to intervene.

"Take it, Quicksilver." Rose shook the little metal box again. "Go ahead. Take your bounty up front. I'd trust you. Just kill him for me. I'm begging you." Tears streamed from the prostitute's eyes, mixing with the blood on her face.

Marcus almost reached out to take it. Almost. His fingers twitched, but his arm didn't seem to want to respond to the signal from his brain. More than that, though, he suddenly realized he didn't want Rose's bounty, or anybody else's, for that matter. He didn't want to spend the next day, the next week, the next year, in the saddle running down murderers and thieves. A moment before he kicked his way into this room, all he'd wanted to do was to make love to Amanda Grenville. And that was still all he wanted. To make love to her, to tell her that—*Amazing!*—he was in love with her, too, and to see where life took them from there. If it took them anywhere.

If life had anything to offer a broke bounty hunter and a beautiful woman with money-green eyes.

A profound emotion coursed through him just then. If it was relief, Marcus didn't know. He wasn't sure if it was love. All he knew was that he felt different. He wanted to be different. And he wasn't afraid anymore. Better to die of a broken heart in the risky pursuit of happiness, he decided, than to go on the way he had been for the past decade, in the risky pursuit of criminals and lowlifes.

Amanda was totally focused on Rose now, as she sat smoothing back a lock of blood-caked hair from the prostitute's forehead. Marcus smiled at her, even though his words were directed at Rose. "You keep your money for now, honey," Marcus said softly. "We'll talk about this tomorrow, when you're feeling better."

"That's right. Tomorrow." Maybelle snatched the box out of Rose's hand and stuffed it back under the mattress. "We'll talk about what to do with all that cash you've saved tomorrow. I can think of half a million better uses right now than wasting it on a man who's already got a price on his head. And anyway, Marcus isn't in any condition to be traipsing off after Scobey tonight, Rose, for two hundred or two million dollars. You can see for yourself that he's hurt, too."

"Will you sit down and stop fussing over me, brat? It's just a scratch."

They were back in their own room now, and Amanda was fluttering around him, half panic-stricken butterfly, half grim-faced nurse. As soon as she realized he'd been hit, she'd been on him like a stamp on a letter. It wasn't that he minded the attention so much, but every time he tried to unbutton his shirt her hands got in the way.

"You've got to get that shirt off, Marcus," Amanda insisted, fumbling with buttons, trying to brush his hands away. "Here. Now hold still. Let me help you, for pity's sake."

He gritted his teeth when, in her helpful enthusiasm, she accidentally whacked his upper arm. "It's just a scratch, dammit."

"Cats scratch, Marcus," she snapped. "Bullets don't. They wound. Now take that shirt off this minute, and let's get that bleeding stopped before you faint or something."

"Before somebody faints." Marcus had already noted that most of the color had drained from Amanda's face and her eyes were brimming with unshed tears. He caught her hands in his in an effort to still them.

"Take it easy, brat, all right? Sit. Sit down." Marcus gently tugged to bring her down next to his seat on the bed. "If you want to help, the best thing you can do is go downstairs and get a pitcher of water and some clean rags from Maybelle. A bottle of whiskey wouldn't hurt, either, and maybe a needle and thread if she's got some handy."

Amanda blinked. "A needle and thread? Marcus, for heaven's sake. Don't you think this shirt is a little beyond mending?"

Marcus laughed as he began to shrug his arm out

of the blood-soaked sleeve. "I was thinking more of mending me, darlin'."

"Oh." Her face grew paler still, taking on a faint green tinge that matched her eyes. "I don't think I'm going to be much help to you in that case. I've never sewn a stitch in my life."

"Well, I've done this once or twice before, so don't worry about it. Go on now." He winked. "The sooner I get this patched up, the sooner I can get on with more important business."

Shocked, Amanda drew back her head and stared at him. What was he thinking? The man was sitting here almost bleeding to death, and he was already talking about getting back to the dangerous business of being a bounty hunter. She was about to tell him that she wouldn't allow him to go when there was a knock on the door.

"Are you two decent in there?" Maybelle called.

"More or less," Marcus said, shrugging off the rest of his shirt. "Come on in, Maybelle."

"I figured you'd be needing these," she said, laying a pile of clean rags on the washstand. "And this." She handed a full bottle of whiskey to Marcus as she passed him on her way back to the door. "It's on the house, Marcus. Just Rosie's and my way of saying thanks."

"How is Rose?" Amanda asked. "Is there anything more we can do for her?"

Maybelle shook her head. "Sleeping. Crying. Maybe a little bit smarter now about who she goes upstairs with. She'll be fine in a day or two."

From the door, Maybelle looked back and sighed.

"Thanks for not taking her up on that fool offer of hers, Marcus. Rosie's been putting that money aside for years so she could start a little restaurant some-day, and I'd sure hate to see her throw it all away just for the sake of revenge."

When Marcus merely nodded in response, May-belle narrowed her gaze. "You're not gonna take it, right? You're not having second thoughts about it, are you? About taking her money and—"

"Of course he's not," Amanda said hurriedly, re-calling Marcus's comment about getting back to business and alarmed that he might indeed be having second thoughts. She rose quickly from the bed in order to usher Maybelle out of the room. The less the subject was discussed, the better. "All Marcus is thinking about right now is getting a good night's sleep."

"Well, that's good. I'll be going then." May-belle's gaze lingered on Amanda a moment, and then she crooked a finger to beckon her closer and whispered, "I guess you know how lucky you are, honey, to be out of this infernal business, don't you, and to have a man who loves you so?"

"A man who—?" Amanda stood there blinking, not certain she had heard the woman right.

"You heard me," Maybelle said with a laugh as she read Amanda's bemused expression. "He'll tell you himself soon enough. Just give him time. It takes some men longer to speak their hearts." She shrugged then, and her smile twisted a bit sadly when she added, "Not that I've been lucky enough to hear those words myself, mind you. But who knows, huh? Maybe one of these days. Maybe one of these years. Well, anyway. If you're smart and you learned anything at all in that sporting house you were in in El Paso, you'll treat him right and keep him close to home. Good night.''

Amanda stood in the doorway, watching Maybelle's skirt swishing down the hall and then disappearing around the corner. It was all she could do not to run after the woman and implore her to explain just how she knew that Marcus loved her and exactly what she meant by treating him right. If Maybelle meant there was a right way to make love, then there must also be a wrong way, Amanda assumed. How in the world was she supposed to know the difference? And what if she—?

"If you're through playing doorstop, darlin', I could use your help a minute," Marcus said.

He was trying—not all that successfully, Amanda noticed—to uncork the bottle of whiskey clamped under his wounded arm, using his teeth while his other hand pressed a cloth to the bleeding wound. Blood was still streaming down his arm, but he didn't appear at all alarmed about it. Not nearly as alarmed as Amanda was.

Plus, now she couldn't think straight. Marcus loved her! Maybelle had said so, although how the woman knew that, Amanda didn't have a clue. Marcus loved her! And he was sitting there, grinning at her like an idiot while he was bleeding to death.

"Oh, no, you don't, Marcus Quicksilver. I didn't die on you, and I'll be damned if I'll let you die on me." She stomped to the bed, tugged the bottle away none too gently and extracted the cork with a distinct pop.

"Now what?" she asked, then eyed the bottle and decided that a little swig—for medicinal purposes only, of course—might help to clear her head. She upended it and let the liquor burn down her throat and flow like hot lava into her veins.

"I hate to tell you this, Marcus," she said, swaying slightly, "but my experience with injuries doesn't go much further than hangnails, and all this blood—first Rose and now you—is starting to... starting to make me a little woozy."

"Sit down," he told her calmly.

She did, then leaned against his uninjured arm and sighed forlornly. "Are we supposed to drink this for courage, or use it on your arm, or what?"

"Courage first," he said, reaching for the bottle and taking a long pull, then handing it back to her. "Go ahead. Take another little nip and then douse this for me." Marcus held out a folded cloth now, glad his hand was steady—well, fairly so—in light of what he knew was coming when he cleaned the wound. Scobey's bullet had only carved a minor groove in the flesh midway between his shoulder and his elbow, but the whiskey treatment was bound to make it feel like an amputation with a dull and rusty saw.

Considering the green tint in Amanda's cheeks, he thought a warning might be appropriate. "And then cover your ears, Duchess, because I'll probably be using some language never intended for them."

Her hands shook badly when she poured the whiskey onto the cloth, and there was a distinct tremor in her voice when she said, "I've heard it's beneficial to think pleasant thoughts when one is in great pain. Perhaps you could think about..."

She fell silent a second, her lips nearly white and her eyes wide with dread as they followed the whiskey-soaked rag, which Marcus had begun to move closer to the wound. Slowly closer. Slower. Hell, what was the rush? He was in no hurry...

"Perhaps you could think about making love with me," she said.

And then, just as Marcus was about to happily change his mind and take his chances with blood poisoning, Amanda covered his hand with hers and forced the medicinal rag into searing contact with his arm.

"You just go ahead and swear, Marcus," she said, almost blithely, pressing what felt like a branding iron against his biceps. "I'm not listening."

Marcus clenched his teeth and nearly gagged on every four-letter word he knew. Then he sat with his wet eyes closed, breathing hard, feeling the fire in his arm slowly subside from white-hot to a dull, throbbing red. After a minute, Amanda eased up the pressure on his arm, then stroked his back and leaned her head gently against his shoulder.

"There," she said with a sigh. "Did you think about making love?"

He shook his head, and a few beads of sweat dripped onto his knees.

"What were you thinking about, then?" she asked. "Something pleasant?"

Marcus's sigh was closer to a groan. "Sort of. I was thinking if we ever have a ranch, Amanda, I'm going to put you in charge of cutting steers."

"I could do that."

"Yeah. I know you could."

She was quiet a moment, and then she laughed. "I don't know whether that's an offer of employment, Quicksilver, or a proposal of marriage. But either way, I accept."

Chapter Fifteen

Damned if it wasn't a proposal of marriage, in a mush-headed, mouth-full-of-oatmeal sort of way, Marcus realized.

Amanda was winding a long white strip of cloth around his arm now, her lips set in a strong, determined line and her touch as skilled as if she'd been patching him up her whole life, instead of gluing together delicate porcelain dolls and matching halves of broken teacups and cookies.

For a minute, Marcus tried feeling sorry for himself, tried feeling as trapped and panicky as a wolf fully prepared to chew off its own foot to regain its freedom. What had he done? No. What had *she* gotten him to do? Married! He didn't want to be married. Did he?

It occurred to him that his reaction had been the same a dozen years before, with Sarabeth. Even though he'd known and loved her all his young life, it had taken him completely by surprise when he heard himself babbling something about forever and a family and a farm, and the next thing he'd known Sarabeth was smiling and saying yes and pressing her cheek to his heart the way Amanda was doing right now.

Only it hadn't been forever. It had only been a few sweet months. One morning Sarabeth had kissed him goodbye, galloped the plow horse into town with her dark hair streaming out behind her, and the next time he saw her she'd been pale and cold and neatly combed in a pine box at the mortuary.

"I was married before," he said now, his voice low, roughened by a grief he hadn't let himself feel in a decade. "You need to know. It was a long time ago. In Illinois. My wife was killed in a bank robbery. The man who shot her was my first bounty." He paused for a moment to draw in a breath. "I brought him in dead instead of alive."

After a moment of silence, Amanda said very softly, "Good. I'm glad. I'm glad you didn't bring him in alive, Marcus, and glad that you found your own justice. I expect that helped to ease your sorrow some."

Marcus shook his head. "No. Maybe some. I don't know." He lifted his hand now and stroked her head as he might have stroked a kitten curled in his lap.

Amanda nestled closer against his chest. "I'm glad you told me about being married, too. I guess it doesn't surprise me all that much. It would probably surprise me more if you hadn't been. Did you...do you have children?"

Marcus shook his head. "We didn't have a chance. We weren't married more than a few months before Sarabeth died. About all we had were dreams."

"And those died, too, I guess."

"Those died, too."

"Marcus?" She hesitated a moment while her cheek rubbed softly against his chest. "Are you trying to tell me you're still in love with your late wife? Is that what you're trying to say? That you'll never marry again?"

"No," he said firmly, even more forcefully than he'd intended. "That's not it. What I'm trying to say is you didn't even know me a week ago. This has all been…I don't know…accidental. Sudden. I'm an honest man, Amanda. A fairly decent one, too, considering what I do for a living. I don't have any dark secrets, but there's a hell of a lot you just don't know."

"Well, I'm listening."

Marcus let go of a long sigh. "It's not that easy, darlin'."

Angling her head now, Amanda held his gaze with hers, while her lips tipped up in a grin. "Are you trying to discourage me, Quicksilver?"

He laughed softly. "Maybe."

"I was only joking about that proposal of marriage, you know." She frowned and then added, "Well, half joking. But is this your way of politely easing me out of the notion?"

"It's my way of telling you I can't take care of

you. Not the way you're used to, anyway. And for sure not the way you deserve.''

"The way I'm used to!" Amanda pulled away and sat up beside him. "The way I deserve! What sort of life do you think I had back in New York, for heaven's sake, if I wanted to escape it so badly?''

She launched herself off the mattress now and started pacing back and forth beside the bed, kicking her skirts out of her way with each step, using her hands to punctuate every other word.

"What I'm used to is being unhappy in that gilded cage my grandmother kept me locked in all my life,'' she said, shaking a fist vaguely eastward. "What I'm used to is having things—things and more things—I don't even want and comforts I don't need.''

Amanda halted now, standing before him, her hands held out in supplication, a sheen of tears glistening in her eyes. She took in a deep breath before she continued. "What I deserve is happiness, Marcus. And I've been happier this past week with you than I've been in all my life. Happier without things, without any comforts to speak of. I've been smarter and stronger and in a million little ways more independent than I ever imagined I could be. I've been...I've been me.''

He started to speak, but she stopped him with a raised hand and a determined *Shh.*...

"As for taking care of me, Marcus Quicksilver, just who do you think got me off of that burning train? Who was it who spirited me away the other night from that awful Raze and his dirty, 'poke'-minded companions? Who took care of me these last few days when I lay nearly dying of a fever in that bed you're sitting on right now? Go on. Answer me. Who was that?''

But she didn't wait for an answer before adding hotly, ''And don't tell me you were just doing it for the reward money, either. Because if it was just my dear old granny's five thousand dollars you were after, I'd be all the way back in New York in my gilded and locked little cage by now.''

True enough, Marcus told himself. Maybe it had been about the reward for ten or twelve minutes, back at the train depot in North Platte. But it wasn't anymore. How Amanda Grenville had worked her way under his skin and into his heart, he wasn't sure. But there she was. Here she was, standing before him like a persistent, implacable lawyer before the judge's bench.

God almighty, he couldn't give her anything except his love. And maybe, if what she was telling him was true and not just some sudden and misguided sense of freedom and adventure... Maybe...

He angled around, stretching his legs out on the bed, leaning back against the iron headboard. ''Come here,'' he said, patting the space beside him. ''You've about worn me out with your speeches, darlin'. Just lie down next to me and be quiet for a while.''

Her little quirk of a smile was far from victorious

and even faintly skeptical, but there was no hesitation when she moved to fit herself against his side and lay her head on his shoulder. There was just the warmth of her and the softness of her hair where it fell over his bare chest and the feathery feel of her breath against his cheek. She fit against him as if she'd been created just for that purpose, Marcus thought. For all he knew at that moment, perhaps she had been.

"Then you talk, Marcus," she said. "How's your arm?"

He flexed his biceps under its cotton wrapping, stifled a small groan and replied, "Tolerable."

"Well, in that case..." Amanda snuggled even closer. "Then don't talk at all. Just kiss me."

She couldn't quite tell then if it was a sigh of grim resignation or one of delightful anticipation that issued from his lips, but Amanda could certainly tell that Marcus Quicksilver was going to do exactly as he'd been told—for once!—when he caught her chin in one hand, then angled her head and covered her mouth with his own. From the instant this kiss began, she knew it was different from the ones that had preceded it.

Warmer. Wetter. Deeper.

And her response was different from when he had kissed her before. In the past, she had merely felt her skin heat up and her insides turn to jelly. But now—now!—every inch of her skin felt on fire, and her stomach and other, deeper places seemed to have melted. Completely liquefied. She thought she might drown from the inside out. If she didn't burn to a crisp first.

Different, too, because his fingers—instead of smoothing along her throat or arms—were insistently working along the buttons down the back of her dress. No sooner had he begun, it seemed, than she felt the warm spread of his hands on her skin.

His mouth left hers and he sat her up, which was an easy task now, since she was as limp and boneless as a rag doll. Just as easily, his powerful arms separated her from her dress and underskirts and camisole, and divested him of trousers and boots with the same agility and speed. Then those arms brought her close against him again.

He brushed her hair away from her ear, and his lips were hot and moist when he whispered, "This is preamble, darlin'. All this kissing and touching. This." One hand slid up the side of her rib cage and cupped a breast. "And this." His thumb moved back and forth across its rigid center, sending waves of sensation cascading through her. Inexperienced as Amanda was, she knew enough to realize she was in the arms, beneath the hands, of a master. Or a magician. Every touch felt magical.

"Feel good?" he asked, though the question was unnecessary judging by the soft, mewing sounds she was making every time he touched her. Marcus couldn't remember any woman feeling so warm or coming so alive beneath his fingertips. Not Sarabeth. Not even the most practiced whore in the territories.

Nor could he remember ever feeling so warm and so alive himself. Hot. Burning with life and desire.

With some reluctance, Marcus reminded himself that as warm and eager as Amanda was, she'd never done this before. He'd warned her of the consequences earlier, but now he wondered if anyone had ever warned her just what to expect the first time she made love. In all probability, they hadn't, he decided.

He raised up on an elbow now and looked down at her lovely face. In the amber glow of the bedside lamp, her lips shone wet and rosy from his kisses. Her skin was flushed a petal-pink, and those green eyes were a lustrous emerald shade. He leaned to drop a kiss on each languorous lid.

"Amanda. Amanda," he whispered, loving the musical sound of her name on his lips. Loving her. "Are you sure this is what you want, darlin'? Because it's not too late to…"

But it was clearly too late—for Marcus, anyway—because she responded by reaching up to thread her fingers through his hair, silencing him by bringing his mouth down to hers, inviting his tongue into its depths, and making him forget there was any warning to be made, any caution to be given. Making him forget there was anything else in the world but the warm give of her mouth and the sweet, nearly stunning taste of her.

It took every fiber of his will to hold back, to go slow enough to pleasure her…slower…a century to tantalize her eager mouth…a millennium for feasting at each succulent breast…an eon or more for her deep, delicious core. And when at last he sensed Amanda was ready for him, when she moaned and arched beneath his body like a bow stretched, quivering, to its limit, Marcus took her with a fierceness he was no longer able to control. Thrusting. Meeting her thrusts. Driving the headboard again and again against the wall and finally driving both of them over the long-sought edge of passion.

"No. Stay," Amanda breathed a moment later, when Marcus murmured that he was too heavy and began to move away. She twined her legs around him more tightly, savoring the weight and feel of his muscular body on hers, his damp chest rising and falling in concert with hers, all the while glorying in the utter and simple miracle of a man inside a woman, of Marcus Quicksilver inside her.

"Stay with me always, Marcus. Please." She glided her palms down the warm slickness of his back, reveling in the feel of the hard muscles beneath the smooth cover of his flesh. "Stay like this. Just like this. Always."

He sighed and shifted his weight slightly, brushing his lips against her neck. Amanda sighed, too, and then she felt her lips curve into a languid smile.

"I didn't know," she said dreamily, "I hadn't any notion that making love was so…that it could be like…like…" Frustrated for want of a word to describe what she'd just experienced, Amanda blew a puff of breath at the damp lock of hair pressed across her forehead. "Well, like…"

"Like the Fourth of July?" There was the faintest hint of a chuckle in his voice.

Amanda nodded. Yes. That was what it had been like. It was the perfect description of the dazzling fireworks that had exploded inside her. Why hadn't anyone ever told her? she wondered. Even Bridget, when she tried to communicate the business of where babies came from, had focused on the physical facts, without so much as a mention of the accompanying fireworks. Why was such a brilliant experience kept such a dark secret?

"It's not always like that," Marcus said quietly now, as if reading her thoughts. Then he jerked up his head to gaze down at her. His dark eyes delved into Amanda's then, and his tone deepened with concern. "I didn't hurt you, did I? I wasn't thinking all that clearly toward the end, and I'd hate myself if I thought for a minute that..."

"Shhh..." Amanda raised her head to kiss his lips, lips that were so taut with worry now. "You gave me more pleasure than I've ever known. More than I dared ever imagine." She grinned, a little sheepishly, but at the same time moved her hips sensually beneath him, then watched with a kind of primal satisfaction as a flame ignited deep in his eyes. A flame that burned for her. Just for her.

"I confess," she said with a sigh, "that I'm looking forward to a lifetime of this particular pleasure now, Marcus."

"I am, too, darlin'."

It was the truth, as Marcus had never spoken it

before. Already he was wanting her again, unwilling, perhaps even unable as his blood rekindled, to cool the hot magic of the moment by talking about what the future might hold for the two of them, or telling Amanda how a lifetime could be cut very short, like Sarabeth's, or stretch out very long and unpleasant, very different for a woman named Mrs. Amanda Quicksilver from the way it was for Miss Amanda Grenville.

Later, after loving her again, when he had turned out the lamp and Amanda lay spent and dreamy in his arms, he whispered a bit about some of those old dreams of his. Soft musings about a ranch. A family. The future he had planned so long ago, before his world broke apart. The future that he'd ignored so long, that perhaps could be a reality once more. He wasn't sure if she heard him completely. Her murmured responses and occasional tender touches might have been just the aftermath of their intense loving. It didn't matter much. They'd have plenty of time to talk it all out later.

What mattered was that Marcus knew he had to do more than make love or merely dream to make a life for them. He hadn't been looking to turn his life inside out and upside down, but he wasn't someone to hide from facts. And the fact was that he wanted to spend the rest of his life with Amanda, and he thought, that given an adequate chance, he could make her happy. He'd die trying, Marcus knew that. But a man without a dollar in the bank and only dismal prospects for the future had no business asking any woman—heiress or pauper—to marry him.

He'd been a damn good bounty hunter—one of the best—for a long time, he thought, even if it hadn't exactly been a life he chose. Or if he chose it, it had been by default, when no other way of life had much appeal. At any rate, he was done with that. Retired.

Or almost. He figured his hunting skills just might stand him in good stead one last time. He'd had a plentiful bounty right under his nose for the past day or so, and he hadn't even realized it. Frank Scobey, who was wanted in New Mexico for murder and in Wyoming for robbery and probably elsewhere for God only knew what crimes, had to be worth at least two or three thousand dollars by now, by Marcus's calculations. That wasn't a fortune by Grenville standards, but it was plenty for a Quicksilver stake. And Marcus doubted Scobey had gone far after that fall from Rose's window.

All Marcus needed was a horse and a gun and a day or two to bring Scobey in. It wouldn't take long. Then he'd have something more solid than dreams to offer Amanda.

Just before dawn, Marcus eased away from Amanda's side, slipped into his clothes and walked quietly to the room next door, where Rose was sleeping alone, snoring through her broken nose. Reluctant to wake her in order to ask her for the loan of her two hundred dollars, he lifted a corner of the mattress and slid the little metal box out from underneath it.

Rose stirred when the coins jingled. "Whazzat?" she murmured.

"I owe you, Rose," Marcus whispered. "I'll be back in a day or two, with Frank Scobey's head and a bit of interest on your investment."

Uncertain if she'd comprehended, he thought briefly about leaving her a promissory note, but decided he'd probably be back—with Scobey's head and ten percent interest on Rose's two hundred—before she even knew it was gone.

Chapter Sixteen

The knock on the door woke her. Amanda opened her eyes, smiled sleepily at the sudden, sensual memory of the night before, then shrieked in surprise when a purple-faced Rose opened the door and came stomping into the room.

"See?" the prostitute shouted over her shoulder to Maybelle, who followed just a few steps behind her. "I told you he wouldn't be here. Didn't I say so? Didn't I?"

Looming over the bed then, with her dyed red hair and discolored face and flashing eyes, Rose looked less like a woman than like some dark, crazed bird of prey. She glared at Amanda. "Where is he?" she demanded, in a voice all the more shrill and birdlike for her broken nose. "Where's Quicksilver?"

In sleepy bewilderment, Amanda blinked down at the vacant space beside her on the bed. Instinctively she reached out a hand, only to discover the coolness that signified a considerable absence. "I...I don't know where he is," she said, pulling the covers more tightly around her naked body. "Perhaps…"

"Perhaps my ass!" Rose snorted. "I knew it! Oh, didn't I just know it! What did I tell you, Maybelle? The son of a bitch is gone. Vamoosed. Skedaddled. And he took my two hundred dollars with him."

"What?" Amanda exclaimed.

"You heard me."

Rose followed that vehement statement with a high-pitched string of curses that Amanda did indeed hear loud and clear. If she hadn't been quite awake before, she decided, she certainly was now. She had no idea where Marcus was or how long he'd been gone, but she didn't for a second believe that he had stolen Rose's life savings.

If he wanted money so badly, all he had to do was cash her in, for heaven's sake. Of course, Rose had no way of knowing that. She still thought Amanda was a runaway from a fancy house, after all.

"I'm sure there's a good explanation, Rose," Amanda told her calmly.

"Sure there is. Theft! That's about as good an explanation as there is."

Maybelle stepped closer now. "She's right, Rosie. You're jumping to conclusions faster than a frog on a hot rock. Me, well, I just don't see Marcus Quicksilver as a thief. And anyway, we haven't looked everyplace in town yet. Come on." She clasped one of Rose's flailing fists and urged her toward the door. "We'll go ask around. I'm willing to bet we'll locate Marcus and your money both."

When the door closed behind the two women, Amanda sat and stared once more at the empty space beside her, while memories from the night before swirled like warm mist through her brain. The recollections alone—of Marcus's mouth on her, of his hard strength inside her—made her heart beat faster all of a sudden, and her body tighten with desire.

She thought about all the things he had told her during the night—all his plans and dreams—when his voice was like a soothing lullaby, when she was too sleepy and sated to do anything but smile in the dark, to lie close to his side and just listen. In hindsight, she wished she had said something—anything—about her longing to share in those plans and dreams. She wished she had told him that life with him felt absolutely right, as if her twenty years in a gilded cage in New York had been merely a dream, as if her real life were truly about to begin. With him. But she'd tell him that today. As soon as she saw him. As soon as he returned from wherever it was he'd mysteriously disappeared to.

But Marcus didn't return. Not that day. Not the next. Or the next.

He hadn't vanished without a clue, as it turned out. The boy in the livery stable went on at great length describing the roan gelding and the barely used saddle Marcus had bought for eighty dollars in gold coins. Two or three people had even witnessed him riding out of town shortly after sunrise. East, as they all recalled.

And it hadn't taken long for Maybelle to discover that Marcus's gun—the one stashed behind the bar, which he had bartered for their room—was gone. But all of those clues led nowhere, and Amanda's hopes, so high at first, sank slowly and then finally vanished from sight. She was miserable.

Rose, on the other hand, seemed to grow more philosophical about her loss with each passing day.

"It ain't the end of the world," she said on the third morning, as she sat across from Amanda at a table in the rear of the saloon. "I'd've probably just lost my investment anyway, if I'd started up a restaurant. And you—honey, you're a lot better off without him. We're all better off. Men!"

Rose grunted with disgust and lifted a hand to test one of the multicolored bruises on her face. "Who needs 'em? Right? If they're not beating you up, then they're stealing you blind. At night they're whispering all those pretty things in your ear, then next morning they've upped and disappeared."

Amanda couldn't deny that Marcus had whispered pretty things in her ear, or that he had upped and disappeared. She was nodding her head in sad agreement when Rose suddenly looked toward the saloon door and said, "Uh-oh. Here's another one we sure don't need."

"Who's he?" Amanda asked.

"That's Jubal. He owns this place." Rose laughed, a little forlornly. "Us, too, I guess."

Jubal strode to the table in back as if he did indeed own both the place and the women in it. "I'm back," he said. "What the hell happened to you, Rose? And who the hell is this?" He stabbed a finger toward Amanda.

Amanda felt like telling him precisely who she was and how she was accustomed to being treated, but Rose spoke first.

"She's that sick girl who arrived just before you left, Jubal. You remember. The one the fella traded his gun for. Only now the gun's gone, and he's gone, too." Rose shrugged, as if to say, "What did you expect?"

Obviously Jubal hadn't expected that. He stood there a moment, gnawing on his lower lip and flexing his right hand, looking as if he were about to slap Rose, but instead he slapped a hand down on the table directly in front of Amanda. "Then you best be gone, too," he said to Amanda. "Today. Right now."

"Aw, give the poor girl a chance, Jubal," Maybelle called from behind the bar, where she'd been washing glasses all morning. "You can't just throw her out on the street."

"Damned if I can't," he bellowed. "You're out, missy."

But then the angry gaze that had been focused on Amanda's face dropped to her chest and held there. "You're put together all right, I guess. What do you think, Rose?"

"I think she's real pretty," Rose said without hesitation. "Real refined for a working girl. Besides, Jubal, Maybelle and I have been telling you for the past year we could do with some time off."

Jubal continued to inspect Amanda's chest. "Here's the deal. You can't stay here unless you're willing to go to work for me upstairs and pay for your room and board."

"Unless I..." Amanda's jaw slackened, and she couldn't finish her sentence. All she could do was sit there, gazing dumbly, first at Jubal, who'd stalked to the bar, then at Rose across the table.

The prostitute shrugged again and then offered Amanda a weak but encouraging grin. "Well, honey, it's not such a bad idea. You already know the business. And Jubal's not half as nasty as he looks. I mean, it's not like you've got much of a choice, is it?"

Of course she had a choice. The fact was, she had two choices, Amanda decided while she stood in the center of the street, unmindful of the puddle soaking the hem of her dress. Two directions. West, where her grandmother so eagerly awaited her return and where Angus waited to marry her. And then there was east, the way Marcus Quicksilver had ridden out of town.

When Amanda looked west, the suggestion of mountains in the misty distance should have appeared formidable to her, she thought. But it didn't seem half as daunting as the flat, seemingly endless stretch of plains that greeted her when she looked to the east. There was nothing there. Between the vast sky and the flat earth, there was no one. It was as if Marcus had disappeared into thin air. As if she, too, would simply disappear if she followed.

She had walked determinedly out of the saloon a moment before, resolved to do something about her plight, instead of just sitting around feeling bemused and sorry for herself the way she had been for the last few days. She would find Marcus if it took her the rest of her life.

A man didn't simply up and leave, the way Rose had claimed. Other men, perhaps. Not Marcus. Not the man who had taken such good care of her, who had made sweet, long love to her and who had whispered all those precious dreams about a future that they were meant to share. There had to be some reason he had disappeared. There had to be some explanation for his absence.

But there wasn't. At least none Marcus had bothered or cared enough to give. Amanda's heart felt as flat and empty as the plains that stretched out before her. Rose was right. He'd upped and gone.

Perhaps someday she'd feel anger, she thought. Now she merely felt numb as she picked up her soggy, mud-stained skirts and walked listlessly toward the telegraph office.

After she sent the briefly worded wire—collect—to her grandmother in Denver, Amanda lowered herself onto a chair by the window.

"Might take a while for a reply, ma'am," the telegrapher said.

"That's all right. I'll wait."

The young man cleared his throat. "Might take a day or more."

"It doesn't matter."

"Suit yourself, lady." The young telegrapher went back to reading the dime novel he'd had to put aside when Amanda came in.

It didn't take a day, but a mere six hours, for a private coach to hurtle into town and pull to a stop in front of the telegraph office, where Amanda was still staring out the window. And it barely fazed her when she recognized the two men, both in dark suits and bowler hats, who climbed out of the coach.

The Pinkertons, Lincoln and Douglas, entered the office and approached Amanda warily, from two sides, as if they expected her to scratch out their eyes, or at the very least to bolt. When she did neither, but merely sat gazing at them blankly, each man reached out for one of her arms.

"Let's go, Miss Grenville," Lincoln said.

Douglas snickered. "Or should we say Mrs. Green? Where's that 'husband' of yours, anyway?"

"Gone," she answered, barely above a whisper. "Take me home, gentlemen. Please."

Marcus ran a slow hand along his horse's lathered left flank. He knew if he didn't slow down he might just as well ride the animal straight to the glue factory. Either that or he'd soon find himself walking the rest of the way back to Amanda.

After loosening the cinch, he pulled the saddle off

the gelding's wet back, then proceeded to rub him down with the saddle blanket, thinking he could have used a good rubdown himself right then. And as those thoughts led unerringly to Amanda and the feel of her warm body in bed and the aching anticipation of more of the same, he gritted his teeth and swabbed the horse all the harder.

It had been a long three days.

He'd found Frank Scobey easy enough. Just as Marcus had suspected, the bastard had been camped out only a few miles east of town, nursing his busted ankle. Then, after Marcus introduced himself with a fist in Scobey's face—on Rose's behalf, his version of an eye for an eye—the fellow had also had to nurse a busted nose.

He probably should have waited to take out the prostitute's revenge, Marcus thought, since he'd had to listen to Scobey whine and complain all the way to Sidney where he'd planned to turn him over to the local authorities and maybe claim a down payment on his bounty.

No such luck. The marshal was out of town, and since the jailhouse had burned down only the day before, the deputy had refused to take responsibility for such a valuable criminal.

"Hell, just get a fifty-pound kid to sit on him a day or two till the marshal gets back," Marcus had said disgustedly. "How far do you think Scobey's going like this?"

But the chickenhearted deputy couldn't be persuaded, so Marcus had found himself taking his blubbering long-haired prisoner all the way back to North Platte, where the sheriff was more than willing to take Scobey off his hands, but not forthcoming with any cash. The man had told him in no uncertain terms that he'd have to file papers—in lousy triplicate—in order to see a penny of his reward.

If he'd had any reservations, any qualms or lingering doubts about getting out of the bounty hunting business, Marcus realized they were gone now, as he leaned back on his saddle and watched the worn-out gelding grazing. He felt worn-out, too, in a way.

It had been a long ten years.

Fate had ended his marriage to Sarabeth and had turned him from a farmer into a hunter. Then fate had intervened again and changed all that. Amanda had changed all that, with her big green eyes and her intrepid spirit and her generous heart.

Marcus wasn't going to tempt fate any more by wasting time, he decided. He was going to marry Amanda the minute he got back, by God. They'd scare up a preacher and have Rose and Maybelle as witnesses. And if a cigar band was the best he could do for a wedding ring, then so be it. If he knew Amanda the way he thought he did, she'd be delighted by the bright paper band. There would be plenty of time to worry about money later on, after he made her his wife.

Six hours and a dozen plodding miles later, Marcus walked into the saloon, intending to take the stairs three at a time and propose to Amanda before he'd even said hello to her. He only managed to make it as far as the first stair, however, before Rose was on him like a duck on a June bug.

"Where's my money, you thieving rat?" she shrieked as she pasted him across the cheek with the flat of her hand. "Where's the two hundred dollars you stole from me?"

Marcus used one arm to deflect her fists while he reached in his back pocket for four of the five remaining double eagles. After living on nothing for over a week, he figured twenty dollars would be plenty to see him and Amanda to Denver.

He slapped the coins in Rose's hand. "Here's eighty, Rose. And when Wells Fargo comes through with my bounty for Scobey, I'll send you the rest. Plus another twenty for the loan." He winked at the prostitute's surprised expression. "I'm much obliged."

"You got him?"

"I got him, all right. He's sitting in a cell in North Platte right now, breathing out of his mouth, since his nose just sort of happened to get in the way of my fist."

Rose's bruised face lit up and, after a whoop of delight, she threw her arms around Marcus' neck. "I knew you'd do it. I knew you didn't steal my money, Marcus. Honest."

He glanced around the room now. "I didn't expect to be gone so long. How's Amanda getting along? She's upstairs, I reckon."

"She's gone."

Marcus blinked. "What? She moved out of here? Where is she?"

"Gone," Rose said again. "None of us figured you'd be back. What did you expect, Marcus?"

He'd expected to be upstairs now, with Amanda in his arms, he thought bleakly. He'd expected her to wait for him till the goddamn cows came home or hell froze over or both. He drew in a long, slow breath. And then, as quickly as his anger subsided, he began to worry.

"The little fool," he muttered. "She's liable to get herself killed, trying to travel all alone."

"Oh, she wasn't alone," Rose said. "She took off in a fancy coach with two slick men. Danny down at the telegraph office said she wired Denver, and next thing he knew here came the coach and those two black-suited, bowler-hatted fellas."

The Pinkertons! Marcus lowered himself into a chair and braced his elbows on the table, trying to make sense of the information. Amanda had given up on him, obviously, and had wired her grandmother in Denver.

He slammed a fist on the tabletop. "Why the hell didn't she wait for me?"

"Wait?" Rose exclaimed. "She did wait, Marcus. She waited three long days, and then I guess she just plain gave up hope." Rose shrugged. "And I guess she decided she didn't want to go back to whoring anymore, which was the only choice Jubal gave her if she wanted to stick around."

"He what?"

"You heard me. Jubal came back and told her she'd have to start earning her keep upstairs with Maybelle and me. That's when she walked out."

"Damn," Marcus muttered. That hadn't occurred to him when he took off after Scobey. He'd thought he'd be coming back the very next day with cash enough to pay for the balance of their room and board and reimburse Rose, with plenty left over for a down payment on a good piece of land. Of course Amanda had taken off when she faced working off their debt upstairs in bed.

He stood up. "I owe you a hundred twenty dollars, Rose, and twenty on top of that as interest on the loan. As soon as I get paid for Scobey, I'll be wiring it to you, all right? In care of the telegraph office, so your friend Jubal can't get his hands on it. It shouldn't take more than a week or two."

"That'd be right decent of you, Marcus," the prostitute said. "Don't you be too hard on her for picking up and leaving, you hear? The way I see it, she only did what she had to do to stay out of this infernal business. When it comes right down to it, you ought to be thanking your lucky stars that she took off."

Marcus did thank the stars overhead the following two nights, as he slept under them on his way to Denver. He thanked them for putting a fair-haired, high-spirited beauty in his path at a time in his life when he could truly appreciate her, and at a time when he had enough years left to make some of his old dreams come true.

And the same time he was being grateful, he also prayed to those stars that he wouldn't get to Denver too late, only to discover that Granny Grenville had managed to talk or wrestle Amanda onto an east-bound train to take her back to her gilded cage in New York. He didn't relish having to spend a good portion of Frank Scobey's bounty on a long trip east in pursuit of the woman he was going to marry, come hell or high water or any other disaster, natural or otherwise.

But the disaster that met Marcus when he arrived in Denver wasn't anything like he'd expected. He'd have preferred fire or flood to the headline he read when he picked up the morning paper. In bold, black letters, a banner headline proclaimed *Heiress to wed McCray today.*

Chapter Seventeen

Honoria Grenville scowled at the fully laden tray that Bridget, her maid, was trying to balance on her hip while she used her free hand to close the door to Amanda's bedroom.

"She still hasn't touched a bite, I see." Honoria lifted a silver warming cover and counted the four slices of bacon she had requested earlier from the hotel dining room downstairs.

"She ate a few corners of the toast, ma'am," Bridget said, "and she drank the coffee. Same as yesterday and the day before. She'll be the skinniest bride ever to walk down an aisle, I fear."

"If she has the strength." Honoria snorted. "God knows she has the will. I've never seen such a stubborn creature in all my years."

"Yes, ma'am." Bridget curtsied and maneuvered the tray around her employer. "I'll be taking this downstairs, then," she said.

Honoria stood there a while, tapping her cane contemplatively on the Oriental carpet, staring at the closed door, wondering what was going on in her granddaughter's head.

She'd won, hadn't she? Amanda had gotten her way. The stubborn child was going to wed Angus McCray this very day. She ought to be happy, for heaven's sake. Not moping around and refusing to eat, the way she'd been ever since the Pinkertons brought her back.

And what a sight she'd been. Pale as a fish, and smelling not much better. Angus, whom Honoria had summoned to greet her, had been quietly appalled, kissing Amanda's cheek while keeping a safe distance from her dirty clothes. Honoria doubted the Scot would have proffered even that wisp of a kiss if not for the Grenville fortune.

Amanda meant nothing to him. It was only the money, as Honoria had suspected all along. And then the scoundrel had admitted as much while they waited for Amanda's return. He was going to marry her or else.

"Or else what?" Honoria had demanded.

"Or else I'll sue Amanda for breach of promise, Mrs. Grenville. Here. In Denver. And I'll win. I'm a very popular fellow."

Honoria sighed now as she prepared to enter Amanda's room. She would do anything for her granddaughter in order not to lose her. That fact had become quite clear to her these past agonizing days. Why the child wanted McCray was beyond comprehension, but if the marriage kept Amanda from running away again, then marriage it would be.

"You need to eat to keep up your strength," she said as she walked into the room, jabbing her cane at the floor for emphasis.

Amanda looked up from the hands that were folded in her lap. "I know, Grandmother." She forged what she hoped was a smile. "I'll eat. Eventually."

"You can begin with your wedding cake this evening. That is, if you still insist on this foolish alliance."

Amanda's reply was a less-than-enthusiastic nod. Insist? She was more insistent than ever. Marrying Angus McCray had once signified independence. Now, however, it signified just the opposite—a loss of independence, a loss of self, even, perhaps, a loss of life. Marrying Angus, Amanda had decided during the past few days, would be a kind of suicide. A blessed end to a life that held little joy or hope or love for her without Marcus Quicksilver.

Her emotions had swung wildly ever since Marcus left her. She'd gone from rage to desolation so often that she felt dizzy most of the time. Now all she wanted to feel was nothing. Which was what she felt for Angus. Nothing. She couldn't wait to take her vows and make that void a permanent condition.

When she heard a soft tap on the door, she dearly hoped it wasn't her fiancé—again—come to inquire about her, to give her a dry peck on the cheek, to speak in a voice that wasn't Marcus's, to move in a way that wasn't Marcus's, to torture her by simply not being the man she loved.

But when her grandmother called, "Yes? Come in," it wasn't Angus who opened the door, but Bridget, with a silly grin on her face and a message in her hand.

"A gentleman downstairs asked me to give this to you, ma'am," she said to Honoria.

"I don't have time for any more rude questions from newspapermen, Bridget." Honoria sputtered and stabbed her cane at the floor, then pointed it at a trash basket. "Throw it away."

After one hesitant step toward the receptacle, Bridget stopped. "He didn't strike me as a journalist, ma'am." Her hand fluttered up and covered her heart. "He was ever so handsome. Quite a manly man. He said his name was Quick— Oh, dear. Now what was it?"

"Quicksilver?"

Amanda was out of her chair immediately, her heart in her throat. No sooner had Bridget said, "Yes, that was the name," than Amanda was snatching the message from her hand and opening it with quaking fingers.

If she expected to read a heartfelt apology or a declaration of love for her or a request for her hand, penned in a flowery script, she was bitterly disappointed when she read instead the fierce scrawl that said simply:

Regarding financial matters. M. Quicksilver.

He wanted his reward. Not her. Not her. It had been the money all along.

After Amanda sagged back into her chair, her grandmother took the note from her limp hand.

"Financial matters!" she exclaimed after she had read it. "Who is this M. Quicksilver?"

"A bounty hunter," Amanda answered in a weak voice.

"And just what is he to you?" her grandmother demanded.

"Nothing," she said, shaking her head sadly. "Nothing at all."

Honoria Grenville sincerely doubted that as she stood staring at her granddaughter. Amanda had come to life—bright, effervescent life—at the mere mention of this man's name. She had never seen the child look so happy or so hopeful. By heaven, it was the way a woman in love should look on her wedding day, Honoria thought. She wasn't so old that she had forgotten or so blind that she couldn't recognize that glorious glow.

But it was gone now. That beautiful glow of love had disappeared, and her granddaughter looked more desolate and defeated than ever. It had something to do with this bounty hunter, she was certain.

Honoria crumpled the message in her fist. "Well, we'll just see about this." Her cane thumped on the floor. "Where is this Quicksilver, Bridget?"

"Down in the lobby, ma'am." The maid giggled and curtsied eagerly. "Come. I'll show you the way."

* * *

The hotel lobby was swarming with people at midday. But the frock coats and the full skirts parted for Honoria Grenville and her ebony cane, in much the same way the seas must have parted for Moses.

"There he is, ma'am." Bridget was bobbing along beside her. "Over there. See! The man is ever so—"

"I see him," Honoria snapped. "Be still, Bridget. Better yet—" she thumped her cane for emphasis "—go back upstairs."

Crestfallen, the little maid did as she was ordered, but only after sending a long, soulful look in the direction of the man, who was just then leaning against a marble column. Casual as his stance was, with his hat pulled low and his gunbelt slanted across his lean hips, there was nothing casual about the set of the man's jaw or the hard determination of his mouth. Quicksilver meant business, whatever that business was.

Honoria could see that clearly as she continued toward him across the lobby. His message had pertained to financial matters, yet the bounty hunter—if indeed that was what he was—didn't strike her as a man who gave as much as a tinker's damn about money. She'd spent too many years recognizing dollar signs in people's eyes, most recently with Angus McCray.

As she neared the man, she became aware of something else in his expression. Her heart skipped a quick little beat when she thought she recognized the same despair and desolation she had just witnessed a few moments before in Amanda.

"Mr. Quicksilver, I presume?"

He shifted off the marble column, then touched the brim of his hat as he straightened to his full height.

"Ma'am," he drawled. "I appreciate your seeing me so soon."

The grandmother had those money-green eyes, too. For a moment, Marcus's heart seized up and his head spun. Then he reminded himself why he was there.

"As my note said, Mrs. Grenville, I'm here to discuss some financial matters. Specifically—" Marcus reached into the pocket of his shirt to withdraw a paper "—expenses incurred during this past week, while I was baby-sitting your granddaughter."

The old woman narrowed her gaze on the list and glared so intently that Marcus expected the scrap of paper to go up in flames.

"You're not here about the five-thousand-dollar reward?" she demanded, her fierce green eyes searching his face now with the same intensity.

"No, ma'am. I didn't do anything to earn it. But I did spend money on your granddaughter's behalf. It's all there on the list. One horse. One Mexican saddle. Used. A few tickets."

"This is all you want? A hundred forty dollars?"

"That's it." A hundred twenty for poor old Rose, Marcus thought, and twenty for enough whiskey to put a certain poor old bounty hunter to sleep for a couple days.

Mrs. Grenville contemplated his list for a minute, as if she were checking his arithmetic, which irritated the hell out of Marcus, since he could have asked for—and probably could have gotten—five or six times what he'd written.

"Amanda is miserable," she said at last. "Is she in love with you, Mr. Quicksilver?"

"I doubt it, ma'am," he answered through clenched teeth. "Not if she's marrying Angus damn McCray."

"Are you, sir, by any chance in love with her?"

A bitter laugh broke from Marcus's taut lips. "In love with that brat?" He laughed again. "You must take me for some kind of fool."

"Are you, Mr. Quicksilver?" Her cane ticked on the side of his boot, and she smiled, almost slyly. "I know my granddaughter is some kind of fool. What I need to know is, are you, as well?"

Marcus shook his head now. There was no way he could deny he was probably the biggest fool the good Lord had ever made. It was probably etched across his forehead, he decided, the way the old woman had read him so perfectly.

"I'll have your money for you, Mr. Quicksilver," she said. "It may take me a few hours to arrange, so if you'll be good enough to wait at my private railroad car, I'll see that someone delivers it to you this evening."

"Much obliged, ma'am."

She started to turn away, then stopped. "Oh. One thing, if you don't mind my asking. If you had earned the reward for retrieving my granddaughter, what would you have done with it? I'm just curious."

The question caught Marcus so off guard that he blurted out the truth, about the choice piece of Montana or Wyoming, before he even realized he was speaking. He felt his face turn hot and ruddy then, so he shrugged. "Well, hell. That was just some damn fool dream. And to be honest with you, Amanda was the best thing about it. Goodbye, Mrs. Grenville."

"Goodbye, Mr. Quicksilver. Thank you for taking care of my granddaughter. I'll go arrange for your cash now. My private car will be at the depot. Please feel free to pour yourself a glass of sherry while you wait."

It had started raining later that afternoon, which suited Amanda's mood perfectly. But by early evening, when she and her grandmother entered the coach to drive to the Presbyterian church, the heavens had opened with a fury. Lightning and thunder ripped across Denver, and a stiff west wind blew the rain in thick gray sheets. Dressed in her ecru wedding gown of alençon lace, Amanda stared glumly out the window of the coach until her grandmother leaned across her to pull the curtain down.

"They say rain is a sign of good fortune on a

wedding day, dear, but I don't want you getting all wet and taking a chill."

It made no difference to Amanda. The lowered curtain offered just as interesting a view as the downpour beyond it. And if she took a chill—a fatal one—that didn't matter, either. Nothing mattered.

Her grandmother hadn't breathed a word about her meeting with Marcus. Well, there hadn't been time, had there, with all the hushed, behind-closed-doors meetings she had had afterward with lawyers and bankers? But Amanda didn't have to ask. She knew very well that those meetings had been to arrange for the five-thousand-dollar bounty that Marcus had demanded and apparently gotten from her grandmother. More than once she had overheard the word *threaten* issuing from Honoria Grenville's lips.

It should have made her angry, she thought, but instead it merely made her numb. When the coach pulled to a stop, she knew her heart should have leapfrogged into her throat, but it didn't. The fact that she was about to enter the church where she would walk down the aisle and vow to love and honor and obey Angus McCray for the rest of her life seemed like a death sentence. And she welcomed it.

"Here we are. Out with you now, child," her grandmother said. When she leaned across Amanda to open the door, a cold rain slanted inside the coach.

With a sigh, Amanda gathered up yards and yards of silk and alençon lace, and began to clamber out.

Blinking in the rain, she cast a forlorn, wet gaze toward the wide bricked archway of the church.

"This isn't the right place, Grandmother," she exclaimed, edging back onto the seat. "There's been a mistake."

"Yes, I know, my dear. And it's about to be corrected. Now get out."

"What?" Amanda looked at her grandmother, then out into the pouring rain, then back again. Honoria Grenville wasn't known for her smiles, but at the moment there was the oddest grin on her face. "Get—get out?" Amanda stammered. "This isn't the church. Where's Angus?"

The grin on her grandmother's face flattened to a sneer. "Mr. Angus McCray isn't your concern anymore. He's not your fiancé, either. I gave him a choice this afternoon. If he wanted to proceed with this wedding, then I informed him in no uncertain terms that I would cut you off without a penny."

Amanda drew in a breath. "Or?"

"Or," the older woman continued with an emphatic thump of her cane, "I would pay him twenty thousand dollars in gold if he would agree to disappear this very evening."

"And he chose the gold." Amanda's voice was hollow, empty of all emotion.

Her grandmother gave a small but distinct snort. "I wasn't the least bit surprised."

"No. Nor am I, I suppose." It was her fortune that mattered to people. Not Amanda herself. Why would Angus be any different? Her shoulders sagged back against the damp leather of the seat. She sat there a moment in bleak silence, then said, "I'm turning into an expensive proposition for you, Grandmother, aren't I? How much did it cost you to buy off Marcus Quicksilver?"

"Good Lord. I nearly forgot." Honoria reached into her handbag and withdrew an envelope. "Here." She pressed it into Amanda's hand. "Now give me a kiss, child, and then do as I tell you. Get out of this carriage."

"But I—"

"You heard me."

Amanda stood in the rain, feeling confused and abandoned. After she climbed out of the coach, her grandmother had slammed the door and called for the coachman to drive on. One minute Amanda had been on her way to the Presbyterian church to get married, and now she was...

Where in the world was she, anyway?

The rain was coming down so hard she could hardly see her hand in front of her face. Then, not too far ahead, she made out a dark rectangular shape with little squares glowing the length of it. A house? When she stepped toward its shelter, only to trip over something metallic and rigid, she suddenly knew where she was. The railroad yard. And the rectangle looming before her was her grandmother's private car.

No sooner had she realized that than a bolt of lightning split the wet black sky and thunder shook the ground beneath her feet. Amanda raced for the shelter of the train. She scrambled up the metal stairs at the rear of the car and burst through the back door, out of the storm and into the warm, golden light.

What the—? Marcus dropped his glass of sherry and reached for his gun. But he stopped before it cleared leather, the second he realized who had just crashed through the door. His heart soared in that second, and then it landed hard, when he saw that she wore a wedding dress—a soggy one—and clutched a wet envelope in one hand.

"Hello, brat." He figured she'd come to give him his money, along with a piece of her mind, before she tripped down the aisle with McCray. Fine. He could endure it. He could take whatever it was she intended for him. He'd had enough of the old girl's sherry to keep his heart afloat now, and when Amanda stormed out, there's be enough sherry left for him to drown himself temporarily.

"I see you brought my money," he said, gesturing toward the drenched envelope in her hand.

She looked down at it as if she'd forgotten it was there. And then her dazed expression turned to fury, and she flung the envelope in his direction. "Here's your money, Quicksilver. I hope you choke on it."

The wet vellum fell apart when it hit the floor, and a few bills trickled out, not far from Marcus's feet.

"You better count it!" Amanda screamed. "Just to make sure it's all there!"

"It's there," he said. "I can see the hundred and two twenties. Tell your grandmother I'm much obliged."

Amanda stared at the scattered bills and then at him. "It isn't five thousand dollars?" She blinked. "You didn't ask her for the reward for bringing me back?"

"Bringing you back!" Marcus shouted as he rose from the chair. "Hell, you scrambled back to marry McCray the minute my back was turned."

"You left me, Marcus. You abandoned me!"

He was about to bellow that a mere three days didn't constitute abandonment and that he'd left her only to try to scratch up a little cash to put a half-decent roof over her head, but he stopped when he saw tears mixing with the raindrops on her face.

"Is that what you thought, darlin?" he asked softly. "That I'd walked out on you?"

She sniffed. "It's what I believed. Everybody believed it. Rose. And Maybelle. There didn't seem much point in waiting anymore." She sniffed again before adding, "Or in living. I decided marrying Angus was the next best thing to suicide."

"Sui—" Marcus started to exclaim, but before the word could leave his lips, the railroad car lurched forward unexpectedly and sent him reeling along the aisle, so fast and so uncontrollably that he literally bowled Amanda over. The next thing he knew, he was sprawled atop a wet heap of wedding dress with a flailing woman inside it.

He moved his hands over her, as much for the

pleasure of touching her as to check for injury or to defend himself from her feisty fists. She wasn't hurt, thank God. At least not physically.

"I'll never leave you again, darlin'." He bent his head to kiss her sputtering lips. A gentle, hesitant kiss, because he was half afraid she'd take a bite out of him and half afraid he wouldn't be able to stop once he started.

She gazed up at him, still a little stunned from the fall, perhaps a bit startled by his words, perhaps not comprehending them. "Never?" she whispered.

Marcus shook his head. "Never. I promise you." He thumbed raindrops and tears from her cheeks. "Marry me, Amanda."

Those money-green eyes lit with instant joy, and a warmth like burgeoning spring filled them as she breathed, *"Yes."* Then her damp brow furrowed. "Marcus, the train's moving."

"Uh-huh." He kissed her again, long and slow and deep.

"Where do you suppose it's going?" she murmured, catching her breath.

Marcus laughed. "Darlin', I don't care."

Epilogue

The train had stopped. Marcus opened one eye and gazed into a tangle of blond hair. God almighty! It hadn't been a dream. Amanda was here, her warm body curved into his as if the two of them were a single being. Inseparable now. One.

The way they had been most of the night, making love again and again while the wheels clattered and the car swayed and the whispered pledges of love they made were more warm breath than sound.

The only sounds now were Amanda's soft exhalations. Last night Marcus had said he didn't care where the train was heading, and he'd meant it then. But now he couldn't help wondering just where the hell they were.

He slid out of the curtained sleeping compartment, located his clothes one by one, all the while smiling at the memory of taking them off. He put them on quietly now. His gunbelt, too. God only knew who or what might greet him when he stepped outside.

What greeted him, though, was not danger but a peaceful valley whose green rolled east as far as he could see. To the west, the lush grass carpet climbed until it gave way to trees and mountain peaks. He drew in a deep breath of clean, cool air. Wyoming, he guessed, from the look of it and the length of their night journey.

If it hadn't been for the train, Marcus might have believed a genie had spirited Amanda and him away to paradise sometime during the night. He gave the metal siding a thump with his hand anyway, just to make sure it was real, then swung down from the little iron-railed balcony onto the solid ground.

From this vantage point, he could see it wasn't much of a train. Just a locomotive, a tender, and the Pullman Palace car, like an elegant caboose. When he caught a glimpse of a man and a young woman deep in conversation by the engine, Marcus felt a little lurch of relief. The presence of others somehow proved again that he wasn't dreaming.

"Oh, good morning, sir." The young girl had seen him, too, and she bustled toward him now, curtsying to a stop.

"I'm Bridget, sir. Mrs. Grenville's personal maid. We crossed paths in the hotel lobby yesterday. And, saints preserve us, now we're here." She gestured toward the mountains, where the morning sun was working a gold-and-purple magic.

Marcus remembered, although it seemed a thousand years ago, perhaps a thousand miles away.

"Mornin', Bridget." He stood quietly a minute,

rubbing his chin, trying to make sense of everything, or at least to think of a question that wouldn't make him look like a pure fool to the little Irish maid.

Fortunately, Amanda floated out onto the balcony just then, sparing him the embarrassment when she exclaimed, "Bridget! Is that you? Good Lord! Where in the world are we? What's going on?"

Amanda gave a tug on the sash of her blue velvet dressing gown, then prepared to descend the metal steps, but by then Marcus's hands had encircled her waist, and he lifted her down.

For a moment it seemed they both forgot about Bridget and the train and the green valley as they gazed into each other's eyes.

"Mornin', darlin'," Marcus said softly, thinking how perfectly her eyes matched the verdant grasses around them. "How'd you sleep?"

The pink flush he'd anticipated crept over her cheeks. She flicked a tiny glance toward Bridget, then grinned up at him like a woman who'd been well loved and answered, "Very well, thank you. And you?"

Marcus laughed. "Oh, yes, ma'am. I've never been one to nap, but—" he angled his head toward the Pullman car and his hands moved smoothly up the blue velvet from her waist until his thumbs were discreetly snug beneath her breasts "—I can see lots of napping in my future."

Her grin widened, turning slightly sultry in the process. "Your *immediate* future?"

He was about to answer with a husky yes when the all-but-forgotten little maid cleared her throat.

"Excuse me, Miss Amanda. I've got a message from your grandmother."

Amanda sighed, and some of the glaze evaporated from her eyes. "What is it, Bridget? Go ahead."

"Oh, dear," the young woman said. "I want to be sure I get this right." She began searching through the pockets of her skirt until she finally came up with a folded sheet of paper.

Marcus wasn't at all sure he was in the mood to hear a proclamation from the cane-wielding Granny Grenville just then. There was no going back now. Amanda was his, whatever the old woman said. But he kept silent and kept a firm grip on Amanda while Bridget perused the note.

"Mrs. Grenville requests that you act as her agent in locating and purchasing some choice acreage here in Wyoming, or Montana, perhaps. She says that's up to you, Mr. Quicksilver. Money, of course, is no object, she wants you to know."

Not for her, Marcus thought as he felt his spine stiffen. Not an obstacle, either.

"Mrs. Grenville also requests that you... Oh, how did she say it?" Bridget glanced back at the paper before she continued. "She requests that you represent her interests on this property in the future."

That sounded a lot like hired help to Marcus, but he bit his tongue while Bridget consulted her paper again.

"Mrs. Grenville says that any and all profits from this property will be considered payment on it."

"In other words, it's a loan," Amanda piped up, snuggling closer to Marcus. "How sweet of her."

"Yes, miss." Bridget bobbed automatically. "Mrs. Grenville says quite explicitly she believes Mr. Quicksilver would prefer that to an outright wedding gift."

Hell, yes, he did. Marcus felt his backbone—and his pride—limbering a bit. He didn't want someone to give him a dream, but he was willing to work his backside off to pay for one himself.

"And, Miss Amanda, your grandmother says finally that, if you've changed your mind, I'm to accompany you home."

"Thank you, Bridget." Amanda nestled even deeper into Marcus's arms. "That won't be necessary. Please tell my grandmother that I *am* home."

* * * * *

Let's Celebrate!

LOVE & LAUGHTER™

invites you to
the party of the season!

Grab your popcorn and be prepared to laugh as we celebrate with **LOVE & LAUGHTER**.

Harlequin's newest series is going Hollywood!

Let us make you laugh with three months of terrific books, authors and romance, plus a chance to win a FREE 15-copy video collection of the best romantic comedies ever made.

For more details look in the back pages of any Love & Laughter title, from July to September, at your favorite retail outlet.

Don't forget the popcorn!

Available wherever
Harlequin books are sold.

 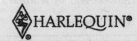 HARLEQUIN®

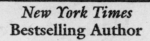

HARLEQUIN AND SILHOUETTE
ARE PLEASED TO PRESENT

Love, marriage—and the pursuit of family!

Check your retail shelves for these upcoming titles:

July 1997
Last Chance Cafe by Curtiss Ann Matlock
The most determined bachelor in Oklahoma is in trouble! A
lovely widow with three daughters has moved next door—and
the girls want a dad! But he wants to know if their mom needs
a husband....

August 1997
Thorne's Wife by Joan Hohl
Pennsylvania. It was only to be a marriage of convenience—
until they fell in love! Now, three years later, tragedy
threatens to separate them forever and Valerie wants only to
be in the strength of her husband's arms. For she has some
very special news for the expectant father...

September 1997
Desperate Measures by Paula Detmer Riggs
New Mexico judge Amanda Wainwright's daughter has been
kidnapped, and the price of her freedom is a verdict in
favor of a notorious crime boss. So enters ex-FBI agent
Devlin Buchanan—ruthless, unstoppable—and soon there is
no risk he will not take for her.

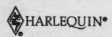 

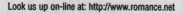

As Seen on TV!

Free Gift Offer

With a Free Gift proof-of-purchase
from any Harlequin® book, you can receive
a beautiful cubic zirconia pendant.

This stunning marquise-shaped stone is a genuine cubic
zirconia—accented by an 18" gold tone necklace.
(Approximate retail value $19.95)

Send for yours today...
compliments of ◆ HARLEQUIN®

To receive your free gift, a cubic zirconia pendant, send us one original proof-of-purchase, photocopies not accepted, from the back of any Harlequin Romance®, Harlequin Presents®, Harlequin Temptation®, Harlequin Superromance®, Harlequin Intrigue®, Harlequin American Romance®, or Harlequin Historicals® title available at your favorite retail outlet, together with the Free Gift Certificate, plus a check or money order for $1.65 U.S./$2.15 CAN. (do not send cash) to cover postage and handling, payable to Harlequin Free Gift Offer. We will send you the specified gift. Allow 6 to 8 weeks for delivery. Offer good until December 31, 1997, or while quantities last. Offer valid in the U.S. and Canada only.

Free Gift Certificate

Name: _____

Address: _____

City: _____ State/Province: _____ Zip/Postal Code: _____

Mail this certificate, one proof-of-purchase and a check or money order for postage and handling to: HARLEQUIN FREE GIFT OFFER 1997. In the U.S.: 3010 Walden Avenue, P.O. Box 9071, Buffalo NY 14269-9057. In Canada: P.O. Box 604, Fort Erie, Ontario L2Z 5X3.

FREE GIFT OFFER

084-KEZ

ONE PROOF-OF-PURCHASE
To collect your fabulous FREE GIFT, a cubic zirconia pendant, you must include this original proof-of-purchase for each gift with the properly completed Free Gift Certificate.

084-KEZR